Rebecca K. Busch was raised in Northeastern Michigan. Later she moved to Boulder, Colorado, where she earned her degree in English Literature at the University of Colorado. She continues to be an avid reader and currently lives in Denver, Colorado.

For my fellow dreamers

Rebecca K. Busch

DRAGON WING

AUSTIN MACAULEY PUBLISHERS
LONDON · CAMBRIDGE · NEW YORK · SHARJAH

Copyright © Rebecca K. Busch (2018)

The right of Rebecca K. Busch to be identified as author of this work has been asserted by her in accordance with section 77 and 78 of the Copyright, Designs and Patents Act 1988.

All rights reserved. No part of this publication may be reproduced, stored in a retrieval system, or transmitted in any form or by any means, electronic, mechanical, photocopying, recording, or otherwise, without the prior permission of the publishers.

Any person who commits any unauthorized act in relation to this publication may be liable to criminal prosecution and civil claims for damages.

A CIP catalogue record for this title is available from the British Library.

ISBN 9781787106819 (Paperback)
ISBN 9781787106826 (Hardback)
ISBN 9781787106833 (E-Book)

www.austinmacauley.com

First Published (2018)
Austin Macauley Publishers Ltd.
25 Canada Square
Canary Wharf
London
E14 5LQ

Acknowledgments

Thank you to my mother who saved the first version of this story, which was written when I was 13 years old. Without it, this book may have never been written.

Thank you to my dad, who was my first sounding board for the book. To Julie, the best big sister anyone could hope for – and my first reader. Thank you to my brothers for protecting me and, at the same time, helping me to be a stronger person.

Anna, thank you for all your support over the years. All of my friends and family, I'm blessed to have you in my life. To those who encouraged my higher self – thank you for helping me connect to my inner spritely being.

Thank you to the entire team at Austin Macauley for seeing potential in me and my project.

Prologue

There is no more promising sound than that of a healthy newborn cry. New life brought into the world, completely pure, untainted. That first explosive wail signals relief and joy in all those who can hear it.

It was an early, cold, winter morning that the Northwood's heard this same pure sound. While the child stretches out its lungs for the first time, the midwife and her nurse hold each other in a shaky embrace, muffling horrified sobs. Their trembling hands still clutching dirtied rags. The harsh smell of blood and burnt flesh will stain the air for years to come.

Down the hall a small boy of the age of five curiously peeks into the room that he was strictly told to stay out of. Large yellow eyes scan the room before brazenly entering. He sees her on the table. Body torn and burned, eyes glassy and lifeless, her mouth ever so slightly turned with a twitch of satisfaction. He should be crying, but he's not. He stands in front of his lifeless mother, perfectly still, with a stoic stare.

With his wife's blood still on his hands, the father holds the child, oblivious to the world around him in this moment. The baby's wing affectionately wraps around his hand. He feels the smooth hard scales on his fingers, but only feels the softest part of love in his heart. A perfect love.

"Sigrun," he says, "child born of fire."

Chapter 1

I hear them fighting again. I cannot understand exactly what they are saying, they are down the hall in our father's den, but with my heavy bedroom door shut the words are muted. The tone of what I do hear sounds like this is one of their more serious battles.

An angry chill has infiltrated my home despite the warmth of the summer night air. Frigid tension has my insides wound into an icy ball, heavy and crushing. I venture out of my room to seek comfort in the kitchen and a late night cup of tea. There are a few exchanges between them as I tip-toe down the hall. Hostile words from Merik and frustrated ones from Father, but it is still not enough to understand the conflict. Quickly, I scurry down the stairs before I am discovered eavesdropping.

The kitchen is quiet. I was hoping to get a solid night sleep but this argument could go on for hours. Normally I would be annoyed, like I usually am when Merik has these fits, but honestly I probably won't sleep much tonight anyway.

The fire is dying down in the kitchen hearth so I throw another log in before putting the kettle on. I'm not hungry but I look through the cupboards anyway. I pick up a chunk of bread but set it down again. I don't want to eat, I am just restless.

The kettle doesn't even have a good steam going when I hear a loud slam from upstairs, and the shatter of glass.

Moments later Merik is at the bottom of stairs. He stops suddenly when he sees me. He wasn't expecting me to be down here. His yellow eyes squint with contempt, but I don't know why. I try to mask the startled and confused expression on my face, to be calm and unaffected. Goosebumps rise up on my flesh and betray me. His mouth twists into a grimace and he storms out the door without a word.

As soon as he is gone, I start breathing again. I hadn't realized that I was holding my breath until then. Merik's moods are difficult to keep up with, but whatever has him upset tonight must be very serious.

I take my tea upstairs, anxious to get back to the safe space of my room. I walk up to my father's den and look through the crack of the doorway. He is standing in front of one of his book cases. His back is to me and his hands are clutching the shelves in front of him. He looks as though he is steadying himself. I cannot see his face but I feel his energy, he is defeated. I want to go inside. I want to talk to him and give him comfort, reassure him that Merik will get over this just like he does everything else. I raise my hand to push the door open, but I stop short of it and slowly bring my hand back to the warmth of my cup. I really don't know what to say, and I'm not sure if I would be a comfort to him. Instead, I slink back to my room and quietly close the door.

Chapter 2

This is taking forever. At least, it feels that way. We have been standing here listening to the Headmaster drone on all morning. Stuck in the sunniest part of the square, no shade, no breeze, just standing shoulder to shoulder sweating, and waiting. I probably wouldn't mind it so much if I didn't dislike the Headmaster so much. The Headmaster and his wife are the only two in the village who are in charge of our formal education, and neither of them has ever been kind or accepting of me, or really any other child for that matter.

He is a twitchy man with a lanky build, large eyes, and a long nose. The Mistress on the other hand is a rather fat woman who waddles on the ground like a flightless bird. Ugliness has settled into the permanent frowns they both wear. He paces in front of the group, hands clasped behind his back, clucking about in his usual fashion stopping every so often to scratch at the red hives he almost always has on his neck. Likely from the raspberry tea his wife makes him drink.

I'm not sure if it is better, or worse for my attention span, knowing that this is the last time I will have to endure his lectures.

"Sig," Jae whispers, "are you going to the bon-fire tonight?"

"Of course," I whisper back. "Are you bringing the wine?"

"Of course!" Jae's excitement raises his voice above a whisper, which catches a glaring look from the Headmaster. I immediately feel my cheeks flush.

"Great," I mutter. "He already thinks I'm trouble."

Jae chuckles quietly at my embarrassment.

I look into the crowd. I see my father's white hair. He is standing toward the back. He gives me a smile and a nod. Reassuring me that at least I am not in trouble with him. I smile back.

I continue to look around to see if Merik is here. I do not see him anywhere, which doesn't really surprise me. I didn't hear him come home last night, and I don't know where he is or when he'll be back.

The Headmaster finally ends his speech and sets us free. With a joyous shout, we all fly straight up into the sky. It's official, we are no longer children in the eyes of the community, but we will be enjoying one final summer of adolescent freedom before we submit to adulthood.

I perch on a tree branch, and Jae lands next to me. "Hey, you coming?" he asks.

"Yeah, I'm just going to check in with my father." I look around for him, but he is no longer in the crowd. "Looks like he already took off. I'll just run home, I have to grab a few things anyway. I'll meet you there."

Before I leave, I hear a flutter come up behind us.

"Hey, guys," Ainia wriggles between us. "Are you coming?"

"I'll be there in a bit," I say, "I'm just going to run home first."

She nods at me. "Okay, see you soon," she says discharging me as she turns her attention to Jae.

I shake my head at her dismissal. She does not mean to be rude, but when she is in Jae's presence her manners flutter away as easily as she does. Jae is beautiful, and if he wasn't my best friend I would probably be intimidated by him like most of the other girls in the village.

Ainia has always been infatuated with Jae, even when we were small children. I am the only one she has confided in, but everyone in the village knows how much she likes him. The way she flounders around him is anything but subtle. Jae seems to be the only one ignorant to her feelings.

Why he has never pursued her has been a bit of a mystery to me. Ainia is also very beautiful. Her long blond hair and striking blue butterfly wings set her apart. Even her family name, Darlington, is charming. The match between her and Jae, as far as the community is concerned, would be favorable.

"Jae, are you coming?" she says playfully. She pulls on a long feather of his wing with her thumb and index finger.

He looks from her to me and shrugs his shoulders. "See you later, Sig, hurry up," he says with a smile. They both spring from the branch and take off.

I take off in my own direction, down to my house. Our home is nothing grand, but it is spacious enough for us, and it is safe within a large hollow tree. The familiar smell of spices greet me as soon as I open the door. I walk upstairs to look for my father in his den.

He is sitting at his table looking out the window. It is odd to see him just sitting and staring, usually he is writing in his book, or grinding plants, he hardly ever sits still. His full head of silvery hair and milky white moth wings glow in the sunlight. He looks like a shining pearl held by a luminous oyster. His face is relaxed, but his eyes are focused. It is obvious he is still thinking about his fight with Merik. His intensity is concerning to me.

"Dadda?" I say quietly, trying not to startle him.

He smiles and looks at me, "Hello petal."

I sigh at his pet name for me. It irritates me when he refers to me as something soft and delicate, something that is the antithesis of me. Normally I would argue with him about it, but today I choose to ignore it.

"Are you alright?" I ask him with concern.

"Yes, I'm fine," he pauses and sighs, "your brother has taken off again."

"Yes, I know," I walk closer to him. "I heard you fighting last night," I confess.

"I need you to keep an eye on him, darling. He has never been as strong as you. He is more susceptible to the poisons of this world," he gazes out the window. "He is searching for something he will not find, and I fear he is lost in his own mind."

His request confuses me. I know that physically Merik's thin wasp-like wings make him more vulnerable, but what does he mean by poisons of this world? I don't understand, but I nod to my father's request. I can see his concern for Merik. It has been mounting for years now.

"Is that what you were thinking about?" I asked

"Actually I was thinking mostly about your mother," he pulls a stool up to him and motions for me to sit. "Come here, and sit with me for a moment."

He does not speak of my mother very often. He knows that his sadness brings me guilt.

"You are so much like her."

"Dadda, I don't look anything like her."

"I didn't say you looked like her, I said you were so much like her. You have her strength and her courage."

"How do you mean?" Everyone always speaks of my mother's beauty and kindness. She had a softness and a lightness, she was loved by all. Whereas, I am tough and edgy and I spent the majority of my childhood merely gaining acceptance. I never felt a likeness to her.

"Sigrun, she knew that bringing you into this world would take her out. She knew. We both knew, and we made that choice together."

I feel warmth on my face and heat building in my body unlike anything I have felt before. It is not from the sunlight, but from within me.

"You are part of something bigger," he continues, "I saw you in my dreams before your mother even carried you. She was aware of the pain she would endure to bring you into the world, and that she would never be here to know you." He stops for a moment and calmly puts his hand on mine. Instantly, I feel the heat in my body begin to settle. "She chose your life over her own because it was that important. To know she would die and still make the decision to go forward," he shakes his head at the memory, "she was the bravest women I'd ever known, until you were born."

He has never shared this story with me before. Why he told me now, I do not know. My heart is heavy. I swallow hard and blink back tears.

"But I don't understand what you mean," I use the back of my hand to wipe the tears that did break free. "Why am I important?"

"I know you don't understand, but you will," he wipes my face with his weathered and scarred hands.

I desperately want to ask more questions. I want to know everything about her, about me. What was the vision he had? Why was I burdened? Before I can coax the words out, he speaks again, "And now, to cheer you up, a gift."

In his hand, he holds a small object wrapped in a cloth. I feel the lump in my throat begin to subside. The heat in my body is completely gone now and I smile at my father's gesture.

"You didn't have to get me a gift," I say shyly.

"Go on, open it," he urges. He sits perched at the end of his chair.

I unfold the cloth to reveal a small pendant the size of a marble, which hangs from a silk cord. The marble is made of polished, clear crystal, but inside of it is a tiny, white, baby rose bud. It is beautiful and unlike anything I have ever seen.

"How did you do this?" I ask, "How did you put the rose in the crystal?" I touch the pendant and the rose opens into a small bloom. I gasp in surprise and wonderment before he has a chance to answer.

He takes the ends of the cord, carefully, and ties it around my neck as he explains, "This is a very special object, and its magic works only for you. It feels your heart, and it will guide you when you are lost." The marble feels cool against my skin. "It will constantly change as you do, and it may surprise you at times. It is a part of you and you should always keep it with you."

"This is, amazing. I don't know what... or how... I mean," I stumble through my own words. Finally, I stop and look at him and simply say, "Thank you. I love you Dadda."

"I love you too, Sigrun." He hugs me tightly. "Now go on, get out of here. Go meet your friends, and take this with you," he hands me a small envelope filled with a tea like substance. "If you are going to drink that swill that Jae calls wine, make sure you mix some of this in it, you won't feel so terrible tomorrow."

"What wine? I don't know what you are referring to Dadda," I respond coyly. I smile and snatch the envelope out of his hand, and kiss him on the cheek, "But I'll take it anyway."

As I dart to the door, he calls out, "Sigrun, remember what I said about Merik."

"I will, Dadda."

"I'm very proud of you child."

I smile at him before I leave his den.

I run into my room and change out of my dress and put on a light cotton summer shirt and shorts. I glance at my reflection in the mirror. My wavy brown hair looks wild and unruly, though it usually does. I am not beautiful like Ainia is. She is delicate and fair. My features are stronger, more muscular. I do think my eyes are pretty, though. They are violet, which is not a common color, and they stand out against my dark green wings. My new accessory shines in the sunlight streaming through the window. It is the most beautiful thing I own.

I grab the envelope with the tea and put it in my pack before I fly out the door. I look over my shoulder back at the house, and feel a little confused about everything that my father has told me, about Merik, about myself. I shake my head. I'll worry about that later. For now I am just eager to celebrate with friends. Looking forward again, I head toward the creek.

Chapter 3

By the time I make it to the river, the party is well on its way. There is a good-sized fire roaring down by the shore, and judging by the laughing and shouting the wine is in vast supply. As I scan the crowd, looking for my friends, I see something out of the corner of my eye, a blur of blue and gray heading right toward me. Before I can turn my head, I am hit hard on the side and knocked down to the ground.

"Rule number one Sig: always pay attention to your surroundings," the assaulter preaches.

The snickering voice is familiar. It is Vidar, one of my classmates. He is standing over me with a few of his minions. I am not injured but his tackle knocked the wind out of me. I am struggling to breathe.

"Vidar, you are such a louse!" I finally manage through my gasps. He smiles at me and extends his hand to help me up. It is actually more sportsmanlike of him than normal.

"I'm just playing with you, Sig, for old time's sake. No hard feelings, huh."

I take his hand, stand, and dust myself off. By this point, I look up and notice that everyone is staring at me.

"One of these days Vidar, I'm really going to give you the proper beating you deserve," I say as I start to walk away.

"I look forward to that, Sig," he shouts after me.

I look back at him and see he is still smiling at me. His gray eyes are still focused on me while his friends, Soren and Ragnar, punch him on the shoulders in victory. Unfortunately, Vidar is quite handsome and his gaze is transforming my annoyance into embarrassment.

I finally see Jae and Ainia, they are heading toward me. "Hey, are you alright?" Jae asks. "He hit you pretty hard," Jae is speaking to me but looking over my shoulder. He is staring at Vidar. Jae has always been a bit protective of me.

"I'm fine. He just surprised me, that's all," I protest.

I hear a humming behind me. In a flash of teal and green, my friend Malyn lands next to me as well. She is very petite, but her hummingbird wings make her incredibly fast.

"Sig, are you okay?" she asks while tucking her short red hair behind her ear.

"Yes! Yes! I am okay! I would like to move on to other things please," I head toward the fire to warm up. Jae follows me. "Oh, here," I hand the envelope my father gave me to him. "My father wanted you to have this," I say with a sly smile.

"Oh yeah," he looks at the tea. "Is this what I think it is?" he asks with a smile.

"Uh-huh. No headaches tomorrow," I smile at him.

"Your old man is the best."

"Yes, he is," I say in agreement.

Malyn and Ainia have fluttered off somewhere and Jae and I are sitting by the fire alone. I can feel he is looking at me.

"Hey," he breaks the silence, "what's that?" He points to my pendant.

"Oh, it's a gift from my father."

"Wow, I've never seen anything like it," he reaches out to touch it. I can feel him coming in close to me, my neck tightens up. He extends his finger to touch the marble and a small volt of electricity generates from the marble shocks him.

"Ouch!"

"Oh, are you okay?" I start seriously, and then I cannot help but to laugh, "I'm sorry, I didn't know it could do that." That is the truth, I had no idea that my pendant could do that, but my father had said that it would surprise me.

"Yeah, I'm fine," he puts his finger in his mouth to soothe the burn. "I just wasn't expecting that," he starts laughing as well, but still looks at me with curious eyes. He sits back and looks around. "Do you want to get out of here for a bit? I want to show you something," he says.

"Sure, should I get the others?"

"Not this time, come on, we don't have much daylight left."

He stands up and then takes my hand to help me up. As we start to fly, I realize he is still holding my hand.

We fly down the river a considerable ways. Flying so fast, it is almost like a race, but without the care of winning. The trees around us are a blur of green. I glide low enough to stream my fingers in the cool water. The sun has softened, and everything is glowing. It has turned out to be the most beautiful summer day.

We finally arrive at the waterfall. The waterfall is not an uncommon place for us to go. Often fairies fly here to collect certain fruits and flowers that only grow in this place, but it was the first time Jae brought me out here.

"You brought me to the waterfall? Why?"

He hovers over the water's edge, and dips his toes in the water. He turns back to me and takes off his shirt. I immediately, and awkwardly, look around at everything but him. We have played together all our lives and I have seen him shirtless many times before, but looking at him now it was different. I see everything: the golden streaks in his brown hair, the graceful beauty of his broad wings. Almost overnight he has developed a more muscular body. It was obvious we are no longer children. At some point, he became a man.

"Come on, Sig, I know you can swim," he says as he shoots up into the air and somersaults into the water.

"Show off!" I shout. "Just because I know how to swim doesn't mean I want to go swimming."

He surfaces and slicks his wavy, wet hair out of his face. "Sig, come on. Quit being a stick in the mud. Trust me."

I look at him and he has his hands stretched out toward me, waving me in.

"Would you look the other way please?" I say self-consciously.

"Sigrun, hurry up," he says ignoring my request.

Timidly, I walk into the water, wishing I had worn clothes made of a more robust fabric. The thin cotton clings to me. In an attempt to protect my modesty, I use my wings to cover up.

I reach out to take his extended hand. Suddenly he grabs me and playfully dunks me under the water. The water is cold. It is a shock that I feel all the way to the top of my head. When I make it back to the surface, he is laughing. It has become clear to me that, though I see him as a man, he still regards me as a little girl.

"What's wrong with you? Water went up my nose," I say, coughing and hacking.

"Sorry, Sig," he says through his laughter, "I just wanted to get the hard part over with."

"How very thoughtful of you," I say with shivering sarcasm. "So was this it? Can I get out of the water now?"

"No, follow me and hold your breath," he takes a deep breath in and dives into the water. I see him swim under the waterfall. I pause for a moment, not sure what to do, and then I hear him shout through the veil of water. "Hey, it's fine, you coming or what?"

I take a breath, dive into the water, and head for the waterfall. The water was cold, and the closer I get to the waterfall the darker it becomes. Then I feel the force of the waterfall beating down on my back and wings. I feel Jae's hand on my wrist. He helps me find my footing. We are in a tight space between the waterfall and the stone cliff behind us. It is very loud with the waterfall crashing and the echo off of the stone.

"Now what?" I shout, wiping water from my eyes.

"We're almost there," he shouts back.

"Almost where?" Looking around at the small space we are standing in, I cannot see any other way out but the way we came in. "Where are we possibly going to go from here?"

He smiles, "Hold your breath, and make it a long one." He ducks under the water, and then comes right back, "Oh and tuck your wings back tightly, you don't want to get stuck."

Stuck? I nod though I am incredibly nervous. The idea of getting stuck underwater did not sit well, but Jae has never put me in danger before so I agree to follow him. As soon as I duck under the water line, I see a tunnel. It is dark in the tunnel and it seems to go on forever. At least, it feels that way because I have no idea when I might get my next breath. I keep swimming forward, pushing myself hard. My chest is starting to feel like it might explode, and the tunnel is too tight for me to turn around. I start to panic. Just then, the darkness in the tunnel starts to lift. There is a light coming from the other end. I push myself even more. I swim harder than I ever have. I see Jae ahead of me, he has reached the end and I watch him swim to the top. I finally make it to the top myself, and I take in my first deep breath, my chest is throbbing, but the rush feels good.

Looking around for the first time, I realize it was all worth it. Jae has found a cavern behind the waterfall, and it is the most spectacular thing I have ever seen. The rock around the pool had been smoothed down over time, forming dark glass-like surfaces. The walls and ceiling are covered in crystals, of all different colors and it is incredibly bright. Even the water in the pool is warmer. The cavern floor is covered by extremely fine sand, it feels like liquid silk wrapped around my toes. I grab a handful of it so see it up close. It shimmers like crushed gemstones.

"Oh my goodness, we are inside a giant geode," I say in awe. "This is amazing, it is so bright. How is it so bright? Where does the light come from?" Looking up, the ceiling appears completely closed in, so I can't figure out where the light source is coming from.

"It is hard to see," Jae explains, "but there is a very small hole up at the top which allows a single beam of sunlight to shine through." My eyes follow his finger as he points upward to explain, "That single beam reflects onto one crystal, which then reflects on ten others, and then those ten reflect on ten more, and ten more, and so on."

"I can't believe this place has been here all along. How did you find this?"

"I had come out to the waterfall one day…"

"By yourself?" I interrupt.

"Yes," he smiles at me, "I was swimming and before I knew it I was under the waterfall, and saw the tunnel. I guess you could call it curiosity, but it was more like something was pulling me here, and once I saw this." He pauses for a moment and looks down, "I knew I had to bring you here."

The splendor of it is overwhelming and I hug him tightly.

"Thank you," I say still holding onto him, "I'm so glad you did."

When I look at him again, he looks different. His eyes are softer, like he doesn't have a care in the world.

The light in the cavern starts to dim and takes my attention away from him. Jae sees me notice the dimming light and spoke before I could express my concern.

"It is the setting sun outside," he explains, "the last time I came here I brought a candle. As soon as my hands dry, I'll light it."

I swim over to one of the steps and hoist myself up out of the water and sit on the smooth step. I am self-conscious because my water soaked clothes are clinging, outlining my shape. Awkwardly I cross my wings around my torso. Jae grabs the candle from behind a rock on the other side if the cavern. Once he successfully lights the candle, the room is as bright as it was when we first arrived.

"There now we can stay here for a while," he says as he makes his way back over to me. He tries to hop up next to me, but the way I have positioned my wings takes up most of the room on the step. "Hey, move your wing would you. Make a little room," he says while tugging on my wing that is wrapped around my body.

"Oh, sure, sorry," I move my wing away, and cross my arms across my body instead.

As he gets out of the water, the water beads up on his feathery wings. He gently shakes his wings to dry them. My scaly wings hardly absorb any water, so they always dry very fast.

"So, what's going on with your brother?" Jae always gets straight to the point, and since Jae is an only child he has always been intrigued by my family dynamic.

"Oh, he's gone again, but I don't know where," I try to sound casual about it. I don't want Jae to know how much it bothers me, or how bad it was this time.

"I think the only thing worse than not having a brother is having a brother like Merik," Jae says.

"That's not true."

"Oh yes, it is. He is never around, and when he is, he is so mean to you."

"Well, I think he just has a tremendous amount of pressure," I defend.

"To do what?"

"To follow in my father's path. Not everyone can be a healer, even if your parents were. Everyone expects him to be, because in every generation of the Livingstone name there has always been a healer. I think he is drowning in everyone's expectations," I know I am struggling to make my argument. It is a weak point that I am making, but I still feel like I have to defend, or at least explain the bad actions of my brother.

I look at Jae. His eyebrows are raised like he is waiting for me to continue. It is clear he is not going to let me off with this weak explanation.

I sigh and finally speak the truth, "My mother's death was hard on him." I look into Jae's eyes and I see a glimpse of compassion, "He loved her so much, and she died because of me." I know Jae wants to interrupt, but I hold my hand up so I can finish my point, "I feel sadness, and guilt, for my brother's unhappiness, and I think he resents having a monster for a sister and that the monster is loved by our father." I realize all I want for Merik is to come home and to love me also.

Jae lifts my chin with his hand, "I don't ever want you to call yourself that word ever again. Do you understand me?" His usually warm eyes are burning. The intensity of his stare makes my throat feel like it's closing. I can't speak, so I look away and I nod.

After an awkward pause, I change the subject to something less serious, "What are we going to do after the summer?"

"I don't know," he sounds as lost as I feel, "but that is what this summer is for, right? Figure out who we are, who we want to be."

"Yeah, I suppose. I am surprised that you don't have this all figured out already," I joke with him.

"What do you mean?" he asks.

"Well, you are the village golden boy. It makes sense that I, the village misfit, would be shiftless and uncertain, but I thought for sure that you would have all the details put together. Including a little wife with two-point-five kids, and your very own love nest," I say with a jest.

"Wow," he laughs, "I don't know about all that."

"Oh, come on, are you saying you haven't thought about it?"

"Well, sure I've thought about it but," he seems nervous and starts to fidget with a rock that is near him, "I just haven't mapped it all out or anything."

"Well, what about Ainia?" I ask.

"What about Ainia?"

"She is beautiful," I say fishing for information.

"Yes," he says quietly, without looking up, "she is very beautiful."

His affirmation of her beauty unexpectedly nips my heart. It is the first stab of jealousy that I have ever felt.

I experience envy all the time. I have always been different from the other girls. I have often wished to have their beautiful feathers or bright delicate features, but I never felt this kind of sting. I quickly try to snap myself out of this self-pity.

"But," he continues, "she isn't the only pretty girl in the village."

I start to feel even worse. I begin to uncomfortably fiddle with my pendant. I wish I had never started this conversation.

"I think you are beautiful," he says. That comment shocks me, and I nervously laugh. With the exception of my father, I have never been called beautiful before, unique maybe, but never beautiful. The compliment makes me somewhat uncomfortable. I feel hotness on my face.

"Hey," Jae changes his tone. He is looking at my pendant, "The rose, the rose in your necklace, it's pink now."

"What?" I look down and sure enough the white rose has changed to a subtle shade of pink.

"It's pink," he says again. "Almost like it's blushing," he is smiling at me.

His attention makes the rose flush even more. I quickly cover it with my hand.

"Huh, well that's funny," I say as nonchalantly as possible. I hop off the rock and back into the pool, "Well, we should probably get back."

"Yeah, you're right," he says jumping back into the water. Before I could dive down, he grabs my shoulders and looks into my eyes, "Sig?"

"Yeah," I squeak out. His sudden intensity makes me nervous again.

"This place, can we keep this between us? Like, it's our place?"

"Sure. Yeah," I feel relieved that he wants to keep this place a secret. I start to pull away, but he pulls me back in, the room feels like it is closing in around me.

"One more thing," he begins looking at me in a very serious way. Not knowing what he is going to say or do next I hold my breath, "We're always going to be friends, right? No matter what?"

I breathe. I'm not sure what I feel, but it resembles disappointment. I don't know what I was expecting him to say, but the fact that he will never see me in any way beyond platonic makes me feel a little sad.

"No," I say with a small sigh. His brow furrows and his mouth twists down. "We'll always be *best* friends," I say finally. This makes him smile showing off all of his gleaming white teeth.

He dives down and is off through the tunnel. Standing there for a second by myself I look around one more time at the beauty of this place. He could have brought anyone here, but he brought me, and even though we are just friends, it makes me feel good. I take a deep breath and head through the tunnel.

******

While we were in the cavern, the night had come. The moon is full, and the reflection on the river is so clear, it looks like two moons are stacked on top of each other. By the time we make it back to the camp site, the party is in a roar of activity. Some kids are playing instruments and dancing, while others are huddled around the fire.

I find a spot by the fire so I can warm up. My hair is still wet, and has given me a chill. Jae leaves me by the fire to get something to eat.

Behind me, two familiar figures land in a very sloppy fashion. In a tangled up ball of blue and teal, Ainia and Malyn giggle their wings free of each other.

"Hey, Sig." Malyn slurs.

"Where did you fly off to?" Ainia chimes in. She also seems to have found her way into a wine bottle.

"And why are you all wet?" Malyn asks while touching my hair.

They are both looking at me with inquisitive eyes, and I actually don't know what to say. I can't tell them about the cavern, and I don't want Ainia to think I am keeping any secrets. I also know she would be hurt that I was with Jae and she wasn't invited.

"Oh, I, uh, just went for a swim, in the creek. Yeah, I just felt like going for a swim, that's all," I stutter out.

"Alone?" Ainia asks. Her blue eyes stare into mine. I swallow hard. At this point, I figure she has already seen Jae, and noticed his feathers are still wet.

"No, I wasn't alone," neither Malyn nor Ainia change their expressions. It was clear I would have to continue. "I was just with Jae," I say in a cavalier tone. Ainia narrows her eyes a bit, and I instantly feel like I am on trial.

"Oh," Malyn sounds disappointed, "Vidar had taken off for a little while too, so I thought maybe…"

"Maybe what?" I ask. She shrugs as though suggesting I had run off with him. I am appalled by the thought, "Eww, no! I would never. I can't stand that guy."

"Okay, okay, I was just throwing it out there. He's not that bad," she sounds a little defensive.

"Malyn," Ainia coos, "would you be a darling and grab some water."

I know sending Malyn away is just a way for her to be alone with me for a minute.

"Sure," Malyn chirps.

"Thank you sweetie, take your time."

As soon as Malyn is out of earshot, Ainia moves in very close to me and tightly grabs my shoulder.

"Okay, what happened? Tell me everything, what did you say? What did he say?" The interrogation is like rapid fire. I don't even know what to answer first, or what she means with her questions. Is she mad that I was with Jae? Does she think something happened between us? Or, is she worried I told him about her feelings?

"Well I… nothing happened," I start, "what do you…"

"Did he say anything about me?" She cuts me off, and I am glad she does. Now I am sure that she really is just curious to see if he took me aside to talk to about her. The thought of him ever being interested in me never entered her mind.

"Oh. Well, let me see," I can see that she is impatient. Unfortunately, the majority of our conversation had nothing to do her, which would crush her. "He, ah… oh, he said he thought you were beautiful."

It is the truth he did say that. I figure the fact that it was prompted by me is irrelevant.

"He thinks I'm beautiful," she beams, "and, what else?"

"Oh, um," I am trying to think how to spin the rest in her favor, but he really didn't give me much else to work with. "He said he hasn't really mapped out that part of his life yet," her posture instantly melts, reading her disappointment I continue, "but, you know just because he isn't ready to start building a nest doesn't mean he doesn't like you, he is just a guy who moves at his own pace. You know, he needs to find himself first." I feel I have done my best to smooth everything over.

"And, he said, he thought I was beautiful?" she asks again, her posture starting to perk back up.

"He said, he thought you were *very* beautiful," I re-enforce. With that, she is back to beaming, and just in time for Malyn's return.

"Hey, May, let's go dance," Ainia jumps up and grabs Malyn's hand. "Come on, Sig, come dance with us."

"I'll be there in a bit. I just want to finish drying off."

I watch the girls flutter over to where the rest of our friends are dancing. Ainia grabs Jae on her way and tugs his arm grudgingly to dance with her. He looks over her shoulder and makes eye contact with me. I know dancing is not his strongest attribute, but I shrug my shoulders at him, and urge him to just go with it.

Turning back to the fire I slide down to the ground and rest my head on a fallen branch. I take my necklace off and stare into the bead, the rose has changed back to white. I hold it tightly in my hand. I start to feel very drowsy. Lying there I go through all of the day's events in my head. Most of it I don't understand, and as I reel through it all my eyelids become very heavy. Finally I succumb to sleep.

Chapter 4

The heat of the fire diminishes and I feel cold and alone. I open my eyes and I am home in my bed. How did I get here? I do not remember coming home. My head feels cloudy, everything is distorted. Then I hear breaking glass and sounds of a struggle.

There is shouting, but I can't make out any of the voices or words. I jump out of my bed, but for some reason my legs don't work, and I fall to the ground. It feels like I have been drugged. I start thinking. Did someone put something in my drink at the party? I don't even remember eating or drinking anything. Everything around me is blurry. I cannot focus on anything.

I struggle to stand myself up. The commotion is coming from downstairs in the living room. I make my way to the bottom of the stairs with a great deal of difficulty. Everything is moving in slow motion. It is like the ground is made of quick sand, like I am sinking into the ground with every step. I finally make it to the bottom.

At first, I don't see anything, it is dark and my eyes are still trying to adjust. I turn toward the fireplace and I see my father on the ground in a puddle of blood. He is barely alive. He sees me and reaches a shaking, bloody hand out to me. I want to run to him, but I still can't move. The breath in my body is shallow like there isn't enough oxygen in the room.

Suddenly, the temperature in the room drops significantly. The cold stings every surface of my body. Even my scaly wings are aching from the cold. I look to the other side of the room and see Merik, he has come home. The relief I feel when I see him is quickly extinguished. He is on his knees holding his side. The expression on his face when he sees me is pure terror. He is laboring to breathe, and every breath he takes is shown by the cold air. Merik also reaches his hands toward me, the same way my father did. As he reaches out, I see the blood on his hands.

My legs collapse again and I fall to the ground. When I open my eyes, I see that I am looking at my own reflection in the floor. The wood has turned to a black glass, like volcanic glass. It is certainly not like anything that we have in these parts of the forest. None of this makes any sense. It is now that I realize that I am dreaming.

Even though I know this is a dream I let it continue. I look at my reflection. My face is different. My image is leaner. There is gauntness in my cheeks. My eyes are no longer violet, but a flaming red. My long brown hair is gone leaving my head bald, but instead of skin my head is covered with scales like the scales on my wings. My expression has so much rage. My image in the reflection suddenly roars. The sound is something that I have never heard before. It is a sound that would come from a beast not a fairy. My teeth are predatory, pointy and sharp with razor sharp canines. My image suddenly pounces, shattering the glass, trying to grab at me. It happens so fast that I don't even have time to scream. Then everything goes dark.

I wake up with a start. I struggle to breathe. Jae is kneeling over me, his face inches from mine.

"Whoa, easy," he whispers. I look around and the sky is still dark, but not for long. The first thing I do is run my tongue across my teeth. I relax a bit when I realize they are all still flat.

The fire has burned down to just a few crackling cinders. The faint glow outlines the shapes of our friends who are all around us sleeping.

"That must have been some dream you had," he continues as he helps me up.

"I think nightmare is a more accurate description," I say, though I'm still fighting for breath.

"What was it about?"

"My father," I pause, "and my brother." A sick feeling creeps into my stomach. The dream felt too real. A surge of panic jolts through me, "Jae, I think something is wrong."

"What do you mean?" He is looking at me with concern.

"I'm not sure, but I feel like my father and brother are in trouble, or hurt," I pause again. Closing my eyes, I search through my dream again. I see the blood soaking through my father's robe. Merik is kneeling on the floor, clutching his side with blood dripping from his fingers. I look at Jae and finally utter, "Or worse."

My voice has a level of gravity that has affected him. His eyes search mine, as though he is trying to see what I had seen in my dream.

He straightens his body and looks up to the sky. "Okay, let's go," he says, "if it was just a dream, and everyone is okay, we can tell your father about it and maybe he knows what it means, and if your father is in danger, I'm going to help him get out of it."

We both take off with urgency. Jae is ahead of me, as he always is, but this time it wasn't competition driving him, it is concern.

My own fear hits me so hard, it pumps through my veins. I am pushing my wings harder and faster than I ever have. My wings are burning from the intensity of the pace. As much as I want to make sure my dream is just a dream, I am terrified to find out the possibility that it is real.

My home isn't very far from the camp, but this feels like the longest flight I have ever taken. On the way, I keep replaying what I had seen in my mind. It was so vivid, and the sensations I felt were so real.

By the time we reach my house, the sun is starting to come up. We land just outside the front door. Cautiously, we look in the window by the door. Nothing seems out of place, and we don't see anyone inside.

Jae grabs my arm before I go in. "Let me go in first," he says.

I nod. The courage that I had mustered seems to be dwindling. My mouth has gone dry and I feel dizzy.

He starts to open the door, and it suddenly dawns on me that we are entering completely unarmed. If someone is inside, the element of surprise would be completely wasted if we don't have any defenses.

"Wait," I grab him, "my father's sword hangs on the wall in the main room." I whisper, "Grab that first, before searching the house."

He nods quickly, "Okay."

His breathing is accelerated and his pupils are dilated. I can tell he is as nervous as I am.

He opens the door quietly and as soon as I am in the room I spring to the wall where my father's sword rests. I gasp when I reach for it. It is gone. I turn quickly, Jae is standing right behind me his eyes are wide. We both freeze, and listen. The house is silent. It is so silent that I can hear my own heartbeat, which is escalating every second.

The rest of the room is all in order. There is nothing that indicates there has been any kind of struggle. My mind reels. Did someone merely break in to steal the sword? Or, maybe my father had simply taken the sword down himself. Could all this panic be for nothing?

Jae puts his finger to his lips, instructing me to remain silent. He points up to the ceiling. He is going upstairs to search the rest of the house. I nod in agreement.

With the sword gone, I need to find some kind of weapon. I settle on a long stick by the fireplace that we use to stoke the fire. Jae grabs a knife from the kitchen. Then we both head up the stairs. Jae and I go into my father's room first. Just as the living room is, nothing has been disturbed. The bed is made. My father hadn't gone to bed last night, which is not all that strange. He has always been a night person. Perhaps he fell asleep in his den while working on a potion, or writing in his book. Despite my rational explanation the sick feeling in my stomach starts to flare up again.

I make my way back into the hallway. The door of my father's den is slightly ajar. A sliver of sunshine peeks through the door. I hold my breath while I look through the crack. I can't see anything except the corner of my father's desk.

There are a few papers scattered on the floor which isn't strange, but something feels wrong. I push the door open. The light from the window in front of the desk blinds me for a moment. My eyes adjust and I see my father sitting in his chair with his head resting in a book on his desk. Just as I thought, he fell asleep while reading. I finally exhale. The sun is shining on his hair just as it had the day before. I put the stick down and walk over to wake him.

"Dadda, wake up," I say quietly. I put my hand on his shoulder. The cold stiffness of his body causes me to recoil immediately. My eyes widen, and I take in the scene again.

Papers are scattered across the room, bottles are knocked over on the desk and floor. Several pages from the book my father's head is resting on are torn, and what at first looked like spilled ink, I now realize is blood. His blood. It trickles from the desk into a puddle of dark red liquid at his feet. I feel wetness on my fingertips. I look down at my hand. Blood drips down my fingers and onto my palm.

Staggering backwards, my heel steps on a broken bottle slicing my foot, but I don't feel anything. I can't breathe. I can't breathe and I want to scream. Without the air in my lungs, I choke on my horror.

Everything feels like it is going dark. The room begins to spin. It takes all that I have not to fall to the floor and vomit. A hand touches my shoulder. I spin around wildly. I find myself looking into familiar brown eyes burdened with pain, and welled with tears. I had forgotten that Jae was even with me. Jae sees the look on my face and the blood on my hand and knows everything.

He holds me so tightly. His arms and wings are binding. When my legs finally give out, he kneels down to the ground with me. I finally draw in a breath and I exhale out a guttural scream of all the pain I feel. I cry and convulse so hard my body feels like it is going to break. My face burns with hot, stinging, tears.

I close my eyes tightly, hoping that when I open them I will wake up. I'm still hoping that this all part of the same wicked nightmare. But, this is real, this is *all* real. I can't speak in words, only in sobs. I cry into Jae's chest until my anguish has taken a turn into hyperventilation. I can't breathe. I can't breathe. My hands desperately clench Jae's shirt.

"Breathe, Sigrun," he is coaching me, "come on, breathe honey," but I can't, I can't. My eyes go dark and I lose consciousness.

******

Time goes by. I'm not sure how much. When I start to wake, everything feels strange. My head feels heavy. I have no idea how long I have been out. I am on the ground outside of my house.

The image of my father's dead body floods back into my mind. The tears instantly return. Jae is sitting next to me. His eyes are red and swollen. His shirt is smeared with blood and sweat from my hands, and tears from us both. My neighbor, Beda Winterborn, is also kneeling next to me. She is an older woman who from time to time would work with my father on medicines. She and her husband, Akin, have been trusted friends of my father's for many years. Her face is distraught with what she has discovered this morning.

"Oh, she's waking," Beda says as she clutches my hand.

"Hey, Sig," Jae says quietly as he attempts to smile. He is still very upset, but he seems relieved that I am awake. I start to sit up, but the rush of blood to my head forces me lie back down immediately. "Take it easy, Sig," Jae orders.

"That's right child," Beda chimes in. "You're in shock. I need you to drink this."

She holds a bottle with a thin milky liquid up to my mouth. It is bitter and chalky which makes it hard to swallow. Some of the drink runs down the side of my face.

"That's good," Beda says to me as she wipes the liquid from my face and then she takes a cool wet rag and wipes the salt from my eyes and cheeks left by my tears. Her kindness makes me think of my mother, more specifically the mother I never knew. The absence of a mother and now the loss of my father seem too much to bear, and the agony swells up inside of me again. Before I start to cry, I gently move her hand away and sit up.

More people are crowding around. My friends have made their way back from camp and followed the commotion.

Jae's father, Falon, and Akin come out of my house, and they both have very grave expressions. Falon sees that I have regained consciousness and he walks toward me.

Falon is the leader of our community. He is very tall with brown eagle wings, white hair and beard. I have always been intimidated by him. However, today his intense yellow eyes have softened. He bends down on one knee so he can speak directly to me.

"Sigrun," he starts, his voice is deep and smooth "I don't think it is a good idea for you to go back into the house until we have things straightened out." He pauses for my response. I can only nod in agreement. "Do you have somewhere you can stay?"

"Yes," I manage to say, although I really have no idea where I am going to go.

"Okay, good," he looks over at Jae, and then back at me, "my son told me you had a dream, can you tell it to me now?"

The devastation of finding my father had completely overwhelmed me and I had forgotten about Merik. He was in my dream as well, and he was also injured. His life might also be in danger, he might be dead. Panic suddenly surges through me. I stand up frantically, but quickly lose my balance.

"Merik!" I exclaim. "We have to find him, I-I have to find him."

"We will," Falon starts to say in a calming tone, but I cut him off.

"No, you don't understand, I think he is in danger, he might be in serious danger."

Beda and her husband are holding me, trying to calm me down.

"Sigrun," Falon speaks very calmly, "we are going to find your brother, I swear to you. I'm sure he is fine. Do you have any idea where he is?" Falon's reassuring tone brings my attention back to him.

I shake my head. "No, no he... he has been gone for two days now, but I don't know where," I reply.

"He takes off all the time," Jae adds.

"That's right," I start again. "He takes off for periods of time, days, weeks, but this time something is wrong," I say urgently.

"Okay," Falon replies, "we'll find him, I promise. First, let's go back to that dream you had."

I tell him the entire dream. I disclose every detail as clearly as I can. It is just as terrifying the second time. I explain the struggle to move, the blood, my father, Merik, even my horrid image in the reflection. By the time I finish, a large crowd is standing in front of my house.

Tragedy doesn't happen often in our village. Most of our people die of old age, warmly in our beds surrounded by our loved ones. This has shocked and terrified everyone.

Ainia comes up behind me and drapes a blanket over my wings. Even though the day is warm, I am shivering.

"Sig," Ainia says in a small voice, "you're going to stay with me, okay?" She is looking at me with her big blue eyes, brimming with tears.

We start to walk away, and I turn back to Falon suddenly, "Wait," I begin, "can you tell me what happened to my father?"

He sighs. I think he was hoping I wouldn't ask for details. "Best we can tell at this point, someone came in found him in his den, possibly stole some items and killed him in the process."

"I mean, how did he die?" I ask more directly.

Falon looks directly into my eyes and without emotion he speaks, "He was stabbed in the abdomen with a long sharp object, most likely the sword that has gone missing." He pauses for a moment. I think he expects me to start sobbing again. When I do not, he proceeds, "But it seems the fatal wound was his neck. It was slit open."

The graphic nature of his death is alarming. I can't think of anyone who would kill my father, especially so savagely. He had no enemies. He was one of the most peaceful men in the village. Everyone regarded him with the utmost respect. The person who could bring forth such a violent end to such a benevolent man was surely not a fairy of our sort.

"Sigrun," Falon adds as I start walking away, "we'll let you know when you can return home."

Home? This was no longer the home that I knew.

Chapter 5

On the day of my father's burial, it was threatening to rain. Under normal circumstances a burial would be postponed due to weather. For fairies with more fragile wings, like Ainia and Merik, heavy storms can be dangerous. The precarious skies should have been a deterrent, but it was obvious the colony wanted to put my father's death behind them.

Falon's older brother Vivek led the ceremony. I have always liked Vivek. He is incredibly wise and even though he has the same intense yellow eyes as Falon, he is not quite as intimidating as his brother. It is fitting that he possesses wings of the spotted owl, a large judicious bird of prey.

I'm sure the service is lovely and heart felt, but honestly I don't listen to a word he says. I just sit under the large heart-shaped leaves of a Homalomena tree with Jae, Ainia, and Malyn.

I probably wouldn't have even gotten dressed this morning if it hadn't been for Ainia. She dressed me in one of her dark blue petal dresses, and brushed my hair while I stared out the window. I haven't looked in a mirror in days.

At the ceremony, tears are shed, people comfort each other, and my life is in tatters. Merik is still missing and my anxiety over it is suffocating. Reconciling the death of my father has not been easy. I still forget he is dead. Even sitting at his funeral it doesn't feel real to me. The service is being held without my brother, and that feels wrong. I have spent a lot of my life feeling alone, but never so much as right now. I know I have my friends sitting next to me, but the void in my heart is overwhelming.

A flash of lightning and a crack of thunder move the ceremony along. A few raindrops begin to fall. The patter of the rain against the leaves drown out the voices. I actually take comfort in that.

I watch my father's body, wrapped in silk, be lowered by Jae, Falon, Akin, and Vivek. It is my turn to cover him with earth and finish the ceremony. I stand up, but I feel like I'm outside of my body, almost like I'm sleepwalking. Once I get to the edge of the grave, I look down at my father's body. I feel dizzy, like I'm going to fall in. I start to blackout and sway, before I fall I clutch my rose pendant and I suddenly steady. My feet feel rooted to the ground. I take the rose that I'm holding in my other hand, I kiss the silky bulb, and drop it into the grave.

A few villagers quickly cover the grave and place rocks as a headstone. The rain is coming down hard now. The rest of the villagers urgently head back to their homes while I stay and stare at the grave well past the end of the burial. I am aware that my friends are leaving and trying to get me out of the rain, but I cannot move, not yet. I can't even look away from the grave.

* * * * * *

Eventually I head back to my house. I have not been there since I found my father's body. Last night I argued with Jae about coming home. I think back on the conversation while I walk in the rain, and how angry he was.

"Sigrun, do you honestly expect me to let you go back there?" Jae shouted at me.

Ainia told him I was intending to go home after the funeral. I just stood there staring out Ainia's bedroom window while he yelled.

"Listen to me. I overheard my father and uncle talking. They believe someone has crossed our borders. Someone is crazy enough and angry enough to kill your father for no reason, and maybe kidnap your brother. You might be next."

I know he is concerned, but his words didn't resonate with me.

"I don't care," I said, continuing my gaze out the window.

"I care!" He shouts again. He ran his hands though his wavy brown hair in frustration. "Just stay here with Ainia," he pleaded.

I finally looked into his eyes. He looked desperate, but I still knew I had to go home.

"No. I'm going home."

"Then let me stay with you."

I shook my head, "No. I want to be alone." I turned my gaze back to the window. He stormed out of the room and started talking to Ainia, but I didn't bother listening.

Now, standing in front of the door, I know I should be afraid to stay in my house, but I'm not. I want this person to come back. It might be the best chance to find Merik, and the only opportunity to get justice.

Beda had gone into my house to clean yesterday. I suppose she didn't want me to come home to blood stained floors. It is dark inside, and the air feels thick. It smells like pine and lilac. No doubt Beda tried to overpower the stench of death. The perfume only makes my head hurt. Everything looks the same as it normally does, and yet feels completely different.

I immediately walk up to my father's den. The desk and chair had been cleaned as well as the floor. The papers that were scattered on his desk are now stacked in neat piles along with his books. It is quiet. All I can hear is the sound of the rain. I look down at the floor and notice I brought in puddles of water with my soaked body. I light a fire in the den and the smell of the burning wood and the crackle of the fire come as a comfort to me. A little bit of warmth on this dismal day.

Once I have a good fire going, I sit in my father's chair. Looking out the window, I see Jae. Since I have not let him in my house he has camped outside. He is standing under the waxy leaves of the ivy plant by the front door. I shake my head, and he thinks I'm stubborn.

Of course, eventually Ainia shows up as well. Wherever Jae goes she soon follows. Jae just stands and watches the house as though he is on guard. Ainia keeps trying to get him to leave.

"She will let us know if she needs us," she pleads with him.

"Well, I'm going to be here until she tells me to leave," he responds. "Even then I might not leave. She needs us, she just does not realize it yet, but she does."

Ainia just shakes her head.

"It's going to get really cold tonight," she says in a quieter tone and crosses her arms over her chest. I can't quite tell, but she looks like she is pouting.

I sit back into my father's chair, and my fingers trace the wooden armrests. The wood is warped and worn yet it feels so smooth. He sat in this chair the last time I saw him alive and when I found him murdered. Even though Beda cleaned the house before I came home there is a dark stain that has seeped into the wood. His blood has infused itself into the chair. Afraid that the sight of his blood would upset me she offered to remove the chair entirely, but I refused. Strangely enough I find it to be a comfort. I figure that if his blood so stubbornly stayed behind that perhaps his spirit did as well.

My finger slowly outlines the stain on the chair, and almost hypnotically I begin to gaze into it. The numbness that I have been feeling for the last few days begins to melt away. I feel the love of my father and the heart wrenching feeling of his absence all at once. I feel extreme grief, rage, and fear. My body feels hot all over, and the sound of rattling causes me take notice that I am trembling so hard that I'm shaking the chair. My pendant is searing against my chest. The room feels stifling and steamy. I can hardly breathe. I have to get out of here. I have to leave right now.

Springing upward, I fly straight up to the skylight at the top of the house. I open the latch and swing the door open. The rainwater pours over me, cooling me as if I were red hot iron. I keep flying up to the sky.

Jae sees me and starts to follow me, but I hear Ainia shout after him, "No, Jae, let her go." She grabs his hand and guides him back down to the ground. I am grateful that she stopped him. I do need to be alone.

I race furiously through the branches. The rain drops are large and forceful. It is suicide to be out in these conditions, but I keep going. Emotion is driving me further and further. Through the rain and the leaves I finally make it above the tree line. The little bit of protection that the trees provided against the rain is now gone, the rain is more fierce than ever.

I fly in place, and watch for the first time the splendor of the storm. Tentacles of lightning stretch out across the sky. They are like magnificent blue and purple fingers reaching out elegantly to touch the trees. So powerful. So beautiful. I feel the charge of electricity running through my body. It is almost magnetic. I know how dangerous it is for me to be up here now, but I'm not afraid. Strangely among the chaos I feel a moment of peace.

In this moment, I realize that I can no longer sit and wait. There is nothing for me here. I have to leave the village, and at least try to find Merik. Maybe we can reconcile, and together perhaps we can find the person who killed our father.

Chapter 6

Jae comes into my house as I am gathering my pack together.

"What are you doing?" he asks. I am so preoccupied I don't even look at him.

"I'm leaving."

"Leaving? Leaving where?" He sounds genuinely concerned.

"I'm leaving the village," I finally look up at him. His eyes are sad and confused.

"Why? Where are you going to go?"

"I'm not exactly sure. I guess I'm going to see if I can track Merik."

"Sigrun, this is totally insane. You don't know where he went. You don't even know which direction to start looking. The rain most likely erased all of his tracks on and off the ground. You won't find him that is if…," he stops himself, but we both know what he is going to say next, "that is if he is even still alive." He has a hard time saying the last part, but I think he has wanted to bring up the possibility that Merik may be dead for a few days now. The search party that Falon put together was short lived and yielded no results. The promise that was made to find him has been dropped like a heavy stone. No one wants to pick it up again.

I turn my attention back to my packing. I gather some food, a water canteen, a few medicinal plants from my father's den, and lastly I take a dagger from a drawer in my father's desk. The dagger is dusty. It is obvious that it has not been touched in years. Our village has not needed such weapons so they just sit, rusting, and gathering dust.

"Are you even going to talk to me Sig?" he asks while following me around my house. I turn to him before I reach the door.

"I have to get out of here!" I explode. "I have to try. I know it doesn't make sense, but I can't sit in this house any longer."

The truth is I had expected this villain to surface by now, but he hasn't, and the waiting is agony. I want Jae to understand how miserable it is for me here, but I don't want him to think I'm looking for trouble either.

"Everything about this house is painful for me. I am drowning here. Don't you understand that?" My tone has changed to pleading. He sighs and reaches for my hand.

"I'll go with you," he says sweetly.

He is being so nice to me and I have been so awful. I feel terrible.

"No," I respond gently. "You need to stay here. You have your own life to figure out, and besides I think it would do me good to get some space."

I know he sees in my eyes that there is nothing he can say to change my mind.

His hand is so warm, it makes it hard to let go. I reach my arms up around his neck to hug him. He strongly puts his arms around my waist and wraps his wings fully around me.

"You come home in one piece," he says, "and soon, okay."

The lump in my throat is indicative of how much I am going to miss him.

"Okay," I quickly kiss him on the cheek and take off through the door. I turn around once and see that he has not moved from the doorway and he is still watching me. He watches me until I fade from sight.

Chapter 7

I really have no clue where to go. Merik never told us where he went on these trips he took. There is no reason for him to head north to the bee colony. The east consists mostly of mountains and plains. It seems wisest to stay close to a water source. Following the river south seems to be the most rational plan.

Slowly flying along the river I look for any trace of him. I search for campfire ashes, traces of food. I even look for indentations in the earth from where he might have slept. But, I find nothing. For miles I fly and search and find no trace of him.

Nighttime is coming and I am exhausted. I light a small fire along the riverbed and fill my canteen with fresh water. I discover some wild blackberry bushes and gather a few berries for dinner. I bite into the first berry and the nectar of it dribbles down my chin. They are sweet and full of juice. I don't realize how hungry I am until I start eating. I eat and drink until my belly hurts. After I wash my sticky hands and face in the cold river water, I finally lie down.

Lying on the ground next to the fire I stare up at the night sky. The stars are so bright. They shimmer like diamonds against the velvety blackness of the sky. The river next to me babbles so gently and peacefully. All this beauty is a waste. I am too exhausted and too distraught to even enjoy it.

In my solitude, I start to think of Jae, and how it would have been a comfort to have my friend with me. We have spent many nights like this together. Camping and laughing and eventually falling asleep to the sound of each other's voices.

Then I think of Merik and how I am going to be a better sister to him once I find him. I am going to be supportive and patient. I am going to obey my father's final wishes, "I need you to keep an eye on him, darling." He had said to me. "I fear he is lost in his own mind." I replay those words over again in my mind for what seems like hours. Instead of admiring the stars, I simply stare off into the night until my eyelids are too heavy to stay open. I assure myself that I will have better luck tomorrow.

* * * * * *

I wake up early even though I haven't been sleeping for very long. The morning light is still dim and the air is crisp. The sun is just barely peeking up above the trees. Today I am going to venture out into the heavier wooded areas. So far I have not found any evidence of Merik along the river.

I cover up the fire embers with dirt and sand, and gather up my things. With my pack slung over my shoulder, I set off into the woods.

By the afternoon, the temperature has risen considerably and the humidity makes everything feel sticky and heavy. It makes me glad I chose to wear shorts.

My initial plan was to search by a grid. I planned to walk the ground as well as fly through the area. It seemed like a good idea in theory, but by the end of the day I am soaked, aching, and I have found nothing except a patch of poison oak. Now shorts seem like a bad idea.

I return to my camp site by the river. My right foot and ankle are starting to swell and itch drastically. I take my pack over to the edge of the water and dip my foot in. The cold water is a huge relief. Soon my leg is mostly numb. Looking through my pack I come across a bottle of Jewelweed. I rub it over my swollen foot and then cover the rash with mud from the river bottom.

This day has been a disaster.

Sitting on the riverside I stare across to the other side. I have never been this far south before. I certainly have never been on the other side of the river. I had not heard of anyone going this far. There had never been a need to. I have no idea what is on the other side but I have made up my mind. Tomorrow I will cross over to the other side of the river.

My leg is starting to feel better. But I am too tired to even eat anything tonight. I just roll over on my side and try to forget about what a pointless day it has been.

By morning, my leg is almost completely healed. Only a faint pink rash is remaining. The itch is bearable so I am certainly able to continue. After a breakfast of the remaining bread I had brought, I set out for the other side.

At first, the terrain doesn't seem much different. However, further south the foliage becomes less dense. The earth is no longer soft but rocky like the side of a mountain. For hours I come across nothing unusual. Just long stretches of land that would be difficult to live on. Trees and plants are sparse and there are only a few species of insects and rodents that seem to live here. There is no reason for Merik to come this far.

Tired, I sit on a large bolder to rest. It is foolish of me to be here. I have no idea where I'm going. I don't know what to look for anymore. For days now I have been wandering aimlessly with only hope to keep me going. I thought this would be easier. The wise thing would be to just go home. How can I return home now? I still have no answers and I have no family to return to. After a while of sitting there with a war going on in my head, I notice how quiet this land is. Then a sound does stand out to me. I hear the sound of buzzing. It is close. It seems to be coming from somewhere behind where I am sitting.

Carefully I walk the ground afraid that I would be easily seen in this non-wooded area if I were to fly. The subtle hum increases and I know I am getting close. In front of me stands a large wall of rocks separating me from the noise on the other side. I put my ear to the wall and I can hear the buzzing more clearly. It sounds like flies. Flies are often attracted to decaying flesh. I feel a sick knot in my stomach. The image of Merik's possibly rotting body flashes into my mind. My heart beat accelerates. The torture of not knowing outweighs the fear of what is possible. Clasping the dagger in my belt I fly up for a better look.

As I reach the top of the rock, I see for myself. It is not Merik. For the first time in days I feel a small swell of relief. Looking around I don't see any possible predator. It seems safe enough to take a closer look.

It appears to be part of some kind of large rodent. It is almost the same size as I am. The head has been cleanly removed, and its brown fur is soaked and matted in its own blood. By the lack of decay, I figure it has not been dead for very long. I walk around the other side of it I see a stick coming out its side. I know I should not linger here. It was clearly killed by something and that something may still be near. Curiosity gets the better of me and I kneel down closer to the look at the stick in its side. The top has been broken, but the wood around the shaft is polished smooth. I take hold of it and with a strong tug pull it free. The bloodied end reveals a sharpened point. It is not just a stick it is a spear.

I drop it immediately. I have stayed too long. This hunter will certainly be coming back.

Before I can stand, I hear a hissing and soft fluttering directly behind me. My senses sharpen. The hairs on the back of my neck stand on end. I slowly stand and turn. Only a few feet from my face is a monster unlike any I have ever seen. It is some type of lizard. It is black and orange with scales similar to ones on my wings but much bigger and much thicker. It is nearly my height, but likely twice as long. It stands on four short but muscular legs with large feet and very sharp black claws. Its head is disproportionately large compared to the rest of its body, and its eyes are lifeless like black glass.

I remain totally frozen staring at the mouth of the beast. I cannot breathe. I cannot move. I feel the pupils of my eyes dilate out of fear. Suddenly the creature's, black, forked tongue springs from its mouth, it flutters mere inches from my face. It is trying to pick up my scent.

For a moment we stand there staring at each other. It as a predator and I as its prey. I figure by its size the dagger I have holstered in my belt would merely enrage the creature further rather than do any real damage. I don't have any other choice but to try and fly out of here.

My legs are coiled like springs. I shoot off the ground thrusting my wings downward to push myself upward quickly. The beast moves as fast as I do. Its mouth opens revealing dozens of needle like teeth. I narrowly escape its jaws but am knocked back to the ground by its massive front foot. Scrambling up to my feet I realize that the creature is too close for me to fly away. I have to put a little distance between us. Panicked I take the dagger out of my belt and grab a rock with my other hand. I throw the rock hard, hitting it in the eye. It moans and turns its head for a moment. I take the opportunity to run into the clearing. The rock doesn't detour it for long. The earth trembles beneath my feet. I can feel it on my heels. I try to fly up again, but instantly feel its dry scaly foot on my back. Its claws drag across my skin tearing it savagely, warm blood pours down my back. I scream out in pain.

Falling to the ground again my head smacks against a rock. I hear the crack of my own skull. I can barely see and what I do see appears blurry and distorted. The lizard is standing over me now. Its black tongue is fluttering around me, tickling my skin. In a last effort, I swing my arm wildly with the dagger, but its hide is so tough it hardly makes a scratch. The lizard's foot stretches across my shoulders and his claws dig into the earth around me. I am trapped. The creature lets out a satisfied hiss-like growl, almost like it is laughing at me. It reveals its teeth. A milky substance drips down from its curved fangs. Its hot steaming breath smells of rotting meat. I am starting to lose consciousness, I'm losing blood. Everything is going dark. Then I hear a shout followed by a loud pop. The creature rears up suddenly and lets out a painful shriek. There is a cracking sound as the full weight of the lizard falls on me. The creature is lifeless. The weight of it threatens to suffocate me and crush my bones. In my delirious and weakened state, I can't wiggle free. I can't breathe and am beginning to pass out.

Before losing consciousness, I hear something else. It is very faint but I hear what sounds like a groan. Suddenly, the weight of the animal is alleviated. I take a deep breath and cough uncontrollably until my lungs adjust. I witness the lizard being pushed off of me. Still too weak to move I look up. The sun is directly above which blinds me. Above me stands a dark figure. It is shrouded in a black cape of some sort. I think to myself, I must be dead, and this creature has come to collect my soul. I close my eyes and pass out.

Chapter 8

My eyes open suddenly. It was daylight when I lost consciousness and now it is well into the night. Looking around I notice I am back at the riverside. How did I get back here? My shirt has been cut away where I was scratched and my body has been wrapped tightly in cloth. My head is throbbing and as I try to sit up my back seizes in excruciating pain.

"Ahh!" I scream without thinking. There is a quick rustling that comes from a few feet away. A dark massive hand presses hard against my chest.

"Don't get up," the voice says. "You are still badly hurt."

The voice is very deep but smooth. He kneels at my side. There is a fire going so I can see him faintly. He is a fairy but not like any I have ever seen. He is incredibly large. Not just in height but he is more muscular than any of the other men in my village. That day at the waterfall with Jae I saw that he had developed a muscular body, but he is long and lean. This man's body bulges out in a way that seems unnatural. He has no hair on his head, his ears are a little pointed, and his skin is a bit darker than mine. His wings are different too. I see now what I thought was a cape are actually his wings. They are wings of a bat. I have never seen a fairy with bat wings before. They appear to be quite thin, but have the mobility of another arm and hand. Everyone I have ever seen mostly has feathery wings, except mine of course. All of this is strange on its own, but besides that his skin has been painted and burned in bizarre patterns all over his body. My first reaction is to fear him, but he clearly does not mean to harm me. If he did, I suspect he would not have saved me.

"It was you," I say after a moment, "you pushed that monster off of me."

He nods. My head starts throbbing again. I put my hand up over my eyes.

"Uhhg. What happened anyway?" I groan.

"In short, you had a fight with a Gila," he replies. I just look at him until he continues. "I had been trying to trap him for a day or so."

"You were trying to trap it?" The idea that he would want to capture such a beast seems crazy to me, "So you put that dead rodent there?"

"Yes."

"Why were you trying to trap that thing?"

He reaches into a small pouch that hangs from his belt and pulls out a small vile filled with a thick milky liquid in it, "To get this."

Immediately I think back to the lizards pointed teeth and the milky liquid that dripped from its mouth. I find it fascinating now that I am safely separated from it by a layer of glass. I reach my hand out to touch the vile.

"It is the venom that is secreted from the Gila's teeth. It is a very powerful poison," he explains.

"Why do you need this?" I ask. I still do not understand why someone would risk their life against such an animal to get such a small vile of poison.

He chuckled a little bit, "You aren't from this area are you?" I shoot him a look that lets him know I don't appreciate his sarcasm. "It is a useful weapon to have," he says finally.

"Well, you're right, I'm not from here. I come from the north," I admit.

I am not sure if I should be offended by his assumption or not. But, he was right I'm not from this area and would not have survived on my own.

"Ah, you're a woodland fairy," he says. I nod. "Well, you need to rest now. We'll talk more tomorrow," he orders.

I want to ask him more questions, find out more about him, but my head is throbbing. I'm finding it hard to keep my eyes open.

He takes a piece of cloth from a bag and walks over to the river. He plunges the rag into the water and rings it out. After kneeling back at my side, he places the wet rag over my eyes and forehead. The cold rag feels good. It soothes my aching head and the coolness of the water seeps into the crevices of my eyes.

Before I fall asleep, I lift the rag a bit to look at him. "Thank you," I say. "Thank you for saving my life."

He just looks at me. He says nothing but turns his gaze to the ground and bows his head to me. He seems uncomfortable with my gratitude. I keep looking at him for a long moment. I am still amazed by his appearance.

"Why do you look at me that way?" he asks finally.

"I'm sorry. I've just never seen anyone who looks like you."

"That's funny," he says smiling, "I was thinking the same thing about you." He rearranges the rag on my head, "Get some sleep."

My body settles into the earth. I rest my hand on my chest and feel my pendant. I roll the marble in my hand until I drift off.

******

By morning, my head is feeling much better. The sun is warm on my face. The wounds on my body still hurt tremendously, but if I use my arms for support I am able to sit up.

I notice that my strange new companion is standing in the river. He is standing very still and holding a long spear. He stares intensely into the water.

For the first time I am able to get a good look at him. He is in fact monstrously big. His back is facing me and I can see that his wings spread down further on his body. Most wings sit on the shoulders, his attach all the way down his back. The outlines of the bones in his wings are visible and they move as easily as the fingers of my hand. He does not wear a shirt, only a pair of very durable looking, possibly leather, brown pants and leather belt to hold his weapons. Even though his legs are covered I can see large muscles protruding from his thighs. His muscular physique is truly remarkable. In an unconventional way, he is sort of beautiful.

His tan skin glistens in the sunshine. The muscles in his shoulders tense and ripple as he suddenly plunges the spear into the water. When he lifts the spear out of the water, a large fish flaps vigorously at the end. The fish shines like silver in the sunlight. He turns to me and raises it in the air, in victory.

"I hope you're hungry!" He shouts as he makes his way out of the water. He smiles, revealing white shining teeth, with sharper, more pronounced canines.

The fire from the night before is still burning. "Did you stay up all night?" I ask.

"I don't sleep much, and never at night," he says while preparing our breakfast.

"Right, the bat thing," I feel foolish for not putting that together sooner. "So, who are you? What is your name?" I change the subject.

He looks at me. For the first time I see his eyes clearly. They are so dark, perhaps even black.

"I am Khalon, a warrior of the Skar tribe from the Southlands," he speaks formally.

"A warrior," I repeat. I can see how he would be placed in that vocation. His size alone is intimidating. Paired with the strength it took to lift the Gila off of me and the precision of his spear he is indeed a fearsome creature.

I sit in silence for a moment and watch him prepare our feast. His large hands work quickly. He removes the head and bones of the fish, and exposes the light pink flesh. I feel my stomach rumble as he puts the meat on the fire.

He works quietly. He doesn't say anything, or ask me any questions not even my name, and I begin to feel annoyed.

"My name is Sigrun," I finally blurt out. I look at him expecting a nice to meet you or sorry, I should have asked, but instead he just keeps his eyes on what he is doing and nods his head slightly. I conclude under my breath, "In case you were wondering."

His reluctance to talk should have been an indication for me to sit there silently as well, but I still have so many questions.

"Where is your family?" I ask. It seemed like an innocent question.

"I don't have a family," he says without looking at me.

"At all?"

He shakes his head, "They died when I was little, but I don't really remember."

"Do you have a family name? Anything?"

He shakes his head again.

In a way, I empathize with him. With the loss of my father, I am an orphan too, but I still have my memories of him. To remember nothing would be such a lonely feeling.

"How did you end up with your tribe?"

"I'm not completely sure. Mantus, our leader, he found me. Kind of took me under his wing, so to speak. He trained me, eventually made me the leader of his army," he tells the story with no emotion.

Looking at him while he speaks I see not only has his body been intentionally branded and tattooed, but he has many battle scars as well. One that demands attention is on his chest. A long diagonal slash where scar tissue has long bubbled over, crosses across his chest were his heart is. At one point in his story, he caught my eyes fixated on it, but he doesn't seem to care. He actually smiles at my fascination with it.

"The Skar tribe?" I divert, "I've never heard of them."

It is not unusual to be ignorant of other tribes since we mostly stick to our part of the land, but something about this tribe makes me think that ignorance could be costly. We have a few retired soldiers in our village, and most of us learn some swordplay, but the stories coming from Khalon sound like his entire tribe revolves around their army.

"You've never heard of us?" he asks. I shake my head, but keep my eyes fixed on his. He breaks our stare and uses his knife to prod the fish on the fire. "Well," he continues as he scratches his chin, "I bet your elders could enlighten you."

I don't know what he means by that so I pursue a different question, "What are you doing out here alone? Are you hunting or scouting?"

"I left," he says, and then looking at my puzzled expression he realizes he will have to elaborate, "I left my tribe, for good. I'm out here on my own because I want to be."

I am more confused now than ever, "Why did you leave?" I persist, "I don't understand. The 'adopted' son of a tribal leader should have no reason to leave. Were you forced out?"

"No. I'm a deserter. I left a while ago." He wipes his knife blade clean on his pant leg.

I can see anger start to rise in him, but I can't stop myself from asking, "But, why?"

"Because I couldn't do it anymore!" He irrupts. His deep voice almost sounds like a growl, "I couldn't burn one more village. I couldn't turn my head one more time while some woman is being raped. I couldn't slit one more innocent throat!"

His eyes burn with primal fury. He looks like a cornered wild animal looking for a way out, and by violent means if necessary. Fear pulses through me, but I keep his gaze. I root myself to the ground and hold myself as straight and tall as I can. This mock bravery seems to surprise him. The rage in his eyes is laced with regret and what looks like sorrow as well. Sorrow for all of the lives pointlessly lost at the end of his sword. I can almost see him silently tallying them in his mind.

Without another word, he stands up quickly and flies up into the trees.

Shaking, I lie my head back down and take my first deep breath since his irruption. I replay the conversation back again in my mind. The horrible images he described attack the forefront of my mind. His deplorable resume makes me reconsider my safety. He is a villain in every possible way. Thief. Destroyer. Murderer.

I should be terrified, but I can't resist this feeling of pity for him, but why? He is by all definitions a monster. There is something in those black eyes that took hold of me. I admit it, I am intrigued.

He was gone most of the day. By the time he had returned, it was getting dark. I had not moved around too much, since my injuries kept me pretty immobile. I had been able to gather a few berries and water from the river, but mostly I spent my afternoon trying to rest. I had managed to build a new fire before his return.

I see him appear from the bushes. In one hand, he carries a sack which looks to be full of something, and in the other, he carries a long stick. I sit very still watching him closely like rabbit would do if a wolf approached. Without speaking, he walks over to where I'm sitting, empties the contents of the sack, and kneels next to me. The sack contains various plants some edible and some medicinal, berries, and nuts. It seems my new companion has been busy gathering supplies all day.

His eyes still have not met mine, but he reaches over to my side to check my bandages. I flinch at his touch, partly from the pain and also the uncertainty of his intentions. He pulls his hand back.

"I'm sorry," he says.

His eyes finally look up into mine. They are hard to read. I'm not sure if he is apologizing for my flinching or for his earlier outburst. Regardless, he seems regretful and sincere.

He pauses with his hand still reaching, but not touching me. I relax my stance a little indicating that he may proceed. He gently removes the bandage around my ribs. The roughness and size of his hands seem to contradict the tenderness of his action. He takes a plant from his recent expedition and tears the thick waxy leaf in half, then squeezes it hard until light green liquid oozes out. He prepares a fresh bandage out of some cloth he has in his bag.

I see the gashes the Gila made for the first time. There are three long scratches that span from my left ribs across my back. The length and shape of them are similar to the scar on Khalon's chest. My wounds have healed considerably, but they are still red and inflamed. As he assesses my injury, I try my best not to make any sound even though the area is still very tender. He applies the gel from plant on the scratches. The coolness feels good, but the pain of just being touched causes me to sweat. Once he tightens the new bandage around my ribs, he looks at me with a confused expression.

"These are healing very fast," he says finally. He sits back. "What else can you do?" he asks.

"What do you mean?"

"Well, for starters, your wings are remarkable. I have never seen anyone with dragon wings before, and I've probably seen more of this world than anyone," he grabs my left wing and stretches it out to look at it. He is so strong I can't pull my wing out of his grasp. He starts examining the scales more closely, "They are incredibly tough, that Gila should have killed you, but I'm guessing that these acted as a shield." He grabs a small knife from his belt. I try to get my wing out of his hand, but it doesn't budge. He moves so quickly I really don't have time to react. He drags the blade across my wing and then it is over. He looks at me, "Not even a scratch."

He lets go and allows me to inspect my wing. He is right, there is not even a mark. I had no idea that they were that tough.

He points to my bandaged ribs, "You have accelerated healing capabilities, and..." He reaches his hand up to my arm and squeezes my bicep hard.

"Hey! What..." I try to squirm free.

Oblivious to my squirming he continues poking his fingers into the meat of my arm.

"You have muscles that you aren't even aware of," he lets go of my arm and I feel my bicep just as he did, trying to understand what he means, but it just feels like a normal arm to me.

He points to my necklace, "Also, that is a very unusual item you are wearing." I wrap my hand around the marble protectively.

"It was a gift," I say quietly.

He ignores me and continues, "So, I'm betting there is more to you than what you are letting on." He is looking at me with a slight squint in his eyes and a smile like he is expecting me to make a confession.

"Well, apparently you know more about me than I do," I say defensively. "There is nothing else that I can do."

"We'll see," he concludes. He notices that I still have my hand on my necklace. "Don't worry," he says, "I'm no thief. I'm not going to steal it."

I relax my hand a little. "Why do you think it is unusual?" I ask him about the necklace.

"It changes when you sleep."

I am surprised. I had never thought that it would change while I was sleeping. How would I have known?

"It does?" I say quietly.

"The flower closes up when you're sleeping and blooms when you wake up," he explains. "I would be careful with it though, not everyone is as," he pauses, "trustworthy as me." He looks at me with a hardened expression for a long moment. Then his eyes soften and he begins to make dinner.

* * * * * *

After we eat, we sit by the fire with full bellies and quietly look each other over. Khalon uses his knife to strip the bark from the stick he brought back to camp. He sharpens the end to make another spear. While watching him, I think what an odd pair we are. I am confused by him, he is fascinated by me. It seems like madness to sit here with a trained killer, but what is even crazier is that I feel like I can trust him. Maybe I even understand him.

His attention on his task allows me the opportunity to really look at him closely without him noticing. In the light of the fire, I see the markings on his body clearly. There are dozens of symbols and characters, and it seems no two are the same. I am particularly fascinated with the large brands on the inside of his forearms. I know that to acquire brands that thick the skin has to be burned at an extremely high temperature for a good long moment. This is a procedure that would require a tremendous amount of pain. The precision of the marks leads me to believe that through that process he never even flinched.

"Those marks," I say, "does everyone in your clan have them?" He looks away from his spear and looks over his body.

"Most of our clan has some markings, yes, but not this many," he says casually returning back to his task.

"Why do you have so many?"

"They are given to warriors after a victory."

"Oh," I squeak out.

Taking into account that his entire body is practically covered, I figure he has never experienced defeat in his life. It also makes me wonder how many people has he killed? I didn't want to pry too much. It was made obvious by his earlier outburst and departure that this is a difficult subject for him. Without saying anything, I sit in silence and watch the fire.

He continues to strip the bark from the spear and smooth the wood down with a cloth. Watching him work is almost hypnotic.

"So, Sigrun," he breaks the silence, calling me by name for the first time, "what brings you down here anyway? You were surprised to find me on my own, so you must have a purpose for being alone as well, and so far away from your village?"

"I'm trying to find my brother."

"Did he run away?"

"Yes…. No...I don't know. He disappears from time to time, but this time something feels wrong."

"Why is that?"

I pause before answering to swallow the lump in my throat. I still cannot talk about my father without feeling it.

"Our father was murdered a few weeks ago," I explain. He doesn't move or change his expression, "And, my brother has been missing since the day before."

He goes back to sharpening his spear, "You know what I think," he says. I lean in like he is going to tell me a secret. "I think you should go home," he says. I lean back again in disappointment.

He touches the pointed end of the spear to see how sharp it is then continues to whittle. His lack of compassion hits me with a throbbing in my chest. My anger stifles the words in my throat.

"You've been out here for what, three, four days?" he asks. "And, you were almost killed. You have no business being out here," he pauses to look at me again. I'm sure he sees my irritated expression.

"Well..." I try to speak.

"Look," he cuts me off, "your father's dead, and your brother might be too, right?" The harsh reality of his logic surprises me, but I manage to nod my head. "How does getting yourself killed avenge your father?"

He has a point. I feel my stance begin to sink.

"You should go home. See if your brother comes home. Maybe, condition yourself to survive out here before you come back."

He tosses the spear at me without warning. My arm instinctively catches it. I look up from the spear to his face, he is smiling. His arrogance angers me. I toss it back at him, and lie down for the night.

******

By morning, I have conceded that Khalon was right. I should go home. I cannot help but to feel like a failure. I had come out here to find Merik, to find answers. Now I will be returning home with nothing but poison oak on one leg and some banged up ribs.

Khalon is already up. I watch him while he packs his gear. He is very careful with his possessions. He cleans the blade of his knife thoroughly before placing it in his belt. He organizes the supplies he has left. Some cloth, remaining medicinal plants, and some food all wrapped and placed methodically. I suppose it makes sense that he takes such care of these items, since these are now the only things he possesses.

I stand and stretch my arms way above my head. Spread my wings far out to the side. The wounds on my back and side hurt a little, but not as much as they should. In fact, the stretch feels good. I flap my wings a few times and that feels good too.

"Looks like you're feeling better," Khalon says.

"Yeah," I say a little perplexed by my rapid recovery. He walks over to me and begins to unwrap my bandages. The scratches are completely healed leaving only pink surfaces. I continue to watch him as he looks over my scars. A strange feeling hits me. Even though he made me so mad the night before I have come to like his presence. I don't know where he is going, but I don't want him to leave, not yet.

"You are definitely fit for travel," he says. He touches one of the pink lines on my side, it tickles more than hurts and I jump, "Sorry," he says through a chuckle.

"So, where are you headed?" I ask.

"Not sure, maybe west."

"Not much for planning are you." I comment rather than question.

"It would seem," he points to my scars, "neither are you."

He goes back over to the fire pit and kicks dirt and sand over the embers. I look around and see that he has pretty much packed up our camp. He is definitely on his way out, and soon.

On impulse, I blurt out, "I think you should come home with me." He stops suddenly and looks at me. I replay my last statement and see how forward it sounds, "I mean you should come to my village with me."

Even though I clarified my previous statement he is still looking at me with an inquisitive expression. I feel myself getting nervous. My face feels flush. I see his eyes focus on my pendant, and the corner of his mouth pulls to a smile. I'm sure the rose is blushing, which only makes my face hotter.

"That's a bad idea," he says finally.

"No, no it's not."

"Oh yes it is," he picks up his spears. They both fit easily in his large hand, and starts walking away. I chase after him.

"Look, listen to me," I almost beg, "okay, you're right I don't know what happened to my brother, but someone killed my father that is a fact. This murderer is still out there." He is moving so fast and I am so much smaller I am practically in a sprint trying to keep up with him. "I need your help. I've never met anyone like you. You can help me. Help train me so I can protect myself," I am shouting at him now, but he doesn't stop. I feel anger and desperation well up inside me. In a panic, I grab his forearm hard, "You don't have anywhere else to go anyway!" He finally stops moving and looks at me. I take this as a small victory. I breathe calmly and remove my hand from his arm, "I am asking you to help me," my eyes search his for hope. His expression is one of sadness, maybe even pity.

He shakes his head and says, "I will not be welcomed into your village."

"Why?" This statement confuses me since I have only ever known my people to be compassionate.

"My tribe has a history with people like yours. I am an enemy to them."

"Not anymore you're not. You are a deserter, remember?" There is silence for a moment. I can tell he is starting to give in, "And, you saved my life. They won't be able to ignore that. We'll get them to come around. Trust me."

He lets out a deep sigh and hands me one of his spears.

"Okay," he starts, "the first lesson is always carrying a weapon out and ready when traveling." I take the spear from him and smile in gratitude. He chuckles lightly, "This is going to be a mistake."

I ignore his remark and take the lead toward home.

Chapter 9

The closer to the village we get the more nervous I become. I realize now that I had not thought this all the way through. Khalon is not just a stranger to my village, he is a stranger who is a warrior for a clan that seems to have a bloody history with our elders. I also have not thoroughly considered housing accommodations for him.

The afternoon sun is just starting to fade when we approach the village. The perimeters are busy with activity. We fly past the women collecting leaves and petals for clothing, and plants for soap. They smile when they see me, but as soon as they take note of my company their smiles twist with confusion. I know Khalon sees their expressions as well. When I glance at him, he raises his eyebrows and smiles as if to say, 'I told you so.' I ignore both his face and theirs and wave boldly and shout a friendly, "Hello."

Dozens of eyes spot us before we make it to my house. The secret was out now, and gossip flew faster than we did in this village. I suspect my companion's presence would be known by all before sundown.

I stop in front of my house. It hasn't been that long since I was here last, but I take in this moment of relief to be back in familiar surroundings. Khalon is looking at my house as well.

"This is your home?" he asks.

"Yeah, this is it."

"It's big," he sounds impressed.

"Well, yeah, I guess it is bigger than some," I say awkwardly, "Umm, okay, so I'll show you your room."

"You want me to stay here, with you?" he says with surprise.

"Sure, for now," I try to sound casual, "It rains a lot up here, you need a solid shelter. We can build you your own nest later if you decide to stay."

I open the door and walk in. The orange afternoon sunlight gives the main room warmth that it had been lacking when I left. The smell of pine has faded and is no longer overpowering the lilac that is wafting through the windows.

Khalon comes in behind me. Even though I do have a good sized home he still has to turn to the side and duck his head to get through the front door. I walk him through the house quickly giving him a very concise tour.

"So, this is the main room, kitchen is over there." We walk upstairs. "My room is here. My father's room and den are over there," I point down the hall. We walk into Merik's room, "And this is my brother's room. I figure you can stay here until he comes home." I know my father's room is empty, but I'm not ready to surrender his corner of the world.

He looks the room over and nods in approval.

"The light is good," I continue, "and this is my favorite part of the room." I walk over to the large window next to the bed, and turn the latch. The window swings open like a door. I take a deep breath in and breathe out as I say, "Instant freedom." When I look back at him, he is smiling. "Well," I say feeling as though I shouldn't linger in here too long, "I'm going to run out and get some supplies. I think the kitchen is empty and we aren't really stocked for company. So, you can just relax, or explore, or whatever." I rush out hastily.

As soon as I make it down the stairs, Jae is walking through my front door. He looks good. His summer tan has already set in. He has obviously been outside a lot since I've been gone. I'm standing on the bottom step when he looks up and sees me. He breaks into a wide smile bearing his bright white teeth, and his brown eyes light up.

"Hey!" He says enthusiastically as we both rush to the middle of the room and hug. He is so warm. He feels like he has soaked up every drop of the sun. "I heard you were back,

I had to see for myself." He pulls back from me to look at my face, but his hands are still on my shoulders, "So, did you have any luck, did you find him?" He is excited and doesn't even give me time to answer. "You look good. It doesn't look like you," he trails off as he notices the pink scars on my side. "What's this?" he asks while examining my side.

"Oh that's nothing," I start.

"She had a little run in with a Gila Monster," I hear Khalon's voice behind me. For a moment I had forgotten he was here. Jae looks up over my shoulder. The mood in the room instantly shifts. Jae straightens his stance and I see the muscles in his neck and shoulders tense up.

"Who is this?" Jae demands while keeping his eyes fixed on Khalon.

"Easy, junior," Khalon growls.

Jae takes a step forward and bumps into me, but doesn't even notice.

"Whoa, guys," I start to mediate. "Jae, this is Khalon, he saved my life. He is my guest. Khalon, this is Jae. We have been friends our whole lives," I speak in a very calm tone like you would to children, but it doesn't seem to ease the tension at all.

"What do you mean your guest? Is he staying here in your house?" Jae questions.

"Yes, he is," I reply.

Outside my house I hear another familiar voice, "Sig! Hey, are you home?" Ainia flutters through the door. "Hi! Oh," she stops abruptly when she sees Khalon, "I heard you had company." She smiles devilishly and twirls her finger around her shiny blond hair.

"You knew about him?" Jae spits.

Before she can answer, Malyn buzzes her way in as well.

"Oh wow, he is big," Malyn says.

It seems everyone had heard about my visitor except for Jae. Malyn is so small and fast she zooms around Khalon taking an inventory of him. She looks like a child next to his grand stature. He impatiently swats his hand at her like she is a gnat buzzing around his face.

"I heard Sig came back with someone that was not her brother," Ainia finally answers Jae's question.

"And, that he is big," Malyn adds. Jae storms out of my house without another word.

"Jae, wait!" I shout after him.

"Come on, Jae, what's the big deal?" Ainia shouts as well. She shakes her head and looks back at me and then at Khalon. "Don't mind him," she says to Khalon, "he is just surprised by you."

"Hmph," Khalon grunts. "I told you. Bad idea," he says to me, only this time he is not smiling.

"Well, anyway," Ainia continues, "I'm Ainia, and this is Malyn."

"Hi," Malyn chirps. "We're not all so bad," she says with a smile.

"I think I'm going to go settle in, and get some sleep. Give you ladies time to catch up," Khalon says before he retreats upstairs.

My head is spinning. This was not the homecoming that I had imagined. I don't know what I want more. To chase after my friend and calm him down, or to run upstairs and reaffirm that Khalon being here is not a mistake.

I decide to stay put with Ainia and Malyn, but I hardly notice what they are saying. I give them vague answers to all their questions and I halfheartedly listen to what they have been doing in my absence. What I picked up is that Ainia has settled into the trade of making clothes, which is truly perfect for her. Malyn, with her speed, has fallen into scouting and gathering.

"Oh I almost forgot," Ainia bursts out. She flies over to the doorway where she dropped a piece of fabric on her way in. "I made this for you, Sig, while you were gone. I think the color will really bring out your eyes."

I had to smile at that. Ainia never stops trying to find my girly side. She holds up the cloth and I see it is a very pretty lavender colored dress.

"You made me a dress?" I ask.

"Well, sort of. See the bottom isn't a skirt it's shorts. See, it's pretty and functional."

I can tell she is proud of herself. She knows I do not like to wear dresses because they aren't very practical. She and Malyn start undressing and redressing me.

"The best part is the top. You know how you always tear the wing holes in your clothes? Well, this ties around the neck and is completely backless so your wings are not constricted. There," she said as she ties the straps into a perfect bow, "you like it?" she asks.

"I love it."

I hug both of my friends and tell them about how I was just on my way out for supplies when Jae showed up. We agree to catch up another time.

I didn't get very far to gather my supplies. I make it out my door only a few feet before I see Beda and some of my other neighbors walking up to my house with their arms full of goods. They brought me food, drinking water, soap, extra men's clothes, towels, and Beda had a bouquet of freshly cut flowers. I thanked them for their generosity. Though I figured that these favors were not only brought out of kindness, I suspect they were using the supplies as an excuse to get a glance of Khalon. Regardless, I am grateful for their gifts.

I put the baskets in the kitchen and listen. The house is completely quiet again. I pause in front of Khalon's door on my way to my room. I don't hear him. I raise my hand to the door to knock, but decide before I touch the door that I should leave him alone for now. He didn't have the warmest welcome in a strange place. I feel bad that Jae acted the way he did. I am embarrassed that Khalon's first encounter with my village was one of hostility.

Moonlight streams in through my window and from the skylight above my bed. Stretching out onto my bed my muscles finally relax, and my headache subsides. The crickets and frogs sing their nighttime lullaby to me as I drift off to sleep.

* * * * * *

The morning trades crickets and frogs for birds singing a new day, and the coming and goings of villagers. I sit up, and though I slept well, I still feel tired. My house is still quiet.

I walk over to my dressing table and look at myself in the mirror. This is the first time I have seen a clear reflection of myself in over a week. With the exception of my clean nightgown, almost every part of me is dirty. The dirt on my face has only been washed away by sweat. My neck, chest, and arms are all smudged with grime, and my hair could certainly use a washing. I will have to make a trip to the river later for a proper bath since I don't have enough water for the soaking tub. In the meantime, I find a rag and enough water to wash my face and arms. I brush my hair out the best I can and tie it back with a ribbon I find in a drawer.

Khalon's door is still closed when I pass it in the hallway. I don't hear a sound from behind it except for the same birdsong that I heard in my room.

In the kitchen, I boil water for tea and dive into the baskets the women brought last night. I find some fresh bread, a jar of honey, and some raspberry jam among other things. Tearing into the bread makes my stomach growl. I tear off a piece of the bread and drizzle honey onto it before shoving it into my mouth. The bread is so soft and the honey is so sweet. It is nothing short of pure delight.

On a tray, I put the largest portion of bread, the remaining honey, and the jam. I find a large cup and pour the tea. Once the cup is on the tray, I make my way back up the stairs. I pause and listen at Khalon's door again, and then I knock softly.

"Khalon?" I say quietly.

I wait but don't hear anything. Timidly I open the door. The room is empty. The bed has not even been touched. I feel panic rise up inside me. Then I notice the large window I showed him last night is wide open. After I set the tray down on the bed, I walk over to the window and lean out to look. I gasp and almost scream as I see a figure dangling on a branch above me. At second glance, I see that it is Khalon. He is hanging upside down from a branch outside the window, and he is fast asleep. I chuckle to myself and shake my head.

"That's right, the whole bat thing," I say quietly to myself.

I leave the tray and decide to let him sleep. I have things I need to do anyway. Find Jae for one, and I would like to take a proper bath at some point.

I don't get more than two feet out my door when I see Jae. I am so happy to see him I automatically smile and assume he must have been thinking the same thing I am. My smile quickly disintegrates when I see he is not smiling at all.

"My father and the other council members want to see you," he says, "and you should bring your friend with you too."

I nod my head and sigh. In my mind I think, can't I have one day of peace.

Chapter 10

I am not looking forward to waking Khalon for this. Once I'm back in his room, I see that he has not moved. He is still hanging upside down on the branch. I lean out the window and touch my hand to his shoulder. He doesn't budge. I shake him more vigorously, "Khalon, wake up."

"What is it?" He groans, "What time is it?"

"It is still early morning."

"What? I just went to sleep a couple hours ago," he shrugs my hand away and covers his face with his wing.

"I know, I'm sorry, but the council wants to see us right now," I plead with him.

He groans again and opens his wing up enough for me to see his face. He has one eye open and it is glaring at me. He sighs. "This can't wait?" he asks.

"I don't think so. Besides I think it might be good to get this out of the way."

He stretches his wings out all the way and yawns so loudly it almost shakes the tree. I back up into the room to give him space to come back in. He climbs through the window and notices the tray I brought up earlier. In one swig, he drinks the tea and snatches up the piece of bread. With his other hand, he picks up the jar of honey.

"What's this?"

"That's honey," I say a little amazed, "you've never seen honey before?"

"Not like this," he opens the jar and smells it suspiciously.

"We have an arrangement with a bee colony not far from here. They collect nectar from our flowers and they give us some of their honey in return," I explain. "Go ahead try it, it's good."

He plunges two of his fingers into the jar and scoops out a huge amount of the honey and ladles all of it in his mouth. His eyes immediately widen.

"Mmm," he moans with his mouth full of honey, "it is so sweet."

Within seconds, he has finished what was left in the jar. He sets the jar back on the tray, but then just stands there looking at his hands, which still have a coating of honey on them. He looks at his hands like a child would, and he simply says, "Sticky."

I can't help but giggle. The biggest man I have ever seen is rendered helpless by sticky fingers.

"Yes, it is very sticky," I say.

I grab a rag and soak it in some water. He lets me wash his hands.

"There you go, all clean," I say.

He splashes some water on his face and walks over to the wall where he has rested his spear.

"You don't need to bring that," I say.

"I am not walking into this without a weapon," he says firmly.

I sigh, "The spear looks a little, aggressive."

"Good."

"No, we don't want them to be afraid of you. We want them to like you."

"No one likes me, and I don't really care if they do," he says defiantly.

"Well, I like you, and all of these things," I point to the tray where the bread, honey, and jam sit, "were brought to us by my neighbors last night. They even brought some extra clothes for you. Though I doubt they are going to fit," I say quietly. "So, we aren't all bad, and it would be nice if you would trust me on this one."

He sets the spear back down.

"Okay," he starts, "but, I'm bringing my knife."

He puts his knife in his belt. I'm not totally thrilled with the compromise, but at least the knife is not so obvious. I start walking down the stairs. I hear his heavy feet behind me.

"You know," he says, "I bet that honey would be really good on that bread."

I start laughing and shake my head.

Outside, Jae is pacing in front of my door. Khalon growls when he sees him. "Not this kid again," Khalon says.

"Don't you ever wear a shirt?" Jae quips.

One side of Khalon's mouth pulls into a sly smile. Jae's remark savors of jealousy and Khalon is relishing in it.

"None of them fit," Khalon puffs his chest up, accentuating his size.

"Okay, can we just get going?" I redirect. Jae takes off first, Khalon and I follow. It seems the entire village is out this morning. Everyone stops as we fly past them. The villagers look more curious than concerned, which eases some of my tension.

The council building resides within a large willow tree on the other side of the village. Inside the willow, there is one enormous room that can fit the entire village population. At the far side, there are three steps up to a platform which holds five large, throne-like, chairs.

Jae's father Falon sits in the chair in the middle. Falon's older brother, Vivek, sits on his right side. On Falon's left side, Beda's husband, Akin, sits. I didn't know that he had been made a council member. It must have happened while I was away. Next to Akin sits Osiris, who is Vidar's father. Vidar clearly inherited his blue jay wings and gray eyes from his father. I see that my father's chair, which is next to Vivek, is still empty. My stomach twists. It will only be a matter of time before they swear in a new member to fill it. The council works better with five members.

"Sigrun," Vivek coos, "it is so nice to see you, and to see that you are well."

"Thank you, Vivek," I say. "Honestly, I most likely wouldn't be here if it weren't for Khalon," I gesture my hand toward my new friend. Both Falon and Vivek shift their yellow eyes from me to him.

"Interesting, how so?" Vivek asks.

"I was attacked by a Gila," I answer.

"A Gila?" Osiris says with surprise, "Where were you that you ran into such a beast?" I can tell in his tone that he is concerned for the village's safety.

"I was down south, on the other side of the river, very far from the village." This seems to comfort him a bit.

"Khalon, is it?" Falon shifts his attention again, "How is it that you defeated a Gila?"

I was curious about this as well since the beast was on top of me at the time he came to my rescue. I also give him my full attention.

"The beast was on top of her when I arrived, since it was distracted I was able to jump on its back, and take it down that way."

"But, their skin is so thick?" Falon questions again.

"Yes, but there is a soft spot at the base of their skull, my spear was able to penetrate its hide. Then I twisted the spear to the side and broke its spine. It collapsed instantly and I was able to roll it off of her before she suffocated."

I can tell by the hush in room that everyone is as amazed as I am by his account. The feat of strength it takes to defeat an animal of that size is something none of us have ever seen, or heard of.

"How incredibly lucky for our Sigrun that you were in the area," Falon says.

"Well, I had been tracking the Gila for a few days."

"Really? Whatever for?" Falon asks in a suspicious tone.

Khalon takes a deep breath in order to stay calm. He does not like the direction that this conversation is heading, "The poison that it secretes is useful."

"Poison? Useful?" Falon's yellow eyes squint, "Where are you from, Khalon?"

"Far south of the river," Khalon stands perfectly still through this interrogation.

"Do you come from a tribe?" I suspect by his tone Falon already knows the answer to his question, but he clearly wants Khalon to say it out loud.

"The Skar tribe," Khalon says without flinching.

The mood in the room instantly shifts from tense to desperate. All four council members sit back in their chairs. They look at each other like they are communicating without speaking.

"I knew it!" Jae exclaims behind us.

"No, no, you don't understand!" I shout out, "He left. He left his tribe. He is no longer a Skar."

I am annoyed that Jae seems to know more about the Skar's history than I do. Khalon still has not moved, and I'm surprised that he is keeping his composure.

"You left your tribe?" Vivek asks.

"Yes. I am a deserter," he turns his head to Jae, "meaning the Skar's despise me more than you do."

Jae looks at him with disgust.

"Jae, he saved my life," I speak slowly and clearly.

"Of course he did, how else could he infiltrate our village this easily? He saved you so you would trust him enough to bring him here. Now that he knows where our village is the rest of his army is probably standing by, waiting to attack."

"What? That's absurd," I argue strongly, "he didn't know that I would be coming along that way. I didn't even know where I was heading."

"It doesn't matter, Sigrun!" He yells, "The fact that you happened to walked into his trap was just lucky for him. All he needed to know is that you are from a different tribe. That is how the Skars survive. They rape, and murder, and take resources from other colonies and move on after they have depleted everything."

My body feels like it is on fire. Jae has never spoken to me this way before.

"That's enough, son," Falon says calmly. "We are grateful that you saved the life of one of our own, and you seem to be an honest man, but my son has a point. Unfortunately, I don't think we are going to come to any conclusions on the matter today. We really just wanted to meet you, Khalon, and hear your side. I think for now I'm going to have to insist that you don't leave the perimeters of the village. I hope you understand."

I am still looking at Jae, but I feel Khalon's body shift away from the council members and face Jae as well. Khalon puts his hand on my shoulder.

In a low rumble, Khalon replies, "Oh, I'm not going anywhere."

His statement was in response to Falon, but Khalon clearly meant it for Jae.

Chapter 11

Jae took off quickly after the meeting was closed. Khalon and I walk out and look at each other. He raises his eyebrows at me.

"I know, I know, you told me so, I get it," I say annoyed, "I have some things I need to take care of. Do you remember your way back to the house?"

"Yes."

"Good. I don't need to babysit you, do I? Promise to be good?"

He doesn't say anything, but he crosses his heart with his finger. I guess that is the closest to a promise that I will get from him.

I start to fly away when he shouts, "What things do you have to do?"

I turn to face him, "Well, for one thing I would like to take a bath. You should think about taking one too." I hear his laughter as I fly away.

More importantly, I want to find Jae. I want to at least try and explain my position to him. I find that he is not at home. Falon and his wife are not at home either. I grab a piece of soap from their kitchen and head down to the river. Maybe it is better that I don't see him right now anyway, clearing my head first is probably a good idea.

I find a good spot at the river where the current isn't too strong. No one is around, so I slip my clothes off and dive into the water. The coolness of the water is a shock at first, but it feels good. It feels clean. I lather the soap up in my hands and scrub my hair vigorously. The soap smells like roses. It is a stronger perfume than I normally use. After my hair and body are clean, I let my body sink down and tilt my head back into the water so that only my face breaks the surface. The foamy lather of the soap slowly washes downstream.

The sun shines through the leaves above me. Everything appears to shimmer. Despite this beautiful day I feel sad. Jae and I have never fought like this before. I keep trying to clear my mind of it, but I can't. Then I think of the cavern, that's where he is. I run out of the water as fast as I can, and shake my wings off. I put my clothes on even though I'm still wet, and head down the river to the waterfall.

The tunnel under the waterfall is much easier to go through the second time. I feel like I reach the end much faster. When I make it to the top, I see Jae sitting on the stone step. His hair is still wet. He must have arrived just before me.

At first, I feel happy that I found him, but he looks so sad and that breaks my heart. He looks at me for a moment and then looks back down at his hands. He is spinning a small piece of a purple crystal. As he does, small rainbow reflections dance around the cavern walls.

I realize now I hadn't really thought about what I was going to say. Normally I would swim right up to him, but the mood between us makes me feel more prudent. I remain standing in the water in the middle of the cavern. I'm hoping he will speak first. He doesn't.

"Jae, I know you're mad."

"I'm not mad," he cuts me off, "I'm upset."

"What's the difference?"

"That guy is dangerous and you don't even see it," he ignores my question.

"Oh no, I am perfectly aware that Khalon is dangerous, but he is not a danger to me or anyone else in this village."

"Sigrun, how can you be so naïve?" He runs his hands through his hair in frustration.

"I'm not naïve, Jae, you weren't there. You didn't see it. He saved my life." I start making my way toward him. I point to the scars on my ribs, "He healed my wounds. He fed me. He gave me a weapon. I had to convince him to come here," I sit next to him. "I went out there to find Merik, and I didn't even find a trace of him. Not one trace and I was really looking. Just as I made the decision to come home Khalon comes out of nowhere. I understand that it might not make sense to you, but I just have a feeling that he belongs here."

Jae looks back at the ground, "Do you love him?" His eyebrows make a hard line.

"What?" I almost fall over, "Where did you get that idea?"

"Well, I don't know," he says defensively, "he is living with you."

"Where else would he stay? Do you want him to stay with you?" I start laughing. My laughter appears to be infectious, because he finally breaks into a smile. "Jeez, Jae, is that what this has been about?"

"Well, no, not really. I was just wondering," his smile fades. He dives back into the water before he speaks again, "I mean I show up after hearing your home, and this guy is in your house, and everyone seems to know about him but me." I open my mouth to speak but he cuts me off again, "Then, from his appearance, my dad tells me it sounds like he is a member of the Skar tribe. I started thinking you were in danger. I panicked." I start to swim to him. He has his back to me, "Honestly, Sig, I thought I was going to find you dead this morning."

I put my cheek on the back of his wing and wrap my arms around him. His wings are so broad I can barely touch the front of his shoulders.

"I'm so sorry, Jae. I didn't even think you would feel that way."

It was the truth. I didn't ever look at things from Jae's point of view. If I was him, I would probably be going out of my mind with worry too.

He put his hand on mine. Still holding my hand he turns around. He looks at me and my nerves come back. I feel uncomfortable being so close to him in such a serious moment. I start to take a step back. He grabs the back of my head gently with his free hand. Then his lips are on mine. Hard at first, probably because I recoil in surprise, but then his embrace begins to soften. His arm finds its way around my waist. His hand is grasping my side tightly. His other hand is still holding mine, but now our fingers have entwined together. I put my other hand on his chest and push, putting a few inches between us until his lips part mine.

"Jae, what are you doing?"

I'm panting now because I stopped breathing as soon as he kissed me. I have never been kissed like this before. My body is shaking, but his feels incredibly still. He looks intensely into my eyes. I think for the first time in our lives he is really looking at me.

"Sigrun?" His eyes are in a squint.

"Yes," I barely reply.

"Did you use my mother's soap?" I burst out laughing, and then so does he.

"Yes," I say. I am grateful for the moment of levity.

He puts his forehead against mine. I close my eyes because the room feels like it is spinning. His nose touches mine. Then I feel his lips again. This time I move mine with his. His mouth is soft and sweet. It feels good, and that makes me feel guilty.

Even though I can't see it I imagine that the rose in my necklace is blushing red.

Chapter 12

I fly back to my house like I'm in a trance. When I arrive there, it seems Khalon has had a busy day so far. He has set up a target on a sapling next to the house. There were already a few gashes in the wood. It looks like he has been practicing his knife throwing. There is a pile of freshly cut fire wood outside of the door. He walks around the side of the house carrying another armload of firewood. He has taken a bath as well. He is the cleanest I have seen, except for the fresh perspiration on his forehead.

"Oh, you're back," he says. "Did you find your boyfriend?" He teases.

"Yes. No.... I mean, I did, but, he's not," I take a breath. He is enjoying watching me squirm. "I found Jae, everything is okay. I think I have straightened everything out," I can feel my brow furrow.

"Uh-huh," he says suspiciously. He looks at my neck and points to his own chest indicating the rose is blushing.

"Ugh," I cover the necklace with my hand and go inside.

This pendant is more of a burden than a gift right now.

It has become rather inconvenient for my emotions to be out on display. I make the decision to stop wearing it for now. I carefully wrap the pendant in the silk cloth that my father gave to me, and hide it all the way back in a drawer.

There is a knock at my door. I slam the drawer shut.

"Come in," Khalon squeezes into the room.

"I hate to admit this but your boyfriend is right."

"He's not my…" I start to say, but he cuts me off.

"The Skars will come here. They will destroy your village," he speaks with certainty. "Whether they come here looking for me or scout you out on their own. They will be moving north soon. Eventually they will find this place. One thing I know is that no one will be safe." His words are chilling.

Images of my friends burning alive in their homes, their throats being slit while their families watch, plague my mind.

"What should we do?" I ask.

"Move your village."

"We can't do that. We have been here for generations this is our home."

"You are outmatched, Sigrun. If you stay here, they will massacre every man and make slaves out of the women and children," Khalon's face is serious. I believe everything he is saying is the truth. It scares me but I know what I have to do.

"Then we'll have to learn to fight."

His mouth breaks into a small grin. I don't know why, but everything seems to be a test with Khalon. Apparently, I have passed.

"First thing we need to do is assess what training the people have had." Khalon transitions into a soldier before my eyes.

"It's not much I can tell you that. We are all given a little bit of basic defensive training. Maybe a third of us are competent with a sword. The majority of our diet is plant based, so we hardly do any hunting."

His face looks grim while I list our deficits.

"Hmm, do you have any allies? Is there anyone we can go to for support?" he asks.

There is not another fairy village anywhere near us. The amount of time it would take to venture to them, plead our case, and enlist their help wouldn't leave much time for us to train. Then I felt the answer creep up on me.

"The bee colony!" I shout out. "They aren't as big as we are, but they have thousands in population, and they all have venomous stingers." Khalon raises his eyebrows in approval. "I think," I continue anticipating Khalon's censure, "we need to bring this to the council." I pause, "I can't do this behind their backs, and we can't leave the village without their authority."

He stands completely still.

"I agree," he says as last, "in order for this to work we need everyone in the village to be on the same side."

I am amazed that Khalon is in agreement on this subject.

"Okay, tomorrow morning we'll go to the council building."

"You know it is not going to be easy to convince them of this," he says. I purse my lips. Khalon has a valid point.

"I know, but there is no other way."

"You will have to make them see that as clearly as we do." Khalon looks out my window. "Well," he says, "let's get something to eat. We can figure this out over dinner, you hungry?" he asks.

I have been so preoccupied all day, and food has not been in the forefront of my mind. All I have eaten was that bit of bread and honey this morning. My stomach rumbles at the mere suggestion of food. Khalon must have heard my stomach because he laughs and says, "I'll take that as a yes."

I laugh and follow him downstairs.

For a while we sit eating in silence. We made a meal out of some boiled greens and pine nuts. For dessert I brought out the jam that Beda brought and some bread. I could tell that I would have to increase our food rations to keep up with Khalon's appetite.

He is so much bigger than the rest of us. He obviously needs more food to keep his strength. Just having him in my house for one day he has just about cleaned out all of the food stores I have.

"So," he breaks the silence, "tell me about your brother."

I swallow hard. The topic makes my throat tense up. I had been distracted the last few days, and have not thought about Merik as much.

"Oh, um, what do you want to know?"

"Why does he take off?"

"Umm," I pause because honestly I'm not quite sure, "well, Merik is, how do I explain him? Moody. I would say he is moody and maybe a little temperamental. I think he never felt like he fit here."

"You don't fit here either, but you don't seem bothered by that," Khalon says while looking me over.

"That's different."

"How?"

"I am physically different, that is true, but Merik never made friends here. He withdrew from everyone, even me." The lump in my throat is growing. I take a drink of water to keep from crying. "My childhood was tough," I continue, "I had to work hard for my acceptance here. Merik is not that strong, and I think the ridicule that he went through having me for a sister hurt him a lot."

"And, you have no idea where he goes?"

"No. He never says. Father never asked and he wouldn't talk to me about it anyway."

"How do you think the death of your father will affect him?"

"I think it will destroy him," I feel one hot tear roll down my face. Khalon is kind enough to pretend not to notice. I think he knows it would embarrass me to cry in front of him.

"Well, you should get to bed," he says, changing the subject, "big day tomorrow."

I nod even though I know I won't be able to sleep, "What about you? Are you turning in for the night?"

"I'm going to get some supplies. You're almost out of food."

I chuckle to myself, "Yes, I know. Well, be careful we're not use to night fairies around here. You might startle some people."

"Don't worry. They won't even know I'm there," he smiles and then walks out the door.

The house feels empty once he is gone. I don't like being alone. It gives me time to think, and I have nothing good to think about.

I wander into my room. I slip into a soft cotton nightgown. The air feels heavy so I open a window. The warm summer breeze is nice but doesn't take the weight out of the room.

Sleep seems impossible. I can't help but to revisit the afternoon with Jae. In one day, my relationship with Jae has completely shifted. I keep replaying the way it felt when he kissed me, even hours later the dizziness rushes back. It would be a lie to say I didn't feel something for him, but it is masked layers of confusion and guilt. What would Ainia say? She would be devastated and furious. She has had a crush on Jae all our lives. The idea of her heartbreak makes me feel awful. I try to shift my thoughts to something else.

I think about how I will tell Merik about our father; what that conversation will be like. I imagine his tears and mine. I imagine him falling to the ground and me falling with him, and through all this tragedy we will at last support each other for the first time in our lives. Before I know it, I am drifting off to sleep. My face cooled by my tear soaked pillow.

I dream about the past. I dream of a memory from my childhood. Merik came home one day when he was about ten years old with a lump on his head and a tear in his wing. His wings are thin like a wasp, they are quite fragile. The physical wounds were easily fixed by our father. The damage to his soul is another thing entirely. The other children surrounded him and began shouting how he was a freak, and how he had a monster for a sister who killed his mother. That was what separated us.

He never outgrew the pain of listening to his mother's sacrifice. Her screams of agony only to bring a monster into the world. The days of sleeping warm under her wing was over for him forever. I hadn't realized it until now how much harder it was for him. I never had those memories of our mother, which was sad for me, but having those memories and then being robbed of their source is certainly worse.

My dreams turn to nightmares. I see Merik surrounded by a circle of children taunting him like ravenous animals. They shout at him, they throw stones. He falls to the ground. I rush in to help him, but can't. We are separated by a glass bubble. He is laying on the ground with his face in the dirt. When he turns to face me, I see that I am looking at my own reflection, but it is the red-eyed monster from my previous nightmare. I jolt awake and find that it is morning.

I can tell it is late in the morning, but the house is quiet. Apparently, Khalon was very busy in the night. The kitchen has been stocked fully with berries, nuts, and greens, and there are strings of fish smoking in the front yard. He didn't make a sound all night long. He was right no one knew he was there, including me.

I decide to go and meet with the council myself. Khalon could use the sleep and it occurs to me that they might be more responsive if I go alone. I put on the purple dress that Ainia gave me and set out across the village.

Halfway there I hear a familiar flapping come up behind me. I land on a tree branch and Jae lands in front of me.

"Good morning," he says enthusiastically and then he looks up at the sky. "Well, good afternoon is probably more accurate," he is smiling at me with those warm brown eyes. I can't help but to smile back. He is leaning against the tree confidently, grinning ear to ear.

"Yeah, I guess I slept in."

"You must have been tired."

He reaches out and grabs my hand. This time the grip feels stronger than friendship. I see him start to lean into me. For a moment I am frozen. My heart and my head are fighting each other. Before his face reaches mine, I pull back and drop my face to the ground forcing his kiss to land on my forehead.

"I'm sorry," I say.

"What's wrong?" he asks quietly. "You took off pretty fast yesterday."

I was in such a fog I hardly remember what I said or did before leaving the cavern.

"I was feeling, overwhelmed. A lot has happened in a very short time and I'm struggling to sort it all out."

I can tell by the furrow in his brow that he is disappointed.

"Is it me? Did I do something wrong?" I chuckle slightly at his question, because it seems absurd to me that anything be wrong with him.

"No," I squeeze his hand tightly. "You are perfect."

He squints his eyes and gives a small grin. I see that he accepts my need for space. This gives me some relief. We look at each other for a hard moment.

Then I hear someone else approaching. Ainia flutters up to us like a rose petal on a breeze. She lands next to Jae. I immediately drop Jae's hand and take a step back putting space between us. I should have realized she would be only a few lengths behind him. I should have been more careful.

"Hey, guys what's up?" she says in a chipper voice.

I breathe again. She obviously didn't see anything. I feel awful keeping these feelings from her, but since I don't even know how I feel, I figure it is best not to hurt her unnecessarily.

"Umm, I'm heading back to the council building," I say.

"You are?" she asks.

"You are?" Jae asks, turning his head back to me.

"What for?" she asks confused.

Jae is asking the same question with his eyes.

"I've decided to ask the council's permission to negotiate an alliance with the bee colony."

"An alliance with the bees? Why?" Ainia questions me.

I'm actually grateful for an opportunity to practice my argument before I reach the council.

"I think we need to strengthen our defenses, right now."

Ainia's eyes widen. Her bright blue irises are awake with fear, "Are we in danger? Does this have something to do with your father's death?" She fires questions at me.

"I think it might have something to do with him, but I'm not sure, and I do think we are in danger."

She holds onto Jae's arm, he doesn't seem to notice, but I feel a pang of jealousy. To overt my feelings I continue, "Khalon thinks that his tribe will be heading this way, and when they do if we don't fight we'll die."

"I told you this guy was trouble," Jae breaks in, "I knew it, the first moment I saw that guy I knew he was bad news, and you didn't believe me."

"It is true they might be looking for him," admitting that is hard for me, "but they would make their way north and find us eventually. You know that is the truth as well." I pause to make sure Jae recognizes my point. "Finding him and bringing him here has given us an advantage that we didn't have before. This way we will be prepared the way no other village has been before. We can learn from him, and we can beat them, but we need help."

I lay my case out in front of the council. The councilmen wear fear and suspicion on their faces. Currently the decision of the council appears to be split. Falon and Osiris are against it while Vivek and Akin see the potential in my plea.

"Maybe we can reason with the Skars," Osiris pleads. "Maybe we can share the lands and food in a similar way as we have with the bees."

"Skars don't share, they conquer," Akin responds.

"Well, we can't move the entire village. It has taken generations to build what we have, and we simply don't have the time to relocate everyone," Osiris argues.

"I'm not suggesting we relocate, Osiris. I'm suggesting we stand our ground," Akin's face is red with frustration.

"We can't win against them, they are warriors, and we are farmers. The mere suggestion is laughable," Osiris' tone is arrogant.

The two men are practically lunging out of their chairs at each other. Falon and Vivek sit back and assess both sides of the argument.

"While we're on the subject, we should get rid of that savage as well," Osiris hisses. The way the word savage stuck in Osiris' throat as he said it made me want to lunge at him as well.

"Now wait a minute," Vivek finally spoke, "no one is getting rid of anyone. We will not stoop to the level of our enemy." He shakes his wings out the way you would if you had been sitting to long and needed to get the dust off. "This is the way I see it," he begins again, "it seems the Skars will come for us eventually whether it is next week, next month, or next year. We can't move the entire village, and even if we did there are no guarantees that it would be any safer. We are not soldiers this is true, but I would rather learn to fight and die fighting than become someone's slave, or worse." He pauses again to look into the eyes of every council member. "I vote to go to bee colony, whether they choose to fight this fight with us is out of our hands, but they deserve a warning of the Skar's movement north as well." Vivek's wisdom and courage resonates in all of us.

Falon, who has been quietly listening, finally speaks, "My brother has a point. I change my vote. Sigrun, you have my blessing to travel north."

"My vote is the same," Akin beams that he is in the majority. "I think, if he is willing, Khalon should train our people. It seems wise to be proactive in this matter."

Osiris sulks in his chair. He does not like losing, "Hmph, well, I still think it is a bad idea, but the majority has spoken."

Part of me feels a little bit smug that Osiris has been overruled. He has always been a little bit of a bully a blue jay through and through, so is Vidar for that matter. Both are very handsome and resourceful, but also cunning. Though he has never been malicious toward me I know he has never wanted me here in the village. His attitude certainly bled into his son, and Vidar and I have definitely had some tense times in our childhood.

It is not very often that I have the upper hand when either of them are involved. The smug part of me wants to rub it in his face a little bit, but instead I politely thank each member before we go over the details of my upcoming journey.

By the time I make it back home, the sun is setting, and Khalon seems to just be waking up. He is still hanging from the branch outside his window.

"Well, it's settled," I start talking while he stretches out. His wing span in incredible. I am amazed every time at his size. "We are going to meet the bees," I say while turning my head upside down to look at his face.

"What?" He says sleepily and confused. He unhooks his large feet from the branch and climbs back inside. "You already met with the council?"

"Yep, and we are going first thing tomorrow," I say with a sense of accomplishment.

"Well, look at you," he says with a smile. "You're pretty tough, kid. That's an intimidating room to stand in by yourself."

He bites into a berry that was left on his table. "Well," he says with a full mouth, "that's fine by me. I've only been here a couple days and I could use a break from certain members of your village."

It doesn't take much guessing to figure he means Jae.

"Umm, well, that brings me to something else," I start.

"I'm going with you," Jae interrupts as he walks into the room.

Khalon squeezes the berry in his hand into a puddle of red pulp and juice that drips from his hand onto the floor.

"Khalon," I start, "it was the only way to get the council to vote unanimously to let us go," I speak to him carefully. "We are all on the same side now, right?" I look at both of them to remind them that this goes both ways.

"Fine," Khalon says, "That's fine with me."

"Me too," Jae agrees.

Though I don't believe that either of them is happy with this arrangement I am willing to take whatever shred of unity I can.

"Okay, we have a big day to prepare for. Even though the bee colony is not that far we have to gather some supplies for a few days at least."

"We should have plenty of food downstairs," Khalon says to me but he is still staring at Jae.

"I'll get water canteens," Jae offers.

"Okay, good," I say, "we'll leave at dawn. Does that work for you?" I ask Khalon considering he usually sleeps in the daytime.

"That's fine. I don't need that much sleep."

"Alright then, I'm going to go through my father's den and see if there is anything we might need. I'll see you both in the morning."

As I head down the hall and into my father's study, I hear Jae and Khalon both exit through the front door. I look out the window to see Khalon and Jae standing toe to toe.

"You can go home, Jae, she's safe with me," Khalon's tone is almost antagonizing.

"I don't trust you."

"But she does," there is a moment of silence between them. "That really burns you up doesn't it?" Khalon digs.

"I've been here her whole life. You've been here a few days."

"And I already sleep in her home, just down the hall, and you sleep across town."

"If you hurt her," Jae starts.

"Settle down junior, first of all she's a big girl she can handle herself. Second, I have no intention to harm her. My interests in her go much deeper," Khalon leans over him, "and it didn't take me years to see that potential. I'll see you in the morning," Khalon steps back into the house and closes the door between him and Jae.

Chapter 13

My father's den is quiet. I go through some of the vials on the wall and put together a few things for the trip. I never spent much time in here by myself before. Merik was the one who showed more interest in potions. I start looking through some of my father's books. Most of it is basic medicinal information, sketches of plants and descriptions of how to use them.

I grab a large book from the shelf, but it doesn't budge. I grab it with both hands and pull hard. I finally jiggle it free, but something that was behind it falls to the ground. It is wrapped in a cloth. I kneel down to look at it closer. I carefully unwrap and see that it is another book, but this one looks different than all of the others. This one is bound in scales. Scales that resemble mine, but they are red in color. I can tell that it is very old, but the material that it is made of has preserved incredibly well. A sense of excitement swells up in me. I've never seen a book bound in scales before.

I feel like I was meant to find this, like this book holds some answer for me. My excitement fades once I flip through the pages and see that it is written in a language that I don't understand. Page after page, I turn them all searching for something I can understand. Finally I see a picture that makes my eyes widen. It is a picture of a circle with a rose in the middle. It looks very much like my pendant, except that flames are drawn around the circle as though it is on fire. Above the picture is one phrase, Օրյեկտ կրակի, and on the opposite page is a paragraph written in the same language.

Երբ մաշված մի երեխայի հրդեհի օբյեկտ շեշտում է հուզական վիճակը: Այն լույսերը կրակը շրջանակներում. Այն տալիս է ուժ է արժանի. Այն ուժեղացնում ներուժ է հաղթահարել չարը.

Երբ մաշված մի երեխայի, որ չար չարաշահման իր իշխանության կարող է ոչնչացնել բոլոր լավ է այս աշխարհում.

I run my fingers across the words hoping for some miraculous insight. I feel desperate to understand what it says. At first, I try to think of who could help me. Someone has to know this language. Then it occurs to me that it might be hidden for a reason. Perhaps what is written on these pages is secret, or dangerous. This validates my decision to keep the pendant out of sight for the moment. At least until I know more about it. Maybe Merik knows. Maybe father showed it to him. I decide to tuck the book back into its hiding spot on the shelf and wait for Merik. I feel a burning in my heart as I walk out of the room.

Chapter 14

The early morning sun is orange and pink. I watch it rise while I brush my hair and braid it back out of my face. I feel a strange sense of purpose and excitement this morning. My mind keeps circling back to the red book in my father's study. I keep thinking about the pendant on fire.

I reach into my drawer where I stashed the necklace. It is waiting for me, safely wrapped in the cloth. The marble is cool to the touch and the rose is as perfect as ever. As I hold it in my hand, the rose blooms slightly like it is waking up for me. I am amazed, just as I was the first time I saw it. I am desperately missing my father. His wisdom and guidance has been stripped from me, and I wish I had some kind of confirmation that I'm making the right choices.

A gentle rapping at my door startles me from my gaze. "Sigrun, are you up?" Khalon asks.

"I'll be out in a minute," I shout back.

I return the necklace back to its hiding spot. It pains me to leave it, but for the moment I feel it is best. I slip into a more practical dark green romper. Ainia's dress is too pretty for this trip. I grab the supplies I gathered from my father's den and head out the door.

It is no surprise that Jae is waiting for us outside. He is perched on a branch across from my house. The sun is behind him so I have to squint to see him.

"Good morning," I say.

He smiles, "Good morning."

He looks beautiful with the sun at his back. His brown hair shows streaks of copper in the sunlight, and the tops of his wings almost glow.

"Did you sleep at all, Jae? Or, did you just sit outside my house all night?" I tease.

Before he can answer, I hear Khalon come up behind me. Jae's smile fades into a tolerant line across his face.

"Morning," Jae says.

"Morning," Khalon rumbles back.

I take a deep breath and realize that for a short trip this may feel like an eternity if these two don't lighten up.

"You forgot this," Khalon says to me handing me the spear he made. "You need to get used to carrying this everywhere you go." I nod in agreement as I take the spear from him. "I can make one for you on the way," he says to Jae. The gesture surprises me.

"Oh, thanks," it also seems to surprise Jae, "but, I have my family sword."

I didn't see it at first with the sun in my eyes, but sure enough he has the sword tucked in his belt.

Khalon nods, "Do you know how to use it?"

"A little."

"Well, maybe we can practice a bit on the trip."

"Sure, that would be, good."

The civility between the two is fascinating to watch. I wonder how long it will last, but I am certainly relieved for the moment.

The awkward exchange is interrupted by Ainia and Malyn, who show up to see us off. Ainia perches next to Jae while Malyn hovers in front of Khalon and me.

"So, you guys are really going to see the bees?" Malyn says. Her greens eyes are wide with excitement, and I can tell she is trying to hide a smile. She is obviously fascinated by the entire endeavor.

"We should only be gone for a few days, but I'm glad you're here," I say to both girls. "While we're gone, I need you to start spreading the word about training. Go to Vidar and Ragnar first, they are very influential. You may have a hard time with Vidar since his father is against this plan."

"Nah, any excuse to throw a knife at something and he will be all over it," Jae cuts in.

"Let's hope so," Khalon says.

"Okay, also," I continue, "we need space to train. Can you two make a clearing and set up targets?"

"Definitely," Malyn says enthusiastically.

"I can't believe this is happening," Ainia says. Her eyes are a little glazed over.

I can tell this is a lot for her to take in. She looks at Jae for encouragement. He puts his hand on her shoulder.

"I know it sounds crazy," he says, "but it doesn't hurt to be prepared."

She looks up at him and smiles slightly. She places her hand on top of his. It seems to be a tender moment between them. I don't like it.

"Well," I break in, "we should get moving. Khalon will start training as soon as we get back, so try to be ready." I fasten my shoulder bag and make sure I have everything.

Ainia dramatically jumps up and wraps both arms tightly around Jae's neck as though she will never see him again. It makes me a little uncomfortable, and I sift through my pack pretending not to notice.

"Whoa, there," Jae chuckles a little, "we are only going to be gone for a few days."

I catch a glance from Khalon. He looks at me and then his dark eyes shift to the two of them. He is smiling and I know that he is figuring out this very unusual situation. Once again, I am glad that I left the pendant in the drawer, because I don't know what color it would be right now.

I give Malyn a quick hug and take off up into the trees. "See you in a few days," I shout on my way up.

Khalon is right behind me, and it takes Jae a few seconds to catch up. I assume it took some coercing to get out of Ainia's grasp.

We travel quickly through the morning without saying much to each other. I had found a map in my father's den of the territory. The route up north follows the river for quite a ways until we reach bee territory then we break west.

We fly well into the afternoon, pushing as hard as we can until we are forced by hunger to stop. We land on a large maple branch. The day is hot, but the thick leaves provide cool shade. All three of us are wet with perspiration. I divide a loaf of bread into three large pieces while Jae passes around a canteen.

"So," Khalon starts with his mouth full, "tell me about the bees."

"Well, honestly I have never been up to the colony myself," I explain. "I have only seen worker bees. I have never met the Queen or a drone. Most of our information about them comes from stories told by our parents and teachers." I feel a little embarrassed that I don't have better firsthand knowledge.

"What's a drone?"

"They are the males who breed with the Queen," Jae explains.

"Wait a minute. One Queen, several…drones?" Khalon questions. Jae and I both nod. Khalon smiles and shakes his head a little, "Well, that's one way of doing it, I guess."

His innuendo makes me blush a little.

"The Queen is the largest from what I understand. She may even be bigger than you," I say looking at Khalon's stature.

"Now that would be a sight," he says smugly.

"The workers are quite small but there are literally thousands of them."

"Maybe even tens of thousands," Jae inserts.

"And, the workers can't speak. Only the Queen and the drones can speak," I say.

"How do they communicate?" Khalon asks.

"Well, they understand what we say, but they can only respond with body language or something like that," I try to explain.

"Hmm, they are perfect little soldiers. Large numbers and they can't talk back," he leans back, "Mantus would probably love to get his hands on them. It's a good thing we are getting to them first."

"They're not soldiers, they're workers," Jae corrects.

"Right now, for our purposes, they are soldiers," Khalon is starting to get agitated.

I jump in, "We can't *make* them fight," I say, "all we can do is ask for their help and illustrate the importance of keeping the Skars out of our territory. The rest is up to them."

Khalon nods to my point, but I know he wants a more concrete plan.

The three of us sit in an uncomfortable silence for a bit until Khalon stands up.

"You know what I think," he says looking at me, "I think the heat is making you irritable."

"What...," I start, but before I can say anything else he has his arm around my waist and we are falling from the tree branch.

He is so strong that he carries me effortlessly with one arm. He spreads his wings and glides down to the river. A small cry escapes my throat as he drops me into the water. Cold water surrounds me and rushes up my nostrils. The water feels cold at first since my body was so warm. I spring up to the surface just in time to see Khalon wrap himself up into a ball and drop right next to me, creating a wave that pours over me.

"What is it with you boys and dunking me in the water?" I cough out. Khalon is laughing so loud it rumbles through the trees.

"Ah, see, don't you feel better?" He says splashing more water on me.

"Not really," I say wiping water from my eyes.

He lunges for me, but I see him coming this time. I duck down into the water so he misses and then snare his leg with my arm pulling him back. He loses his footing and falls back into the water.

"Now I feel better," I say as he comes up to the surface. He looks a little surprised that I got him off his balance, but he laughs anyway.

I look up at Jae. He doesn't seem to be as amused as we are. "Come on, Jae," I wave him to come down.

"Yeah, Jae, come on," Khalon says in a tone that I can't determine from inviting or challenging.

Regardless, Jae stands at the edge of the branch just above the river. He stands tall and perfectly still before allowing himself to fall backwards. He tucks and flips three times before diving flawlessly into the water.

"Show off," Khalon says quietly before Jae reaches the surface. I burst out laughing, because those are the exact words I said to Jae that day at the waterfall.

"I know he is," I say laughing. Jae swims up to me, "Very impressive as always," I say.

He smiles at me. It is the first time I have seen him smile since we left home. I can't be sure if he is smiling because he thinks I am impressed by his performance or if he is just grateful for a moment of flippancy. He stands close to me, his eyes locked in on mine. He reaches out to touch my face, but suddenly I feel something grab my legs and I rise out of the water. Khalon has me on his shoulders. He takes me out of Jae's reach. He flies out of the water taking me with him.

"We should probably move on while it's still light, since I'm the only one who can see in the dark," Khalon says. Now Khalon is showing off. I see Jae's face, he is absolutely annoyed.

Khalon easily lifts me off his shoulders and sets me down on the branch. Jae also lands next to us. He shakes off his wings, sprinkling water on Khalon.

"Sorry about that," he says to Khalon, though it is clear he is not sorry at all, and then turns to me. "Are we ready?" He takes off on our course before I can even answer.

The rest of the afternoon passes quickly. The scenery begins to change and I know we are approaching bee territory. This time of year brighter more fragile flowers bloom in this area. They make the sweetest honey. Unfortunately, these flowers have a fairly short lifespan and come autumn the bees are forced to collect pollen from more robust flowers closer to our village.

Khalon gives the signal to stop. "Do you hear that?" He says. I strain to hear. There is a faint buzzing sound coming from the distance. He must have exceptional hearing if he could hear that over the sound of our wings.

"We must be close," I say a little out of breath. "We should camp here for the night. I think the hive is just over that hill. It would be better to approach in the morning. We don't want to startle them in the night."

"I agree," Jae says. We set down our gear and I pick up a few sticks to start a fire.

"We're going to need some more wood," I say, "I'll get some more." The two of them look a little uneasy about being left alone together, but neither one would ever admit it. "How are we on food and water?" I ask.

Khalon looks over our supplies, "We're good for the night."

"Okay, I'll be right back," I walk away quickly to prevent either of them the opportunity to volunteer to come with me.

As soon as I am away from them, exhaustion washes over me. I'm not sure if it was the heat of the day, the never ending tension, or if it is the just the realization that those carefree lazy days, that summer used to be, are over, possibly forever. Flying down to the waterfall with Jae, building fires down by the river and staying out until sunrise, sleeping under a shady tree on a hot afternoon, all of that, I fear, is gone.

By the time I pull myself out of the trance of my past, I realize my arms are full of sticks. As I creep closer to our camp site, I hear a faint conversation between Jae and Khalon.

"Are you that ignorant that you don't see she's in love with you?" Khalon's question to Jae stops me completely. My heart accelerates and my face feels like it is in flames. I stop breathing to hear his answer.

"What do you mean?"

"You are oblivious. You're a little blue winged beauty."

"Ainia?" Jae questions.

I peer around the tree I'm hiding behind. I can see Khalon's face. He has his eyebrows raised in a dumbfounded expression. My first impulse is to go in there and put a stop to this entire conversation, but the curiosity of Jae's response is too enticing to interfere with.

Jae takes a moment to go over this information. "I would say it is more of a crush," he says finally.

"Oh, so you are aware of it, and you string her along knowingly," Khalon has a way of pulling out information. I could see him being a masterful interrogator.

"I do not string her along," Jae's irritation starts to rise as does his voice, but he quickly stifles his tone, I suspect to keep me from hearing. "It's just… it's complicated," Jae sputters out.

"I think I can keep up, junior."

Jae takes a deep breath, "It would make sense to be with Ainia. She is beautiful and sweet. I know our families would be pleased, and," as he speaks I hold my breath, stuck on his every word, "it would be a lie to say I didn't enjoy the attention I get from her."

The shame on Jae's face makes his confession mildly easier to stomach, but I'm shocked regardless.

Khalon nods as though he is impressed by Jae's honesty. I do not share his enthusiasm. In fact, I am angry. I am angry that he has been aware of Ainia's feelings for him and he has maybe even encouraged her simply to feed his own ego. I am angry that he has put me in an uncomfortable situation with Ainia. Mostly, I am angry that he has made me feel foolish. I realize I don't know if what he has said to me is real or not. Is he just stringing me along also? Am I just one more object to feed his ego? My heart rate is frantic and my blood is boiling.

I decide I have heard enough. I snap a twig so they know I'm coming back. They both turn to me as I approach. Jae's face looks like a little boy who has been caught misbehaving, but I pretend not to notice.

I drop the wood next to the small fire Khalon has started. "Everyone getting along?" I ask trying to keep a light tone.

"Pretty much," Khalon responds. Jae sits quietly.

"Good," I sit by the fire and start to go through my pack. I grab a handful of nuts and dries berries. I eat my dinner in silence, we all do.

I'm grateful that neither of them attempt to strike up conversation. I have nothing to say to either of them right now. I want to stretch out the quiet as much as possible. When Jae finally leans into me and asks, "Is something wrong?" I shut him down quickly.

"I'm tired," I snap.

Khalon takes this opportunity to interject, "I scouted an abandoned squirrel's nest in that tree." He points to a large oak behind me. It seems he has picked up on my irritation. Somehow he knows what I'm feeling, even when I'm not wearing the necklace. "You should sleep there, it's safer."

I would normally take offense to the implication that I needed a safer place to sleep than the two of them, but I feel a need to separate myself. I nod in compliance, grab my pack and my spear, and say goodnight.

The former tenants of this nest left a bed of raw cotton and leaves. The nest is spacious and comfortable enough, but I feel like I'm struggling to breathe. The nest might as well be inside of a cupboard, because the room feels like it is closing in on me.

I lie down. Moonlight is surrounding me. I close my eyes praying for sleep to come. Even though I try to force the thought from my mind I keep going back to what Jae told Khalon. How long has he know about Ainia's feelings? It dawns on me that Ainia has not been subtle with her attention to him. Not to mention that practically everyone in the village knows her deepest desires. I quiet my mind down a little bit. He probably doesn't want to hurt her feelings, and I suppose I understand the attention thing. I certainly have been indulging in the attention he has given me. Just as I start to reconcile my thoughts I think about this morning as we were leaving. I think about how Jae put his hand over Ainia's hand so tenderly, and I remember back to the day he kissed me. He did the same thing to me.

Tears tickle my lashes before they roll down the sides of my face. I stare at the moon. It looks blurry through the water in my eyes, and I get ready for another restless night.

Chapter 15

I wake up before the sun. I look out the hole of the nest. The stars are gone but the sky is still dark.

Jae is still sleeping on the ground next to the dwindling fire. I don't see Khalon, so I look to the branches. He is hanging on a branch just above my nest. I quietly fly to the branch.

He makes hanging upside down look so easy. His feet are longer than ours. He also has an extra set of bones that allow him to curl his feet around the branch. I don't have feet like his so I can't latch on the same way, but I still want to try it. I sit on the branch and slide down until my knees hook on the branch and I allow my body to be pulled down by gravity. It is incredibly uncomfortable. It does not feel normal to look up and see the ground. The blood rushes to my head and makes me a little dizzy.

I turn my head to look at Khalon. He has a faint smile on his face. I suspect he has been awake this whole time. He opens one eye to look at me. His smile spreads across his face. I can't help but to smile back.

"Morning," I whisper.

"Good morning," he whispers back.

"Did you sleep at all?"

"I took a little bat nap."

I can't help but chuckle a little, "A bat nap? What's that?"

"You've never heard of them?" He says in a joking tone. I laugh again. "Did you sleep well?" he asks.

"Not really," I confess.

"Yeah, I didn't think you would."

"You didn't?" I ask a little surprised.

"Well, with the anticipation of meeting the bees I figured you would be restless," he says diplomatically. "I like looking at you this way," he says, changing the conversation.

"I don't know how you can sleep this way. Don't you get a headache?"

"No. To me this feels good," his voice almost purrs.

"Sigrun? What are you doing up there?" Jae shouts.

We must have woken him. Khalon rolls his eyes.

"Well, I'm getting a headache," I say quietly to Khalon.

I'm not sure if my headache is from hanging upside down, or the tension I'm feeling with Jae right now. I straighten my knees and let my body fall down. I twist around. My wings shoot out, and catch the air before I fall all the way down.

By the smile on Jae's face, it is clear that I'm the only one who feels tense.

"Hey there, are you hungry?" he asks. He reaches his hand to my face to move a strand of hair that has come out of my braid. Just the touch of a single finger has me unnerved. He still makes me unsteady in that good way. I shake it off. Keep your head about you Sigrun. I give myself a private pep talk. After all, I am still unsure about his intentions. I move away from his touch.

"Yeah, I saw some cherry trees last night when I went to get firewood. I'll go gather some," I say as casually as possible.

"Okay, I'll go with you," he offers.

"You don't have to."

"I want to," he insists gently. He is staring into my eyes with a certain sense of desire.

Even moments after he wakes up his eyes are bright and his hair is tousled effortlessly. I always feel like such a mess around him. I'm exhausted, I'm sure the circles under my eyes have not gotten any smaller in the last day. My hair is coming out of my braid. My green romper is wrinkled and dirty. He, on the other hand, looks rested and fresh. I have to remind myself that I am still mad. Maintaining my chilly disposition would be so much easier if he wasn't so beautiful.

I sigh deeply and shout up to Khalon, "We're going to grab breakfast. We'll be right back."

I take off before he can respond. Jae is right behind me. I push myself hard to stay in front. I know that my efforts are futile if Jae wanted to he could fly right past me without breaking a sweat.

I see the trees up ahead. At this point in the summer, the fruit is fat and almost overripe, and at its sweetest point. We don't have cherry trees in our village. I haven't had cherries in years.

The last time I had one I was a child. My father had gone with the other council members to discuss our terms with the bees. When they came home, they had bags of cherries and honey. Jae, Merik, and I ate ourselves into a sugary bliss. So, the prospect of this rare treat has suddenly lifted me to a better mood.

We flit between the branches looking for the best fruit. It is a bit of a chore to find pristine berries since the birds have already picked over most of it. We make a game out of finding untouched fruit. For a moment it feels like we are children again, and the only concern we have is winning. The cherries are bigger than my hand, so big that we could stuff ourselves on two of them. So I grab four for Khalon and set them in a pile.

"Sig," I hear Jae call for me. I look up he is standing on a branch near the top. "I think I found you the perfect cherry," he smiles proudly as I fly to him.

I land next to him. He lifts the leaves like a curtain for the reveal. Hanging from a bright green stem is a perfectly shaped, deep red, cherry. It has grown here in its sanctuary, hidden from the birds and insects, like it was waiting for us. A single drop of dew drips from the stem down the perfectly smooth skin. It looks too beautiful to eat. My mouth waters anyway.

Careful not to bruise the delicate skin Jae reaches out and plucks it free from the stem. He hands it to me. It is truly unblemished. "Take a bite." He urges.

"No, I'll wait until we're back at camp," I say feeling a little self-conscious with him watching me.

"Go ahead. You have to be hungry," he urges.

Realizing he is not giving up I take a small bite from the top. The skin breaks open against my teeth and my mouth fills with the sweetest juice. The flesh of the cherry is firm and soft all at the same time. It is so good. I can't help but to close my eyes.

"Mmm, you have to try this," I say to him. I hand him the fruit.

"No, I got that for you."

"I don't care you have to take a bite."

He takes it from me. He takes his bite, just a little bit bigger than mine. His eyes close too, and I know he is experiencing the same pleasure as me.

"That is so good," he says with amazement.

"I know, right!" I exclaim, "It's even better than I remember."

We giggle like we did when we were little. I feel transported to easier times that I miss so dearly. I take another bite, bigger than the first. The juice drips down my chin and I laugh at my sloppiness. When I go to wipe my face, Jae stops my hand and uses his hand instead. He has stopped laughing. He stares at me and his brown eyes are burning. He starts closing the space between us. I know what he wants. My brain is screaming at me to stop him. Another part of me wants him to close all the space between us.

I have almost forgotten that his hand is still on my face. His thumb brushes against my lower lip. The angry side of me screams. He is a scoundrel! Put a stop to this right now! Between the two voices waging war in my head, one of them has already lost. He kisses me, gently. His lips are soft and sweet, and he tastes like cherries. I feel myself melt into him. Not only has my angry voice been silenced the other voice has completely taken over my body.

Jae takes my subtle surrender as a sign of encouragement. His hold on me tightens. He backs me up to the trunk, pinning me hard between him and the tree. All the while his kiss deepens. I feel the velvet of his tongue and my body again feels like it is on fire. Before I know it, I am stifling and struggling to breathe. I find the strength to break our embrace.

"I can't breathe," I exclaim breathlessly.

"I'm sorry," Jae says a little out of breath too, "I haven't had a chance to have you to myself for a few days. I guess I got a little carried away." He kisses the tip of my nose, and puts his cheek to mine. He instantly stands up straight to look at me, "Your skin is so hot, you feel feverish," he looks concerned, "I hope you're not getting sick."

I put hand on my cheek it feels cool to me. "No, I'm fine," the fire in my body has been snuffed.

"Jae, I'm sorry," I say apologetically.

"For what?" he asks. He is holding my hand gently in his. I carefully take my hand back.

"I'm sorry," I say again, "this was a mistake. I can't do this."

I force myself to look at him. His once burning eyes are now dark with hurt and confusion. I try to leave and he grabs my arm.

"Sigrun, wait! What do you mean? What are you doing? I want this. Don't you want this?" He looks desperate.

I hate seeing him like this. I do have feelings for him that has become obvious to me. Why not give it a chance? I shake my head. My own internal struggle proves to me that I can't give into him.

After a moment, I finally say, "I don't know what I want, and honestly," I pause and think about what he said to Khalon last night. By the time I finish replaying it in my head, my tone is no longer apologetic. "Honestly, Jae, I don't think you know what you want either."

His face is the saddest I have ever seen it. I know this is the right choice, but I feel awful. I can bear it no longer. I jump off the branch, scoop up the cherries I gathered, and head back to camp.

Back at our camp sight Khalon is sitting against the root of the tree sharpening his blade with a rock. He runs the rock along the side of the blade slowly. The scraping sound is entrancing and eerie.

He looks up as I approach. He smiles at me when he sees the bounty I am delivering to him. As I get closer, his smile fades and his eyes squint. He knows without a word spoken that something happened between me and Jae. His constant read on my emotions is becoming a little taxing.

I drop the cherries at his feet. "Breakfast," I say as chipper as possible. I instantly regret my over the top tone, it sounds like I'm compensating.

"Where's your friend?" he asks suspiciously.

"Umm, he's just behind me. He'll be here in a minute," I say while avoiding any eye contact.

I start to gather my pack. Out of the corner of my eye I notice Khalon heading toward me.

"Did he do something to you?" He growls.

"No, no, goodness, no. It's fine, I'm fine. Nothing happened," I look at him. He does not seem convinced. I start to panic a little. If Khalon goes after Jae, there is no way I could stop him. I need to calm him down, now. "Really, Khalon, everything is okay. You can, stand down soldier," I joke, and that makes him smile again.

I relax, and he turns his attention back to the fruit. He grabs one from the pile and bites it nearly in half. Red juice pours down his hand and forearm. With his mouth still full, he mutters out, "Mmm. Oh, wow. I could get into this whole plant eating thing you people have going on."

I hear Jae's wings whirring as he makes his way back. His face is a little flush. His eyes are serious. He extends his arm out to me, "You dropped this," he says, and I see the cherry he gave me in his hand.

"Oh, thanks," I say awkwardly.

"Your hands must have been full, trying to carry too much," his voice is chilly.

"What about you, are you not eating?" I ask.

"No. I've had enough," he says.

I have no idea what he means by that. I can't make out his expression. Is it fury, sadness, desire, or some twisted combination of all three?

The only sound I hear is Khalon biting into another cherry behind me. Everything else is silence. The laughter is gone.

Chapter 16

Once we pass over the hill, we are in a sea of bright and fragrant flowers. The fields are full of flowering shrubs and trees, and almost every inch of the ground is covered in wildflowers. The air is thick with floral perfume. The worker bees are everywhere busily flying from flower to flower. They move so fast I almost get dizzy trying to keep up with their motion. We land and decide to go the rest of the way on foot so we don't get in their way.

There are hundreds of them. They are much smaller than we are maybe a quarter of our size. Their heads are mostly covered by large, black, oval eyes that look like they are covered by a screen. They have enormous abdomens, six legs, white gauze-like wings and they are covered with black and yellow fuzz. I'm dying to touch one, but I resist because I also know they have short tempers. Khalon impulsively swats at the ones flying around his face.

"No, no, don't swat at them," I warn. "They might be smaller than us, but they will attack you in numbers and we are definitely outnumbered."

He looks around and puts his arms down by his sides.

One of the bees flies right up to his face and hovers in front of him. Its antennas are dancing around touching Khalon's face lightly. His face is contorted. I know he is uncomfortable with the bee touching him that way. He is trying so hard not to react to its invasive examination.

"It's okay," I insist, "it's just trying to figure out who you are." The bee suddenly takes off and goes back to its task. "See, you don't bother them, they don't bother you," I say optimistically.

He just grumbles something inaudible.

We only make it a few more steps before a much bigger bee stops us in our tracks. He is almost as big as I am. He must be a drone. His body looks very much like the worker bees, but his abdomen is narrower, and he only has fuzz on his upper body. His lower abdomen is smooth and black. He hovers in front of us with his body curled forward keeping his stinger between us and him. His posture is obviously a warning.

"What are you doing here?" His voice rolls out in a low hum.

Jae steps forward a bit with his palms facing the bee, "We are from the Northwood. We have come in hopes to gain audience with your Queen," Jae speaks softly and diplomatically.

"Our treaty with you has not expired. She has nothing to say to you."

"Perhaps not, but we have some things to say to her," Jae continues to bargain.

A few more drones appear and flank the sides of the first drone. I see Khalon start to tense up like he is getting ready for a fight. The muscles in his forearm ripple as his hand tightens around his spear. He slowly raises his other hand to the knife in his belt. I put my hand on his. He looks at me and I shake my head at him to stop.

Tension is swelling in me as well. I know this is dangerous. We could be killed within minutes, but not before Khalon takes out a handful of bees on his own, which would make our treaty null and void. There is a lot at stake here.

"Turn around and go back to where you came from," The drone says. The drone turns and starts to fly away, the others follow.

The relief I feel that I was not stabbed through the heart with a venomous stinger is instantly replaced with despair. We have come quite far. I have been through too much. I will have an audience with the Queen.

"Your entire colony will die if you do not bring us to your Queen," I shout out after him without thinking about how that sounds like a threat.

He double backs to me, "What did you say?" He is so close I can see my own reflection in his black eyes. My eyes are wide. My breathing accelerates.

"I am not threatening you," I soften my tone, "I am here as a friend. I am here to warn you of danger." He has not moved. He remains in front of me keeping me in his lifeless stare. "Please," I decide to come clean with our intentions, "we need your help."

He turns again to leave. I feel hopeless.

"Follow me," he shouts back to us, "and, keep up."

The three of us let out a collective breath and are off the ground. We fly hastily and are really trying not to disappoint our guide, but he is so fast. Trying not to run into any of the worker bees that are zigzagging around the entire area makes this a very complicated task. It is amazing how they navigate around each other so easily. They must communicate in ways that we do not.

Up ahead in the middle of a large field I see an enormous lilac tree standing alone. As we get closer, the hum of the bees gets increasingly louder. The floral smell of the lilac is mixed with the sweet smell of honey. Beneath the long fragrant tendrils of the lilac flowers hangs the hive. It is enormous, bigger than I anticipated. The overall shape is that of an upside down egg, but it also has obvious chambers and even a couple towers with several entry points. It really looks like a castle. Hundreds of bees fly in and out from the base of the tree depositing the pollen they have collected.

The humming of all wings rapidly moving all at the same time is deafening. Khalon, Jae, and I have to communicate through hand signals until we are in the hive.

Once we enter the main room of the hive, the buzz from the outside dies down considerably. The main room is massive. Every wall is covered in honeycomb. Amazingly it is a room with no windows, but it still glows with a warm yellow light. The bees inside the hive are climbing on the comb rather than flying. They carefully tend to each pod. The walls are literally dripping with honey.

I look at Khalon. His black eyes shine with wonder. Taking into consideration his recent infatuation with honey, I watch him closely. Just as I suspected, he reaches out to touch a stream of the golden liquid. I grab his hand and shake my head.

"We shouldn't touch anything," I whisper. "We don't want to offend them, or contaminate anything."

He nods in compliance.

The drone leads us through a winding tunnel until we reach a chamber near the top. It must be the Queen's room.

Inside, honeycomb continues to cover the walls, but instead of honey these pods are filled with eggs. These eggs will someday be the next generation of workers.

The Queen sits in the middle of the room, keeping an ever watchful eye on her children. She really is bigger than Khalon. Her lower abdomen is so large that even if she were standing it would rest on the ground. Her four lower legs are folded neatly beneath her. The bottom half of her looks very much like the other bees, but her upper body looks more like ours. Her middle abdomen is all black and her upper two legs are actually arms similar to ours. Her head is shaped like ours, with a mouth and nose, but her eyes are still the same large black ovals like the rest of them. She has no hair and two antennas coming out of her forehead.

The drone flies up to her and says something to her in a language we don't understand. She nods to him and the drone then stands next to her. She smiles at us slightly.

"What do we have here?" she asks. Her voice is softer than her drone, but it still possesses that humming sound. She almost purrs to us. She addresses me, "Step closer to me child."

I walk towards her. Though her eyes are solid black and unreadable I know she is inspecting me.

"Spread out your wings," she orders.

I hesitate at first, but I do as she asks. I spread my wings out completely. I feel self-conscious about my wings most of the time, but now I'm feeling utterly exposed.

"Ex-tra-ord-in-ary," she stretches out the word in one long hum.

Embarrassed, I fold my wings back quickly.

"Your majesty," I start in eagerly, "we are so sorry to intrude. I know this is a busy time for you." She nods to me so I continue, "I am Sigrun from the Northwood Tribe."

"Sigrun," she interrupts, "the dragon child. We've heard of you. I am very fond of your father, Baron. He is a good man."

The mention of my father makes the muscles in my throat tighten. She does not know of his death, and I for some reason choose not to tell her.

"Yes, I know," I whisper.

Jae looks at me and instead of the hurt expression that he has been carrying all day I see a trace of sympathy in his eyes. I shake my head and try to get back to my original thought.

I jump straight to the point, "Your majesty, we have come to ask you for your help."

"Help you? How could we help you?" she asks. Her tone is almost impossible to read since her face is absolutely expressionless.

I sigh, knowing this will sound crazy, "By forming an alliance with us in case we go to war."

"War?" She is certainly surprised by my request. She actually begins to laugh. The sound echoes throughout the room. "Why would we ever go to war? We are a peaceful colony, and I was under the impression that you were as well."

"We are," I begin, but she cuts me off.

"But, here you are talking about going to war," she sits perfectly still. Her hands are neatly folded in her lap.

"I believe our colony is in danger, and soon so will yours." She tilts her head a bit to the side. I take that as a signal to continue, "You see," I swallow hard, "my father was murdered, and my brother is missing. I believe the tribe responsible is planning an attack."

"Baron has been murdered?" She repeats with surprise and sadness.

"Yes ma'am," I'm struggling to keep it together. I feel my chin start to quiver.

"Tell me everything," she commands.

Khalon steps forward. I suspect he sees me struggling so he has taken the lead.

"Uh, your majesty," he says awkwardly. He is not use to any kind of formal court. "I am Khalon, a former general for the Skar Tribe."

She sits back slightly. She obviously knows of the Skars' reputation.

"Though I don't know for sure who is responsible for the death of Sigrun's father, I do know the Skars are heading north. Their supplies in the south are dwindling and they will be upon the threshold of the Northwoods before we know it. Eventually they will find you as well. Your hive will be ransacked, your eggs will be crushed, and every flower will be dust."

Once again, his powerful imagery has silenced everyone.

I finally speak again, "All we are saying is that we are going to prepare ourselves to defend our lands and our people. We suggest you do the same, and I'm asking for you to join us if it comes to a fight." The muscles in my stomach are tight with anticipation.

The Queen turns to her drone, and they speak again in the unknown language.

She turns back to me, "Is there a chance you are wrong?" she asks.

"No," Khalon interjects, "I know Mantus, and I gather by your reaction you do as well. He's coming."

"Well then, you have my word. If it comes to a fight, we will stand with you," she nods slightly toward me.

I take a breath and relax my body for the first time since we entered their territory.

"Thank you, your majesty," I bow to her.

"Oh, please," she shakes her head, "call me Asherah, and stand up. There is no need to bow to me. In fact, I suspect someday I may be the one to bow to you."

"Ha!" I laugh unexpectedly, and quickly cover my mouth with my hand, embarrassed by my outburst. What an absurd thought, "No, I don't think so," I press my lips together to keep from smiling.

She says nothing, only smiles back.

Chapter 17

Before we left, the Queen instructed her bees to supply us with wax for candles and jars of fresh honey. All three of us have our hands full with heavy bags. Ordinarily this would be enough to last the whole village through winter, but with Khalon around it may only last a few weeks.

We stop for the night figuring we still have half a day's journey ahead of us. We pick a spot next to the riverside. Khalon heads further down the river to catch some fish for our dinner. While I fill our canteens, Jae gets a fire going.

Jae and I do our tasks in silence. I steal a glance at him. He is working vigorously at his task, but his mind seems to be elsewhere. I get the feeling that he wants to talk to me as badly as I want to talk to him, but neither one of us knows what to say. I think we are beyond friendly exchanges at this point, and the thought of getting into yet another fervent discussion turns my stomach.

Fortunately, Khalon appears sooner than I thought with a spear stacked with fish. He smiles at me when I look up. His white teeth stand out against his tan skin.

"Come, help me clean these," he calls out to me. I leave my bags and canteens and join him downstream.

Jae looks over his shoulder at us. Fighting or not, he doesn't like to have me out of his sight.

Khalon releases the fish on the ground.

"What do I do?" I ask.

"Grab your knife," he instructs. I snatch the knife from my belt. "Cut it from here to here," he points with his massive index finger to the underbelly of the fish from the mouth to the tail.

I follow his order. The flesh of the fish is firmer than I thought. I really have to press on the knife hard. Once I feel the pop that I have broken through the skin, the knife moves easier. I slice it down the middle like he told me to. The fish bleeds a little. The smell amplifies once the fish has been cut. My stomach clenches.

I look to him for the next step. "Okay, now cut off the head and the tail," he says. I feel a little relieved once the head is removed. Even though the fish was already dead, I didn't like having its glassy eyes staring at me. "Good, now spread it open to clean out the insides," he instructs. I look at him with a look of trepidation. He laughs at my timidity. "You are going to have to toughen up, soldier," I narrow my eyes at him for using my joke.

I reach my hand into the fish's middle. It is cold, wet, and slimy. The organs are hard to hold onto. They slip between my fingers. I know my face must be scowling, because Khalon irrupts in a boisterous laugh. I finally get it all clean. Khalon takes it to inspect the insides.

"Looks good, nice work, now finish rinsing it in the water and come back so we can do the others."

The three of us sit around the fire eating our freshly caught dinner. The fish flakes apart tenderly. It tastes so good after such a long day.

Once I'm sufficiently stuffed, I find that I am having a really hard time keeping my eyes open. So many long days, so many restless night are taking their toll. I say my 'goodnights' and retire to a soft grassy spot not too far off. I close my eyes and fall instantly to sleep. For the first time in a long time I dream of nothing.

* * * * * *

I wake up late the next morning, but I am still up before Jae and Khalon. I quietly fly down to the riverside.

The water is slow moving at this point of the river. I slip off my romper and venture in for a swim. The water is cold, but bearable. My stomach muscles clinch as the water reaches my waistline. I dive in. Once I am completely submerged, it feels good.

The deepest part comes up to my shoulders. I take my braid out and comb through the wet strands with my fingers. Tipping my head back I submerge my head up to my ears. The rising sun is on my face. I close my eyes and empty my thoughts. The only sounds I hear are the birds singing their morning songs and the breeze lightly rustling the trees.

"What's this?" His low voice startles a scream out of me as I jolt upright. Khalon is standing on the edge of the river with my romper in his hand. A sly smile has spread across his face. I wrap my wings around my body.

"If I have your dress in my hand, what are you wearing in there?" he asks with a devious tone. My irritation is rising. I shake my head trying to think of my next move. "Sigrun, are you naked?" he asks with mock surprise. His grin is now a full blown ear to ear smile. His sharp canine teeth are fully shown and I can't decide if that makes him look more attractive or more conniving.

"Khalon, the gentlemanly thing would be to turn around, so I can get dressed."

"It's too bad I'm not a gentleman," he is really enjoying this.

"Whoa, what's going on?" I hear from Jae, who is now standing next to Khalon. Between Khalon's smirk and my awkward stance in the water he quickly puts everything together. He starts to chuckle. I can't believe it. I can't believe that he finds this funny too.

"This is great to see the two of you bonding," I sputter out with sarcasm. They both start laughing. "Yeah. Good. Really funny," I roll my eyes at them. "Seriously, I'm starting to get cold in here," I shout at them through a slight chuckle of my own.

"Okay, Okay," Jae says winding down from his laugh, "we'll leave you to get dressed."

"You're a better man than I am, junior," Khalon says. Jae gives him a sideways glance, "I'm kidding, relax," Khalon brings my romper over to a low branch and carefully drapes it over.

Before leaving, Khalon gives me a wink and a smile, and instantly my irritation melts away.

After getting dressed and pulling my hair into a tight bun, I make my way back to camp. The boys are already getting into breakfast. Khalon sees me and tosses me a piece of bread.

"Thanks," I say squinting my eyes and trying my very best to look like I'm mad at him. By his smile, I figure he is not convinced.

"Well," Khalon starts as he stands and stretches out. He twists at the waist, first to the right then the left, "how about a little training?" He finishes, but he is not talking to me.

"I said I would help you with that if you wanted," he says to Jae while pointing at his sword.

Jae looks at me and then back to Khalon, "Yeah, let's do it," he says.

Jae springs to his feet and the two of them head toward a nearby clearing.

Khalon snaps a sturdy stick over his knee making it sword length. He points to me, "I want you to watch from up there," he says pointing to a low branch, "I don't want to worry about you getting hurt, okay."

I nod in compliance and shoot up to the branch. From up here I really do have the best view to watch, and I won't be in the way.

Jae draws his sword and stands ready. He slightly bends his knees, his right foot in front. He is holding onto the sword tightly. The muscles in his forearms ripple as he adjusts his grip.

Khalon has a more relaxed stance. He holds the stick casually against his shoulder. "Okay," he starts, "let's see what you know so far."

With that, Jae lunges at Khalon. The muscles in my stomach tighten immediately. This suddenly feels like a crazy idea. Khalon effortlessly dodges Jae's thrust causing Jae to run past him. Jae turns quickly, just in time to raise his sword and stop Khalon's weapon from hitting him on his shoulder.

"Hmm, good reaction time," Khalon dishes out a rare compliment, "again," he orders.

Watching Khalon in this atmosphere is thrilling. For someone so big he moves with surprising grace and ease. The fresh perspiration shines on his body. His massive shoulders bulge with every move.

Jae runs forward again. This time he anticipates Khalon's movement better. Their weapons clash in front of their faces. Jae's eyes are intense and I can't tell if it is anger or concentration. Khalon's eyes are almost smiling. He is enjoying this. Their weapons clash again and again, until Khalon ducks under Jae's swinging arm, grabs Jae's arm at the wrist, and holds his arm behind his back almost to the point of breaking. Jae shouts out in pain as Khalon swings the stick down and stops just as it is about to make contact with the back of Jae's neck.

I know this is a training exercise, but it feels real. The pain on Jae's face is real.

They stand there for a moment, Khalon holding Jae in that painful position with the stick hovering above his neck. If this had been a real fight, Jae would have been beheaded.

"You're dead, friend," Khalon says in a cool tone. He lets go of Jae's arm. Jae sighs in both relief and defeat.

"I appreciate your swordsmanship," Khalon continues, "but that is not what we are training for." Khalon paces slowly around Jae, like a predator circling prey, as he speaks. "This battle will be about ending lives, not showing off. The Skars don't care about footwork. They don't care about form. They only care about winning, and that means they will kill you all if they have to," his already black eyes seem to darken. "If you are going to have a chance, you have to move faster, be stronger, and have the same merciless conduct that they do. You have to cut off this man's head," he points into distance like he envisions someone there ready to attack. Then he swings the stick down like he just beheaded the invisible man. "Then you move on to this man and cut off his arm, and then move onto this one and stab him through the heart," he acts out every step as he speaks thrusting the stick into every imaginary soldier. His breathing has amplified, his eyes are wide. I feel that my eyes are wide also. He finally brings his attention back to Jae who seems to be drinking in his every word. "It has to be fast, dirty, and without any hesitation. Can you do that?" Khalon asks Jae.

Jae stands up straighter. His brow is furrowed with a serious expression. "Yes I can," he says solidly.

Khalon smiles, "Show me," Khalon grabs the other half of the stick he broke. "Here," he says tossing it to Jae, "use this so you don't hold back." Jae sets his sword down. "Again," Khalon orders once more. Jae nods and removes his shirt. He sets it down next to his sword. He swings the stick a few times to get the right grip on it.

I find myself perched so far forward I have to hang onto the branch so I don't fall off. The two men circle each other for a moment. Their eyes locked on each other.

Suddenly they both charge at each other. Just as they are about to collide Jae jumps up. His wings shoot out catching the air. He is flying over Khalon's left shoulder and before Khalon can react, Jae swings down the stick hard across the base of Khalon's neck.

"Ow!" Khalon shouts.

I am watching Khalon closely. He strikes me as somewhat of a sore loser. I fear he might lose his temper.

Once Khalon realizes what just happened, he irrupts in jubilant laughter, "That's good! That's what I need from you."

Jae laughs a little also, but I think he is mostly relishing that he was able to finally hit Khalon.

My tension eases a little. The mood relaxes from here but the training intensifies. Both men go after each other for the next several hours until they can barely raise their arms.

By the time it is dusk, I force them to stop so they can wash up and rest before tomorrow. We have to get an early start to get back home.

Chapter 18

Even though we left early in the morning it is late in the afternoon by the time we make it back to the village. The three of us are exhausted. We decide to address the council tomorrow.

Jae takes off quickly towards his home. He has hardly spoken five words to me since the cherry tree. I feel despondent, I wish I could fix it, but I just don't know how.

Khalon heads up to his shady branch for some sleep. He has hardly slept for days, I know he is exhausted. This has been a real change for him, being awake so much during the day.

"Hey, Khalon," I stop him as he is leaving. He turns to me. "Maybe soon we can make a proper room for you, so you don't have to sleep outside."

He smiles, "Yeah that would be nice. You should get some rest." With that, he heads up into the branches, out of sight.

I should get some rest, but I have to check on something first.

My father's den is just how I left it. The fading afternoon light streams in on orange rays. I make my way over to the bookshelf. Reaching my arm back around the books, I feel the cloth. I grab it and pull it free. I breathe deeply when I see the book is still here.

I take it to my room where I fish my pendant out of my drawer. Sitting on my bed I look over the two objects. They are obviously connected somehow and the book, at least, is meant to be secret. They are not safe here.

I decide to hide them outside of the house, but where? I can't ask anyone else to keep them. I might put them in danger if I do. The cavern.

No one, besides Jae, knows about it. No one would even know to look there. I wrap the book tightly in large, thick leaves which I bond in melted wax to protect it from the water. Then I stuff both items in a cloth sack and fly toward the waterfall.

By the time I make it to the cavern, I have just enough light to stash the sack and briefly admire the beauty of this place. I think about the day I was here with Jae, before all of this madness, when things were simpler. I wish for that day again.

With the book and pendant safe, I feel relieved. I head straight to my bed, and sleep hard for what feels like a week.

Chapter 19

The council is relieved to see us. The news that our visit went so well pleases them. However, it does not diminish the anxiety that we may face danger in the near future.

Malyn meets us outside the council building.

"Hey," she says cheerfully, "welcome back. What was the hive like? What was the Queen like? Is she super big like they say? Was it scary? Ooh, is that honey?" She fires questions at all of us so fast. She talks the same way that she moves, fast and scattered. I can't help but giggle a little, because I don't even know where to start.

"Umm, yes they gave us honey and candles for everyone," I hold up the bags, while I attempt to answer all of her questions. "The Queen is quite big, but kind. It was scary at first, but it went really well, and the hive is much bigger than I thought," I pause to make sure I covered everything.

"Wow," she starts, "hopefully, I'll get to see it sometime." Her amusement makes me smile.

"Well, we've been busy while you've been gone," she darts onto a new topic. "Come on, follow me," before we can even reply she is already up in the air. I look at Jae and then to Khalon.

"Did you see which way she went?" I ask. They are both looking around trying figure out which direction to go in.

"She is so fast," Khalon says with amazement in his voice.

Just as Jae starts to point in a direction he thinks she went Malyn zips in front of us again.

"Are you coming, or not?" she asks a little annoyed.

"Yes, we're coming," I laugh at her. "Malyn, you have to slow down a little bit. You're too fast."

"Oh, sorry," she blushes and smiles, "okay, come on."

We follow Malyn through the woods, until we come across a clearing. Perfectly lined by mature trees is a meadow covered in soft grass.

"I found this the other day," Malyn says to us as we land.

Khalon nods in approval, "This should be just fine," he says.

Off in the distance between the trees I see movement. It startles me at first until I recognize my friends. Vidar, Ragnar, Soren, Ainia, and Ragnar's two brothers and sister have all shown up. The group approaches us casually except for Ainia who pounces on Jae as soon as she sees him. Judging by his grin, he seems to welcome the attention. It bothers me.

Vidar, Soren, and Ragnar saunter over coolly. It is the first time in a long time that I have seen Ragnar and all of his siblings together.

Ragnar's entire family is beautiful. Ragnar is black and orange like the oriole. His mother has shining gray mockingbird wings and a singing voice to match. His father and older brother, Ravi, both have brown and yellow wings like the meadow lark. And his younger brother and sister, the twins, are both like cardinals. Wren, the sister, has slightly more muted colors than her brother but with her short black hair against her faded red wings she is stunning.

I have always had a turbulent relationship with Vidar, Soren, and Ragnar. They tried to bully me when we were kids. That was until they realized I was as strong as them and I hit back. Since then we got on with a mutual respect and understanding, with the occasional cheap shot. To see them all gathered here, realizing they came to help, makes my heart swell a little.

"Hey, guys," I say to them, but I see that their eyes are all drawn to Khalon. They have all heard about him, possibly seen him from a distance, but this is the first time they have been directly in his presence. "Uh, this is Khalon," I say pointing to Khalon, "Khalon, these are our friends. Ainia you know, but this is Vidar, Soren, Ragnar, his brothers and sister Ravi, Remi, and Wren."

Khalon nods at them all, and they all answer with a collective and timid, "Hi."

I enjoy watching the awe on everyone's face when they meet him.

"So, what's first?" The ever eager Vidar asks.

Khalon stands a little straighter, "What do you have for weapons?" he asks.

"Not much," Jae admits, "I think every household has a family sword that has been passed down to each generation, maybe a few knives and daggers. We are mostly farmers and gatherers, we don't often hunt, and we don't fight," Jae's tone is almost apologetic.

"Farmers?" Khalon's eyebrows go up a bit, "What do you use to harvest?"

"We use harvesting blades, sickles," Soren answers.

"And, what do those look like?" Khalon prompts.

"They are long sticks with sharp, curved, blades at the end," Soren answers again.

"What do you use to chop wood?" By this point, we can all see where Khalon is directing us. The morale is improving already.

"Axes," Ragnar jumps in.

"Axes," Khalon repeats, "harvesting blades, you have weapons. We need to stock pile the ones you have and make more. I want you two," he points to Malyn and Wren, "to gather sticks to make bows and I'll show you how to make arrows. Gather any metal you can to be melted down for swords and arrowheads."

"What about us?" Ragnar asks pointing to himself and the rest of the boys.

Khalon smiles a devilish little grin, "Today we are going to work on hand-to-hand combat."

"I think you should just observe for now," he says to Ainia. She nods in absolute agreement.

"What about me?" I say feeling a little left out.

"You, I'm going to work with separately," he says in a way that I cannot decipher what he really means. I notice Vidar and Soren exchange a glance, and Jae's eyes narrow.

"For now," he continues, "I want you to work on your strength: push-ups, pull-ups, sit-ups until you can't move, then do ten more. Then endurance. I want you to do wind sprints back and forth on this meadow until you feel sick."

It is clear to me that he is not fooling around. If Khalon is going to build an army, it will be hard as stone by the time he is done.

I sneak glances at the boys between my sets of pull-ups and everything else. Khalon has them match up two at a time. First he matches them up according to their size. He puts Jae and Ravi together first because they are the tallest. He puts Vidar and Soren together because they are shorter and stocky. Then he switches everyone around to demonstrate the strengths and weaknesses of all statures. Jae and Ravi may have a longer reach, giving them what seems to be the advantage, but Vidar and Soren have lower centers of gravity making them better grapplers.

He shows them quick forceful moves. He shows them how to use their wings as a distraction and then punch their opponent in the throat. Then, he demonstrates a grappling technique that allows you to get behind the other person and break their neck. He explains where all of the soft parts of the body are, and where all of the vital organs are.

Every time Jae takes a hit I hear Ainia gasp. She is becoming a distraction, and I think Jae is embarrassed. After a while, Khalon sends her away to catch up with Malyn and Wren.

I admit I am much more curious about what they are doing than the task I have been given, but I keep at it. I do sit-ups until I lose count. I challenge myself to go lower with every push-up. I run faster and harder than I ever have before.

By the time Malyn and Wren get back from gathering sticks for bows, I am a wobbly, sweaty, mess. I can barely lift my arm to wave.

Khalon calls for us all to gather in the middle of the meadow. When I get closer to the boys, I can tell they are grateful for the break as well. They are all rubbing sore muscles and nursing a few bloody lips, and noses.

"Okay, everyone did well today," Khalon says to us, "I think we can call it a day." I hear a few sighs of relief. "Tomorrow, we'll work on archery," with that he dismisses us all.

The majority take off before he has a chance to change his mind, leaving just Jae, Ainia, Malyn and me. Khalon bends down and investigates the items brought back by Malyn and Wren.

"Aren't you coming?" I ask him.

"Nah, I think I'm going to stay out here tonight and put these bows together."

"Oh, want some company? I can help you," I offer. His eyes light up a little bit.

"Yeah, I'll stay too," Jae says. Khalon's eyes dim.

"Why don't we all stay and help," Ainia offers.

This brings a clever smile to Khalon's mouth, "I think that is a great idea," he says.

Inside my head, I'm screaming. This seems like a bad idea. Jae and I are not in a great place, Ainia is completely unaware of what has really been going on, and Jae and Khalon are barely tolerating each other. All of us camped out around a campfire making weapons all night sounds like my basic nightmare.

I shake my head and surrender, "Well, I'm going to get some things for dinner and clean up. I'm a sweaty mess," I say.

"I'll go with you," Malyn says.

"You are going to have to get rid of those girly habits if you are going to be a soldier," Khalon jokes with me.

"Well, I'm not a soldier yet, and I'm still a lady," I smile sweetly and curtsy dramatically.

He smiles, but says nothing. He simply watches me as I fly away.

Chapter 20

Later that night we sit around the fire and make bows the way Khalon instructed. We make practice arrows and tell stories about our journey to see the bees. I tell the story about the Gila and about how Khalon saved me. I watch the eyes of Malyn and Ainia, especially, and how they widen in anticipation with every gory detail. At dramatic moments, I drop what I'm doing and act out the scene to enhance my tale. At times, I forget that I'm making weapons. I forget that I am preparing myself for an invasion.

After a while sleep catches up to just about everyone. Jae falls asleep sitting propped up against a tree. Ainia, of course, curled up next to him with her head resting on his wing, and Malyn is curled up on the other side of Ainia. I drape one of the blankets I brought over them and return back to my spot by the fire.

Khalon and I sit next to each other in front the fire. We work quietly on our bows for a while.

"You must be getting tired?" I finally ask. "We've been doing so much in the daytime, you aren't getting enough sleep."

"I'm fine," he responds in an assuring tone.

"Well, I was thinking that we could set up torches all along the meadow and we could train at night so that you can sleep during the day."

"Then when are you going to sleep?" he asks pointing out the hole in my logic.

"I can learn to sleep during the day."

"And, I can learn to sleep at night," he counters. He smiles at me until I smile back, "Don't worry, we'll figure it out." He goes back to building his bow. I watch him for a minute. His hands are so big, but he fastens the string of the bow with such precision and ease. He bends the wood carefully so not to break it. Everything he does, he makes it look easy.

Watching his hands leads my eyes to the rest of him. All of his markings and scars so many untold stories – all about pain. I focus on one on his right forearm. It is two curved lines that almost connect to form a narrow oval and a solid black dot within it. It almost looks like an eye.

My hand moves without my telling it to. I reach out and touch the marking. His skin is warm and smooth, and I feel only the slight rise of his flesh where the mark resides. He looks at me. He seems surprised by my touch.

"Tell me about this one," I ask him.

He drops his eyes to the ground and shakes his head, "It is not a good story."

Tightness grabs hold of my chest. I feel what I can only imagine is his shame. Instantly, I regret asking.

He goes back to working on his bow in silence. The quiet between us is more uncomfortable than his unwillingness to open up to me. I have so many questions for him, but I do not want to upset him further.

"So, will you tell me about Mantus?" I ask, breaking the silence again.

"What would you like to know?" he asks without looking at me. I can tell he doesn't like to talk about him, but he is willing.

"I don't know. What does a warlord look like?"

"A scorpion."

"What?" I say with surprise.

"Mantus, he is a scorpion," He finally looks at me. I can feel that my mouth is open and my eyes are wide. I don't know what I expected him to say, but that certainly was not it. "Do you know what a scorpion is?" he asks me.

I nod. "Y-yes," I stutter out, "I've read about them, seen pictures."

"Well, that's what he looks like. He is sort of like the Bee Queen, but only a scorpion."

"Are the rest of the Skars like that?"

"He's the only scorpion I have ever seen, but yes there are others that are 'like' him. They do have fairies like your friends too, with bird wings I mean." I start thinking about how horribly outmatched we are and I feel ill. Khalon obviously sees me turn green. "You okay?" he asks.

"Umm, no, not really, I think it has just become mortifyingly obvious how inferior we are."

For the first time since we started talking he stops working and focuses only on me.

"I find it amazing that you seem to forget so easily who you are," he says to me with astonishment.

"What do you mean, I forget who I am?"

"You're a dragon, Sigrun!" He nearly shouts as he throws his arms up in the air."

"No, I just have dragon wings," I snap back.

"Oh boy," He mutters while rubbing the bridge of his nose. He is frustrated with me, "For starters, you are so much more than just a pair of wings, and someday soon I hope you realize that. Even if that were the only thing different about you, have you ever heard of anyone else with dragon wings? As far as you know do dragons even exist?" He knows the answer to this question already, but he wants me to say it just to make his point.

I bite down on the inside of my cheek and shake my head.

"Neither have I, and neither has Mantus. The best offense is the element of surprise, and you are the biggest surprise imaginable," he says his last sentence with a passion that I am confused by, because there is a hint of tenderness in his voice.

We lock eyes. He almost looks sad, but he doesn't stop looking at me. He speaks slowly, "You are the most special thing I have ever laid eyes on. I would never let him, or anyone, harm you. That is a promise."

I don't say anything, but I slowly change my position so I am kneeling in front of him. He hasn't moved. He is looking at me, and he looks a little nervous. He is perfectly still. So still, that it takes him a moment to react to me once I'm hugging him. I have my arms tightly around his neck. He acts as if he doesn't know what to do with affection. Finally, I feel his hands on my back.

"Thank you," I say quietly, still holding him tightly.

His arms tighten around me. I feel him melt his posture a little. "I didn't mean to yell at you," he says sweetly. I giggle because that is not the reason I am hugging him.

"I am so grateful for so many reasons that you found me that day," I say to him.

He has pulled me into his lap completely. I pull away to look at him. His face is filled with confusion and longing. I wonder if I'm the only person who sees this vulnerable side of him. I look down at his chest, particularly at the long scar. I reach out and trace my finger across it. His breathing picks up a little. I realize I want to look after him as much as he wants to look after me.

"I wish you were wearing that necklace of yours so I could figure out what you're thinking," he jokes.

I narrow my eyes at him, "You are usually pretty good at figuring me out. It has actually been quite inconvenient."

"At the moment, I will admit, I am completely lost," he smiles a little sideways smile, "I would really love to know what that pendant would say right now."

The muscles in my stomach tighten, "I think it would say," I suddenly feel a little shy. I look down at my hands, "I think it would say that I'm a little tired."

"Tired," he repeats with slight disappointment.

I nod.

"Yes, I'm sure you are," he sighs and lifts me as easily as though I were a dried leaf. He sets me down next to him.

"Do you mind if I sleep here next to you?" I ask him while I yawn.

"No, I don't mind. I actually prefer it," he smiles down at me. He grabs the other blanket and wraps it around me, "Will it bother you if I keep working?"

"Ugh-uh," I mutter. My eyelids start to feel very heavy.

He runs his fingers through my hair. It feels good.

"You worked very hard today, you'll probably be pretty sore tomorrow."

"Mmm-hmm," I moan sleepily. I feel his hand lightly stroke my temple. I easily drift off to sleep.

* * * * * *

I wake early. The eastern sun is just peaking up through the trees. The meadow is quiet. Jae, Ainia, and Malyn are still sleeping, but I don't see Khalon.

I stand up to stretch out and my muscles cry out. Just as Khalon said, I am sore. Next to me are stacks of bows and practice arrows. Looking around the meadow I finally see him. He is making adjustments on a shooting target. He has set up a long row of targets along the tree line. He has been busy in the night.

I pick up a bow and a handful of arrows and make my way over to him. He smiles when he sees me coming.

"Morning," he says cheerfully.

"Morning," I return with a smile.

"How do you feel?" He almost looks smug. He already knows that I'm sore by the way I'm moving.

"Well, you weren't lying. I am a bit sore today," I admit while I rub my shoulder.

"Are you up for more?" He challenges with a smile.

"When do we start?" I accept.

"After breakfast."

By the time I finish eating, Jae and the girls start to wake and the rest of our friends show up as well. While they eat and catch up with each other, I make my way over to get my first lesson in archery.

"Have you ever used a bow?" Khalon asks.

I press my lips in a hard line and shake my head. I don't know why I feel embarrassed by my lack of combat knowledge.

"That's okay," he reassures me, "it's pretty simple once you get the hang of it."

He reaches down and grabs a bow for himself. After taking a few steps back, he aligns himself with one of the targets. He stands sideways, twists his body, and raises the bow to eye level. He pulls the arrow back and releases it effortlessly shooting right into the center of the target.

The others have gathered to observe as well. I feel a vibration of excitement rattle through everyone.

"Your turn," he extends an arrow out to me.

I feel nervous. I have all eyes on me and I have to follow that very impressive example. I grab hold of the arrow, but he doesn't let go.

When I meet his eyes, he has a reassuring look on his face, "Most people don't hit the target on their first try, don't get discouraged, because after a few tries you will, okay?" he encourages me. I nod and give him a grateful smile.

I step back and try to remember his stance. He was standing so that the target was at his side and then he twisted his upper body so that he was facing the target. I model this position and my side muscles scream in protest. I am still so sore for all of those sit-ups I did yesterday. I wince, but I fight through it hoping no one notices. I position the arrow's end against the string the way he did, and lift the bow up to eye level. I have a tight grip on the front part of the bow. I pull the arrow back, feeling the resistance of the bow, the arrow head is lined up with the target. I take a breath and hold it. Everything around me stills. I feel my hands steady and release as I breathe out.

The sound is exquisite. All of it, from the thrum of the bow's release, the sound of the arrow cutting through the air, but most of all the pang of the arrow hitting its destination. That's when I knew I hit the target, from the sound. I look down at the wood target and see my arrow sticking straight out from it. It isn't anywhere near the middle but it is on the target all the same.

I look at Khalon. I can't help but to smile, I'm feeling very pleased with myself. His eyebrows are raised. He obviously is very pleased also.

"Alright, let's continue," he says trying to stifle his admiration. Excitement from the others irrupts as they all race to grab bows of their own and handfuls of arrows. "Today we are going to practice short distance, straight shooting,"

Khalon shifts into instructor mode, "We'll do long distance shooting later." He walks from person to person giving pointers and small adjustments that make large improvements.

Shot after shot I hit the target, but I have yet to hit the center. Frustration starts to well up inside me. Khalon comes over to where I'm standing. I smile in attempt to hide my disappointment. He looks over at the target. My most recent shot is only two inches from his first arrow which is perfectly in the middle.

"You're close to the center," he says. His tone is pleased, but he knows that I am not satisfied. I wipe the perspiration from my forehead. The day has gotten hot. "Let's see what we need to do to get it in the center," he has me pick up another arrow and get into position. "Hold that position," he orders. He slowly walks around me and stands so that his front is against my back. My muscles tighten up. He puts one hand on my ribs on the left side, and the other on the underside of my drawn arm. He pulls me gently up and makes an adjustment to my shoulder so it is more in line. He holds me there for a second. His touch is demonstrative and intimate at the same time. I feel my cheeks blush. "Remember how this feels," he says. I know he is referring to my posture, but with the way he is touching me my heart beats faster.

He lets go and steps back. I focus on his arrow in the center. I breathe in, ignore everything around me, and let go. I am so alarmed by the shouts and applause that comes from my friends that I don't realize at first that I split Khalon's arrow right down the center. I blink hard to make sure I am seeing it correctly. I bite my cheeks to keep from smiling, but my efforts are in vain. As soon as I look at my friends who are jumping up and down in excitement, I laugh out loud.

Khalon walks up to me. His eyes have a look of wonder and pride. He smiles but says nothing. He only tucks a loose tress of hair behind my ear and moves on.

Throughout the day everyone does exceptionally well. Even Ainia does fairly well with a bow. However, she does take every opportunity to get Jae to help her with her form. It is strange to see her in all her fragile perfection holding a weapon. Her blue and silver wings shimmer in the sunlight. She seems completely out of place here. Everything about her stands out rather than blends in. Her blond hair is tied back in a perfect low ponytail, and she is wearing a white cotton summer dress, which says to me she has no intention of getting dirty. Observing her makes me more concerned about her. She is not built for fighting. Even though she is taller than Malyn, Malyn has a muscular quality to her and is quite strong. Ainia has never been athletic at all. Her wings are very delicate and difficult to heal, and her frame is so slender. From what I understand about the Skars, one of them could easily crush her. This thought makes me shutter. I decide to talk to Khalon about her position here, I don't want her harmed.

Everyone else is surprisingly enthusiastic. The boys are competitive, of course, but in a jovial way. I have even noticed a little special attention between Vidar and Malyn. It makes me smile. I think she has liked him for some time.

The mood suggests that everyone has forgotten what we are training for. I choose not to remind them. Time slips by, the afternoon light is almost gone, and no one appears to be phased by its absence.

Though everyone did well, Malyn turns out to be the star student. She moves faster and she hits more targets than anyone.

"Okay everyone," Khalon shouts to us, "gather around."

I also failed to notice the day's end had already come. The sores on my hands and the fatigue of my arms are the only indication of how long the day has been.

We circle around Khalon, "Everyone has done well today," he says. We all breathe with relief. "But, targets that don't move are easy to hit." I would feel discouraged, but he has a point. "Over the next few weeks we are going to continue training. I will put together a schedule. You still need to do your harvesting and prepare for winter. I also need to get together with your metal workers and have better weapons made."

"I can help with that," Ravi interrupts, "I do metal work."

"Excellent. We'll talk about that later. Before you all leave, make sure you take your bows with you. They are yours now," Khalon pauses to look the group over. "Take the next two days off, let your bodies rest and I'll see you back here on the third day, at dawn," He dismisses us.

I take a moment to say goodbye to my friends. The majority seem relieved to have a break from all of the physical work, and take off quickly.

"What about you Sig? What are you going to do tomorrow?" Ainia asks me.

"Not sure. I have to get some supplies, restock the kitchen, you know just normal stuff. You?"

"I'm probably going to lay low. My arms are really sore from today," she says while rubbing her shoulder. This makes me giggle to myself since I am pretty sure she doesn't know what being really sore feels like.

"That's probably a good idea," I say diplomatically. Jae and Malyn walk up to us. I turn my attention to Malyn.

"You did really well today," I say to her, and give a hug.

"Oh, thanks," she smiles, but I can tell she is a bit shy about her accomplishment.

"No, really," I reiterate, "I'm really proud of you." She blushes at the compliment. I hold her hand tightly.

I see Jae over her shoulder. He is watching us. I can't quite read his expression, but I feel a bit nervous with him there.

"Okay, I'm gonna take off," I say as I let go of Malyn. "I'll see you guys later," I hurriedly wave to everyone as I head over to where Khalon is to grab my things. They stay there and continue to talk. Even though I don't look back I feel Jae watching me.

My focus at this point is to go home. I am exhausted. I get to Khalon he is squatting down stacking up the remaining bows and tying the arrows up in a bundle.

"Are you heading home?" I ask him.

"Yes, I actually am quite tired myself," he says with a little smile.

"Are you taking these back with you?" I ask in reference to bows and arrows.

"Yes, we shouldn't leave them out in plain sight, just in case."

"Just in case?" I ask, with my eyebrows raised.

"Yes, just in case. Don't worry," he chuckles, "I'm just being cautious."

"Okay. Well, I'll take these for you," I reach out for him to give me the bundle of arrows. He looks at my outreached hand and notices the raw skin from today. He stands up and takes my hand in his. He carefully assesses the damage from the day.

"I can make a balm that will take care of this. I might have to gather some Broadleaf Plantain before I get back to the house," he says, not letting my hand go.

"I bet you'll find what you need in my father's den."

"You think so?"

"Yeah, I'm pretty sure we have it. When we get back, you should go through his vials so you know what we have."

He nods, "Okay, then let's go home," he hands me the bundle of arrows and we start for home.

Chapter 21

Watching Khalon in my father's den is fascinating to me. Someone so big around so many small fragile things would seem like a natural disaster, but he is so careful and precise in his movements. His massive hands go through the bottles easily.

He finds one jar and opens the lid. "Ah, this one," he inhales the aroma of the contents, "I'd say this is fresh enough." He grabs a mortar and pestle and a small bottle of oil. He sets everything down on my father's desk and motions for me to sit down.

"You know you don't have to do this. It's not that bad," I say feeling a little silly that he is putting this all together for a couple of blisters.

"It might not be all that bad right now, but soon you will be training almost every day, and this will get worse," he quickly looks over the sores. "Your hands will toughen up, but this will prevent infection," Khalon often surprises me. At first glance, he is a brute, but under that fearsome exterior he is more wise and caring than I ever would have expected.

I think about the many layers of Khalon while he is crushing leaves in the mortar and adding oil here and there to get the right texture. His precision and attention to his task makes me think of my father, and that makes me smile.

He glances at me, "What are you smiling about?" he asks in a playful tone.

I shake my head, embarrassed that he caught me, "It's nothing, I was just thinking about how you are always taking care of me," he looks at me and says nothing, so I continue,

"It's just I've been a mess since I first met you, and I feel a little bad about it."

"Why does it make you feel bad?" He stops what he's doing and looks at me. His eyes almost look sad. I am explaining myself badly. He has taken this the wrong way.

"Oh no, not bad, just umm," I search for the right word, "helpless. You know, haven't you ever felt helpless?" His eyes are searching, sifting through his past. "What about when you were a child?" I ask, attempting to dig a little deeper.

"I don't remember much from back then. I remember knowing that my parents were gone, and then Mantus found me and brought me into his tribe. It's all kind of a blur."

"Did anyone look after you then?"

He shakes his head, "It is kind of a figure it out or die type of colony. A sure way to weed out the weaker element," he says with a hint of disgust.

He turns his attention back to making the balm.

My heart throbs for him. I hadn't thought about it until now that at one time this mountain of a man was also once a small child, and he has never been given an ounce of affection or sympathy.

In some ways, I empathize with him. My childhood certainly had its difficult moments. When we were kids, Merik used to randomly punch me, hard, or pinch me, for no reason. He knew just how hard to hit me without leaving any marks. He would laugh so hard when my lip quivered and I started to cry. When our father came into the room, he would fall to the ground and cry so I would be the one to get punished. Jae used to get so mad. He never understood why I wouldn't hit him back. "I can't hit Merik," I would say, "He is my brother."

The recent care and affection that has been ladled onto me by both Jae and Khalon shows me the void that was there all those years.

Merik has a family that loves him, and a home to come back to. I know the loss of our mother was hard on him, but our father made up for the loss as best he could. Khalon grew up in a world of pain and emptiness, and yet he has compassion behind it all. How is it that Merik holds more anger in his heart than this man?

Khalon takes my hands, bringing my attention back to him. One hand at a time he gently spreads the mixture onto the raw spots. Then he takes some bandage cloth and rips it to make it the right size. Watching him tie the bandages around my hands with such delicate attention causes another question to spring to mind.

"One more thing I can't figure out," I pause waiting to see if he will cut me off, but he doesn't so I continue, "If you've never been cared for, how is it that you are so good at caring for me?" This brings a smile to his face. He looks at me. His eyes are big and sincere.

"That's an easy one," he says with coolness.

"It is?"

"Yeah," he leans in to me like he is about to tell me a secret. I lean in also. He speaks slowly, "You are the first person I have ever wanted to care for, and the only person I care about," he smiles at me, and I can't help but to smile also. He kisses the bandage on my hand, and leans back, "There, all better."

"Thank you," I say quietly. The words don't seem adequate enough, but I don't know what else to say. This is not the first time he has rendered me silent, and I suspect it will not be the last.

We both retire to our rooms for the night. I think he is as tired as I am, because he goes straight out to his branch and goes to sleep.

Once in my room, I take a moment to look at myself in the mirror. I am dusty and dirty. The edges of my face are brown and smudgy with dried perspiration and dust. My once tidy braid is loose and disheveled.

I fill my washbowl with water and grab a clean rag. Mindful of my bandaged hands I wash my face and arms carefully with the rag. I take my hair out of the braid and look at my reflection. My hair has gotten long over the summer. It is way past my shoulders now, almost to the middle of my back. It is wavy and wild looking, and the summer sun has bleached golden tones into it. My violet eyes are looking back at me. My cheeks have a bronze flush from the sun. I hardly recognize myself these days.

For so long I have thought of myself as the awkward little girl with scaly wings. I've always been strong, but felt defenseless, like a wild thing caged until it became tame. Now I'm starting to see something else behind my eyes, something fierce. I like it.

Crawling into my bed feels divine. The nights have been getting cool enough that I have to use an extra blanket. I stretch my wings out, feeling them pull at my shoulders. I sink into my mattress and finally let my muscles relax.

I sleep late into the next morning. I peek at my hands under the bandages. The sores are much better. I can see that new, tougher, skin is already forming.

I tie my hair back into a ponytail, and put on a pair of light gray cotton shorts and a matching sleeveless top. Looking at myself in the mirror, I feel good. The shirt shows off the recent fullness in my arms and shoulders. I know Ainia would still be disappointed in my color palate. "Why do you wear such dull colors when nature provides such vibrancy?" She used to ask me. I never had a good answer for her, except that I never wanted to stand out any more than I already did. I shrug at my own reflection and head out down the hall.

I peek out Khalon's window and see that he is sleeping late as well. His wings are wrapped around him like a shroud, covering his face to block out the sun. I sneak out of the room quietly so not to disturb him, I know he is tired.

The kitchen is just about bare. I grab the bucket off the outside windowsill, it is dry. There has been no rain since my father's burial. With the bucket in one hand and some empty sacks over my shoulder, I head for the door. My bow rests against the wall and I think about what Khalon said, "Just in case." I pick it up, sling it across my torso. I tuck an arrow in my belt next to my knife and head out for supplies.

Normally I would get fresh water from the town's water supply, a surplus of rain water that is collected in the center of town. However, my food gathering will take me toward the river anyway.

My nose picks up the rich scent of pine so I head toward the pine grove near the river. The trees are showing a few open pine cones. The nuts must be ripe. It won't be long before the birds and other animals will have eaten them all. I stop to gather as many as one of my sacks will carry. I cut the cones carefully at the base with my knife, being mindful of the sap.

I remember a summer morning when Jae and I were children we stopped to grab what we thought would be a quick morning snack. It took two days to get Jae's fingers unstuck from one another from all the sap those branches produced.

I place dozens of unopened cones into my bag. Birds and squirrels will spend hours pecking and clawing them open. The reward to get to those small buttery morsels, but they don't realize that by leaving the cones in a bag for a few days the cones will open by themselves releasing the treasure on their own. Then all that is required is shaking the seeds out and peeling the thin skins off the individual kernels.

I move on once my bag is stuffed. I stop occasionally to gather berries and plants, and dig up a few roots. I fill every bag I have and by the time I fill my water bucket I don't think I will be able to carry anything more. This should keep us stocked for at least a week, even with Khalon in the house.

The riverside is quiet. Only the sound of soft babbling from the water and the quiver of a few leaves reach my ears, even the wind is fairly still. I take a moment after I have filled my bucket and a few canteens to rinse my hands and face with the cold river water. It is easy to forget your troubles here. The sun shines on my shoulders, the smell of pine needles lingers around me, and even the feel of the cool summer grass on my legs gives me contentment.

I close my eyes. Breathing in, long and slow taking in all that surrounds me, exhaling even slower, fully letting go. The once quiet ripple of a few leaves now sounds like moving water. I hear it quietly at first, a distant wave a long ways away, then the wave rushes closer, and closer, crashing into one tree and then the next, until it is upon me. A powerful gust of wind circles around me. I hear everything. Every flit from every bird. A spider stretching its web. The flow of my own blood. When I open my eyes, my focus is different, heightened. I can see the individual blades of grass, the Ghost Ants on the soil working between the blades. I see the smooth stones at the bottom of the river. My breathing picks up a bit. I don't understand how I am seeing everything so clearly. Then something in the river catches my attention. A shiny silver fish stops at the rocks near the shore. It quickly swims around looking for food to eat. I slowly reach next to me for my bow and the arrow from my belt. I line up my shot. The string of my bow presses on my cheek. The fish stills in one spot as though he is waiting for me. I release my arrow and with the splash of the water I lose sight of my target. Walking into the water I feel foolish. That was stupid. I could never make that shot. I reach into the water to retrieve my arrow. I pull it hard to release it from the ground. As soon as my hand brings it to the surface, something silver flips in the sunlight. The fish that I thought I missed is pierced by my arrow. I didn't miss. I shot it straight through. The thrill of hitting a moving target, through water, more than twenty feet away fills me with joy, and I laugh to myself. It is a small victory, but it means that my skills are improving.

I put the fish in one of the bags to take back to Khalon. I'm not sure what he will be more excited about, the evidence of my improvement, or the fish meat he will be having for dinner.

I take the long way back so I can fly by the grain fields, to see how the harvest is coming. Careful not to spill my freshly filled bucket I land on the edge of the field. The grain is tall and the green has all but gone leaving golden stalks behind. I can barely see the tops of my friend's heads from the ground. I set down the bulk of my supplies and head towards them with a canteen of water.

"Hey, Sig," I hear Vidar say over my right shoulder. I turn to look at him, he is casually resting on the dull end of his harvesting sickle. His shirt is off and the sweat on his body and the slight laboring of his breathing indicates he has not been resting long. His blond hair is soaked through. He's been working all morning. He smiles at me and his gray eyes shine brightly in the sun's light.

"You look thirsty," I say with a smile and extend my hand to him that is holding the canteen.

"Oh, you are a darling," he says eagerly reaching for the water I offer. He takes a long drink and then pours a small amount in his hand and splashes his face. Soren, Remi, and Jae come through the tall grass. I am surprised to see Jae here. He doesn't usually work on the harvest.

"What are you doing here?" I ask him.

"I was going to ask you the same thing," he says back to me in a somewhat chilly tone.

"Redwood, don't be rude, she brought refreshments," Vidar says while tossing the canteen to him.

Vidar defending me from Jae? Now that is strange.

"I figured I should help with the harvest since our time will be split this summer," Jae finally answers my question.

"I was just out doing some gathering. The pine trees are ready for harvest as well," I quickly explain myself.

The boys fervently drink up the majority of the water as Wren comes through the grass with a bundle of grain stalks slung over her shoulder. Her short black hair is neatly tucked behind her ears.

"Hey, is there any left for me?" she asks with a smile.

"Just barely," her twin, Remi, says handing it to her.

"I have more," I start to say, feeling bad that I didn't grab more.

"Oh no, this is great, thanks, Sigrun," she says. She drinks the rest of its contents and hands the dry canteen back to me. "We are going to be wrapping up soon anyway," she points to the sky and I realize that the afternoon sun is fading already. The days are getting shorter.

"Yeah, I should get going anyway," I am feeling uncomfortable. With the water in my canteen gone and the day almost over, I have no other reason to linger here.

"I'll walk with you," Jae offers.

This surprises me, since he has been very cold to me ever since that morning I left him in the cherry trees.

"See you later, Sig," Soren chimes as we make our way out of the grain.

"Thanks again for the water," Vidar shouts after us.

I wave back at them and then they are out of sight.

"So, why did you really come here?" Jae asks me.

I don't understand what he is implying and I am feeling annoyed by his tone.

"Jae, honestly I didn't have a motive. I was out gathering and thought I would swing by this way and see how the harvest was going, that's all."

"Oh," is all he says in reply, and he seems almost disappointed.

We walk to the edge of the field in silence. Once I see my supplies, I start slinging bags over my shoulders and situating my bow. Jae stands there awkwardly.

"You look nice today," he finally sputters out. I look at him with squinting eyes partially because the sun is setting behind him, and also because his comment strikes me as odd. "I haven't seen you wear this for a long time," he continues while pinching the hem of my shirt between his thumb and index finger.

"Well, Ainia would say that it isn't bright enough," I attempt to make a joke.

"I think that is what I like about it, it's understated," he smiles at me.

"Understated?"

"Yeah, understated," he says again. I shake my head a little. I know he is trying to pay me a compliment, but it seems somewhat backhanded.

"Thanks. I think," I say the second part quietly. There is an awkward silence for a moment. "Well, I'll see you in a couple of days," I say at last and start to fly up.

"Wait," he shouts out to me, "what are you doing tomorrow?"

"I'm not sure yet."

"Will you come over tomorrow for dinner?"

"To your parent's house?" I ask just to be clear.

"Yeah."

Is that a good idea? I ask myself. Do his parents even want me in their home? All I have been is a source of stress and tension for our village lately.

"You can bring Khalon of course," he says under his breath. He misinterprets my hesitation.

I admire that he is trying to bridge the gap between them, even if his offer isn't the most sincere, it is still an attempt.

"Dinner would be nice. After sundown?" I say finally.

"Yeah, that would be great," he sounds pleased.

"Okay, I'll see you tomorrow," I land just long enough to give him a kiss on the cheek, and then before he can say anything else I take off towards home.

******

Khalon is not at home when I get back. I'm a little disappointed that I will have to wait to tell him how I caught this fish. I prepare the fish the way he showed me in the woods and then roast it over a fire in the kitchen. I leave it on a plate for him outside of his door along with a note that says, "Your dinner was caught with this arrow," I use the arrow to post the note on his door. Standing back I smile to myself at the display I have left for him, and feel anxious for him to see it.

I put the bags of pine cones up in a cupboard until they are ready. After getting everything put away and cleaned, I head to my room to go to bed. The day has caught up with me and I am very tired.

I change into a thin cotton nightdress and crawl into bed. Nighttime can be the loneliest time in this house. Everything is so quiet. The only sounds are the crickets outside and the night breeze. The stillness allows my mind to wander.

I start thinking about the events of today and that, of course, leads to the prospect of what may happen tomorrow. I have eaten at Jae's home almost as much as my own, but this summer has changed everyone. Everything with Jae has been so strange. I have no idea how much his parents know.

Regardless, I don't think we will be able to have simple dinner conversation anymore. Even though I don't think I need Khalon to be there, I think it would be good to have him with me. I want to show as many people as I can the good that is in him.

It takes a few hours, but eventually my drowsiness overcomes my anxiety and I drift off to sleep. Sometime in the middle of the night I wake to thunderous laughter. Khalon has come across my note. I smile to myself and lay my head back onto the bed. Too tired to get up, I decide to tell him about it tomorrow.

Chapter 22

It's early. The sun has barely started to come up. I stretch my arms and wings out. They are still a little sore, but they feel much better today.

The house is silent, I tip-toe down the hall trying to keep the floor from creaking beneath my feet. In the kitchen, I start a fire in the hearth. It has been too hot to have a fire in the house the last few weeks, but this early in the morning the heat feels good against the clinging chill from the night. I set the kettle above the fire and while I wait for it to boil I locate the tea that Beda had brought in one of her care packages. Opening the jar I smell the mint right away and the lemon peel is also strong. It smells fresh. It smells like the best part of summer.

After brewing my tea, I make my way back upstairs to my father's den. In recent days, I have not had much time to just sit alone in the quiet. In the past years, I used to spend hours at a time off in a shady spot somewhere in the woods, or in the cozy warmth of my room reading. Since the death of my father I haven't wanted to be alone in the quiet of his den. Every time I am left to think too long I always start to remember my father. I have been trying to shut out thoughts of him, and I realize now that by doing that I am shutting out the best parts of myself.

I grab a stack of books from the shelves and sit at his desk. So many of them have been written by him, seeing his handwriting brings a lump to my throat, but it is a comfort as well. I run my fingers across the words, feeling the slight indentation of his pen. I take a sip of my tea, it burns my tongue a little but it is so good that I don't care, I take another and start reading.

Most of the books are about medicines, how to make them, how to apply them. I have leafed through the lot of them before, but Merik studied them the most. I go through them setting aside the ones that I have read before, keeping a stack that I want to read again.

The morning light is bright now. The breeze from the window is getting warmer. The steam from my cup has faded. Time is slipping by while I pour over these books. I don't know what I'm looking for but I can't stop searching.

The day before he died, the day he gave me the necklace, I felt like he was trying to tell me something important. Perhaps he was preparing me for a conversation we were supposed to have in the future. A conversation we were never able to have. I know in my heart the answers are in the red book that I stashed, but there must be something else, something I can understand.

"A-hem," the noise startles me and I scream a little. I turn and see Khalon in the doorway. For someone so big I forget that he can be so quiet.

"You just about scared the life out of me," I put my head in my hands and laugh at myself.

"Sorry," he chuckles, "but I have been aching to ask you about this," he tosses something to me. It is the arrow from my catch. Just seeing it again makes me smile.

"It was incredible," I start. He pulls up a chair to listen to my story. "I was just sitting on the riverside looking at the water and all of the sudden my vision was so clear. I could see everything, the rocks on the river bottom, the algae moving, I've never had focus like that. Then I saw something silver. The fish was swimming around the rocks looking for food and I grabbed my bow and took a shot. I thought I missed at first, but when I went to retrieve the arrow the fish was shot through."

He was smiling at me, "Well, I am going to release you from moving target practice. It seems you have that down." By his tone, I can tell he is pleased.

Leaning back he looks at the stacks of books on the desk. "What's all this?" He says pointing to the books.

"Oh, just some of my father's old books," I say casually.

"What are they about?"

"Um, mostly medicine and some history, they are pretty academic," I try to make them sound as uninteresting as possible.

"Are you looking for something specific?"

I believe that he is either curious or trying to be helpful, but I honestly don't know how to answer his question. The whole story is a long and complicated one, and the truth would entail telling him about the red book.

"Nothing specific," I say finally, "just rereading some things, and I guess getting some insight on my father's work."

Khalon nods at my explanation. By the squint of his eyes, I can tell he knows I am not telling him everything, but he graciously says nothing to it.

"What about you?" I change the subject, "What have you been up to?" I didn't see him at all yesterday or last night. He is still new to our colony so I wonder what would occupy his entire day.

"You'll see," he says with a sideways smile. His mysterious nature and playfulness cause me to smile back.

"What do you mean I'll see?" I say as I lightly kick his shin.

He chuckles at my irritation, "Don't you like surprises?"

"No, I don't," which isn't necessarily true, I just want him to tell me his secret.

"Well, that's too bad, because you will have to wait," he smiles broadly enough for me to see his pointy canines.

I shake my head and laugh at him. This might be a good time to break the news about our dinner plans. "As it turns out, I have a surprise for you," I say, his smile fades to intrigue, "we are having dinner with Jae and his family tonight."

His smile is completely gone now, "Am I being punished?" His pitiful tone makes me laugh out loud.

"Oh you'll be fine, you big baby," I tease. Looking at him I realize that I have become used to his bare chest, but for a more formal dinner it might be inappropriate. "I think I might look into getting you a shirt that fits."

He looks down at himself and then back at me, "Good luck," he says with a smile.

"You underestimate me."

"Never," his eyes are serious though he is still smiling.

I stand up and head toward the door, "Come on. Let's get you some breakfast," I glance out the window and see that the sun is quite high, "or lunch."

* * * * * *

The day goes by quickly. After lunch, I met up with Ainia to see if she could put a shirt together for Khalon. As always, she questioned me about every little detail since I last saw her, most of which concerned Jae. I don't have much to tell her these days. My once encouraging attitude regarding her affection toward him has been tainted. His intentions with her and with me have polluted my feelings on the matter.

Once I leave her, I head to the waterside to clean myself up. Khalon is not the only one who needs to look presentable. Even though I have known Jae's parents my entire life I still feel intimidated in their home. Jae's family is the closest thing our colony has ever had to royalty. We have never had a solitary leader, all decisions are put to a vote by the council, but at least one member of Jae's family has always had a chair on the council. Falon's and Vivek's opinions are weighted very heavily.

By the time I make it back home, Ainia has dropped off Khalon's shirt. He isn't very excited about it, but he doesn't put up much of a fight either.

Looking at myself in the mirror I find that I am nervous. I keep fussing with a troublesome tress that won't stay put. I had an illusion that I could come up with a clever little up-do like the ones Ainia often wears. Something pretty and sweet, and trickled in flowers. However, my skills in this arena are lacking. Normally I would not be bothered by what my hair looks like, but tonight I feel pressure to be elegant, which is a characteristic that I am not. After a moment, I relinquish the idea of wearing my hair this way, and shake it loose. My messy waves fall down past my shoulders. I dip my finger into a small jar of solid oil and dab it on my lips to give them a shine. Once I pinch my cheeks to bring the color out, I look at my reflection once again and figure this is the best it is going to get. I stand up and smooth out my purple dress and head down the stairs.

Khalon is standing in the main room waiting for me. The shirt Ainia made fits him well, though I can tell he is uncomfortable in it. It is a very casual, soft cotton, short-sleeve shirt, gray in color, but he looks handsome.

He turns to look at me as I enter the room. His mouth opens a little like he might speak, but he says nothing. Usually when I'm with Khalon I'm flying or fighting, and sweating. This is the most dressed up he has ever seen me.

"Don't stare, it's rude," I say to break the tension.

He smiles, "You look nice."

"So do you," I walk over to him and smooth out the shoulders of his shirt, "Ainia did a good job on such short notice." He says nothing, but continues to smile at me.

"We should get going," I say and walk through the door. The sun has just set and the stars are starting to show themselves. "Shall we walk or fly?" I ask.

"Well," he starts to say as he looks up to the sky, "it is a nice night for a walk."

As the light continues to fade, we see lanterns and candles start to appear in the windows of all the homes. The twinkle from the trees looks like a second starry sky, it's beautiful.

Jae's home is the biggest in the village. It is an old oak tree that has been in his family since our people settled here. The family home should have gone to Vivek, the oldest brother, but he refused it. Apparently, he was uncomfortable with the size of the home, and he opted for a cozier dwelling just down the way.

Khalon stopped walking once we came up the house. He said nothing but I know he was amazed by the size of it.

Jae's mother, Ulani, opens the door before we are even on the steps. It is no mystery why Jae is as handsome as he is. Falon is a striking figure, but Ulani is stunning. Her eyes are a pale gray, almost silver, and against her tan skin they look electric.

"Sigrun," she bursts, "it's been too long since you've been here," she pulls me in for a long hug. It was always strange to me that Falon kept me at arm's length, but Ulani always rushed right in.

I haven't been to Jae's house since before my father died. I know she was at his funeral, but I hardly noticed anything that day. She hugs me tightly like a mother would. It, unexpectedly, brings a lump to my throat. I pull away from her embrace.

"Yes, I know. It's been," I pause and look at Khalon, "an interesting summer," he smiles at me.

"Oh, you must be Khalon," she rushes to him as well. He looks positively frightened. Before he can react, she is hugging him. He has never had such a welcoming reception. He doesn't know what to do. I chuckle quietly as he awkwardly hugs her back, "I've heard a lot about you," she says.

"I'm sure you have," he says to her as Jae come to the door.

"Hey, Sig," he says giving me a hug. "Khalon," he nods to him.

"Jae," Khalon nods back.

I take a breath. At least, they are being courteous.

"Well, come inside," Ulani urges us into the house. "Dinner is almost ready."

I make my way inside.

"You look nice," Jae says quietly to me as I walk past him.

"Thank you," I blush a little. I think Ulani notices because she is trying not to smile, which only make me blush more.

Jae's home is large, too large for a small family, but it is also warm and inviting. A fire is going in the grand living room filling the room with the smell of fresh pine. Falon and Vivek are sitting in the two chairs in front of the fire. They must be in deep conversation, because they don't hear us until we fully enter the room.

"Ah, Sigrun, welcome," Falon says to me as they both stand up.

I hadn't realized that Vivek was going to be here as well. I am glad to see him. He has always been kind to me, though his being here makes this casual dinner feel more serious than I anticipated.

"Thank you for having us," I say.

"Khalon, we are very pleased that you came as well," Vivek says diplomatically.

"Can we get you something to drink?" Falon offers, "Some wine perhaps? I think you kids are old enough now," he says with a smile.

"I would love some tea," I reply. Spirits might relax me too much, and under the circumstances it seems best to stay sharp.

"I'll take you up on that offer," Khalon says.

"Me too," Jae chimes in.

Falon disappears into the kitchen for a moment and comes back with Yoana, Vivek's wife. Yoana rarely speaks, but her eyes tell you everything you need to know. She is quite thin and her wispy hair refuses to stay put in her tidy bun. There is a frailty to her and yet a silent strength.

Falon hands the boys their drinks and Yoana brings me mine. She smiles at me as she hands me the cup.

"Thank you," I say to her. As I take the cup, she puts her hand on mine and unexpectedly squeezes with affection. Then she disappears back into the kitchen.

For the next several minutes the men engage in small talk, but I must admit I'm not paying attention. My thoughts are more consumed with what tonight is really about. There has been a formality in the air since we arrived. I have dined here several times before and never felt so fussed over before.

Ulani comes to gather us for dinner before I get wholly lost in my thoughts. Usually when I have eaten here in the past we sit at the small table in the kitchen which seats about five. Tonight we are taken into the formal dining room. The long oak table is large enough to sit twelve comfortably. The table has already been set and fresh flowers have been placed all down the center of the table. The food has just been brought out. It is a beautiful meal of smoked fish, squash soup, boiled greens and potatoes seasoned with fresh herbs. There is an abundance of fresh bread paired with honey and jam, and fresh cakes for dessert. The mere sight of this feast makes my stomach grumble with hunger.

Ulani instructs us on the seating arrangement. For formal dinners couples are split up to promote a more social environment. I know this is a common custom, but this is the first time that I have attended such a dinner. Falon is sitting at the head with Vivek on one side and Khalon is instructed to sit on the other. I can tell that Khalon is not pleased about being separated from me but he does not argue with it. He politely takes his seat. Next to him sits Yoana and Jae sits next to her at the end. I am seated on the other side between Vivek and Ulani.

The soup is served first then the fish. The start of dinner is fairly quiet. We are all enjoying the meal, but there is a heaviness looming in the air, like everyone wants to say something but no one knows how to start. It isn't until tea and dessert are served that the tension finally breaks.

"Sigrun," Falon starts, "though we love having you for dinner, I will confess that we had ulterior motives tonight."

I am not surprised I had figured as much since we arrived. I suspect he wants to talk more about my father's death and Khalon's arrival in the village. I know it has been on his mind.

"What do you know about your mother's death?" he asks directly. I am stunned by the question. I had not expected this conversation at all.

"Umm, I know she died giving birth to me," I choke out. My face suddenly feels hot. I don't like talking about this.

"Did your father ever tell you anything else about it?" Vivek inquires.

My thoughts travel back to the last time I saw him, and the conversation that we had.

"Yes, he did," I pause to remember. "He said she knew she would die."

Falon and Vivek exchange a look that can only be described as validation.

"What else did he tell you?" Falon presses.

"Nothing really," that was the truth. He never expanded on the conversation. He changed the subject by giving me the necklace and that was the last time I saw him alive.

Then I remember another detail, "Oh, he said he dreamed of me, and that is how they knew that I would be... different." I look at Jae he looks pained by my memory.

"Yes, your father had a gift of foresight," Falon started, "he couldn't see everything and he couldn't choose what he saw. His visions were sporadic and not always clear as to the meaning. Before you were conceived, Baron had a dream that Maia would give birth to a dragon. As I'm sure, you can imagine the first reaction to this news was written off as some kind of bizarre nightmare. Then when you were born, we understood the greater meaning of his vision." He pauses his explanation to take a sip of his tea. It is almost cruel to leave me suspended like this. For the first time in my life I am starting to get answers.

"You see, Sigrun," he continues, "your birth made an ancient prophecy true."

"Prophecy?" I ask.

"Yes, there was a book in which it was written. It had been passed down for generations. Unfortunately, decades ago there was a lightning fire and along with many things that book was lost. We only have the spoken story left."

"Well, what is it?" I'm starting to get agitated.

"That the rise of the dragon era would come again and that peaceful times would come to an end."

I feel sick. My wings have never felt heavier.

"What are you really saying, Falon?" Khalon accuses. His body stiffens. I know he is feeling protective of me.

Falon puts his hand up to ease Khalon. "I'm saying that I feared Sigrun from the moment that she was born. I feared that she was evil and that she would destroy everything that my family helped build," he turns back to me, "Baron was so in love with you from the first time he saw you that I couldn't make him see how dangerous you could be. He wouldn't hear of it. I only allowed my son to be friends with you to keep you close."

This confession cuts me so deeply. I thought of Jae's house as my other home. Now I find out that this was all a facade. I think back to everything Jae ever said to me. Has my entire friendship with him been a lie?

"Did you know about this?" I spit out to Jae.

"No, Sigrun, I swear," his eyes are wide and his face is red with anger, "this is the first I've heard of this." His anger quells mine a bit, but I'm still incredibly hurt. I admired Falon. I never believed that he thought so little of me.

"I have watched you closely your whole life, Sigrun," Falon speaks again. "I had to. No one knew what you would be capable of, not even your father. Jae did not know of my intentions. Your friendship is real."

"If this is a story passed down, why is this the first we've heard of it?" Jae asks.

"To protect you. Telling you kids would have put you all in danger. One of your hot headed friends might have killed Sigrun out of fear, or vice versa."

"Sounds like you thought of doing that yourself," I hiss.

"I did," he says meekly. "There was a time..." he trails off and looks down at his hands. "When you become a parent, you would do anything to protect your family. Your father felt the same way."

"Fortunately for us all that he did," Vivek chimes in. I look at him quizzically.

"Sigrun," Falon speaks again, "I was wrong. I have seen you transform from an awkward child into a remarkable young lady. I have seen things in you that make me believe I have interpreted the prophecy incorrectly. I think our utopia was bound to be threatened, just as is the natural order of life.

Your father's murder proved that, but I think you were born to restore it."

My breathing has escalated, and my body feels hot.

Falon's eyes have welled up. I have never seen this kind of emotion from him. He has always been an exceedingly stoic man. He looks directly into my eyes, "I am ashamed of my thoughts and actions toward you. I hope you can forgive me."

Feeling so many emotions of my own has also brought tears to my eyes. I blink them back, and nod to him. That is all I can manage for the moment.

Vivek puts his hand on my shoulder, "We also wanted to let you know that we fully support you and your efforts to ready our people for what lies ahead. Whatever you need from us you will get."

Chapter 23

"Well that was interesting," Khalon says to me as we walk out of Jae's house. I had to get out of there. Even in a house that big it felt like the walls were caving in on me.

"To say the least. I didn't expect that at all," my heart is beating wildly, I can feel the pulse in my throat.

"Sig, wait!" Jae is running after us, "Don't leave."

"I think it's best I go. I don't know how I feel about what just happened in there," I warn.

"I never heard that story, he never told me. You believe me don't you?" His eyes are sincere.

"I'm not sure what I believe. This was all a lot to digest. Prophecies and Dragon Eras," I chuckle a little bit because when I say it all out loud it sounds absurd.

"You don't believe it's true?" he asks.

"No, I don't," I say with certainty. "I know I'm different, and that I'm the only one with wings like this, but meeting Khalon has opened my eyes. From what he has told me there are others out there who might not look so different from me."

"I wouldn't go that far," Khalon chimes in, "I've never seen anyone like you either."

"My point is," I regroup, "Mantus is a scorpion, we've never seen anything like that here either. That doesn't mean he is part of some prophecy."

"I don't think it's the prophecy you have trouble with, I think it's the idea that you are in the center of it," Khalon says. His attitude on the subject surprises me. I thought for sure he would see it as some silly bedtime story. Instead, he is throwing his weight behind it.

I shake my head. I don't know what else to say.

"Let me walk you home," Jae insists gently. His offer comes as a surprise. Jae has been so hot and cold with me the last few days, I don't know what to expect anymore.

I look at Khalon. He shrugs his shoulder as if to say, "It's up to you."

I nod in acceptance.

"Okay, I'll see you back at the house," Khalon says. He squeezes my hand before he takes off into the night sky.

Jae starts walking slowly so I follow. My body has cooled down and the night air has gotten colder. I shiver.

"Are you cold?" Jae asks.

"No," I lie.

I know he wants to say something but he doesn't. We walk a bit longer in silence before I finally speak up, "Jae, you've hardly said two words to me for days, then you invite me over to dinner where I am beset by your father, and then you offer to walk me home." I stop to look at him. "What's going on?" I ask him directly.

"I know I've been kind of a jerk lately."

I don't argue with him.

"It's just that I opened up to you," he continues, "and I felt rejected." I know he is talking about what happened at the cherry tree.

"I wasn't rejecting you, Jae. You and I," I stop to think carefully about what to say next, "well, it's complicated. I've known you as a friend my whole life. I thought you looked at me like a little sister or something, and then all of the sudden you flipped on me."

He is looking at the ground. "It wasn't all of the sudden for me," he tries to explain.

"Well, you did a good job hiding it from me," I start to think about the other element in this equation. "Then there is Ainia to consider," his eyes fix on mine, "she has had feelings for you as long as I can remember."

"What do you mean?" He is playing dumb and it agitates me.

"Cut it out, Jae, I know you are aware of it."

"What…"

"I heard you," I cut him off before he can lie again, "that night in the woods when you were talking to Khalon I was on my way back and heard that whole conversation."

His beautiful tan skin goes pale. "Sigrun, I can explain," he starts.

"No, you don't have to," I raise my hand to stop him from talking, "I've been able to think about it and I understand. I don't blame you for liking that attention. After all, I admit I like the attention I got from you."

His eyes shine with hope. He leans a little closer to me. Feeling the space between us close once again makes me nervous. I have discovered that he can distract me very easily, so I take a small step back.

"But, I don't want to hurt her," I say finally.

"Neither do I," he agrees.

"This," I motion to the both of us, "would hurt her."

He doesn't say anything at first, because he knows it's true. "I'll talk to her," he offers.

"No."

"Yes, she is a reasonable girl," he starts walking again at a quicker pace.

"I don't think we should do anything yet…"

"And, she is our friend…"

"I think you are getting ahead yourself…"

"I'm sure she just wants us to be happy…"

"Jae, hang on a minute…"

"We're not doing anything wrong…"

"Jae! Stop!" I shout. He looks alarmed by my tone. I put my hands in my hair in frustration, "You are about 100 steps in front of me right now." I take a breath to get grounded again. "Even if these feelings weren't sudden for you, they are all new to me. I'm just trying to understand."

"Understand what?"

"Understand why. Why me? You could be with anyone. Ainia is the most beautiful girl in the village and she is throwing herself at you."

He is shaking his head, "I know she's beautiful, Sigrun."

"Not to mention a good person," I continue.

"I know she is."

I know he is frustrated, but I press him anyway, "So, I'm asking again, why me?"

"I don't know, Sigrun! I just love you," he snaps.

I'm stunned. His words make my mouth go completely dry.

He speaks again with a quieter voice, "I just love you," he pauses to look at me. I feel he is trying to read my expression. I don't stop him so he continues. "You are my best friend. Doesn't it make sense that you would want to spend the rest of your life with your best friend." He reaches his hand out to move the hair away from my face. Then he holds my chin, tilting my face up toward his. It feels like he is about to kiss me, but he stops. "I understand that I am ahead of you. I will wait as long as it takes for you to catch up."

I swallow hard because I know what I'm going to say next might hurt him, "What if I never get there?"

His eyes squint, "Hmmm." He lets go of my face and grabs my hand instead. "I guess I have to keep showing you the way," he smiles. I breathe and smile back. "Come on," he pulls on my hand, "let's get you home."

My house is empty, which surprises me. I thought for sure Khalon would be waiting at the door for my return. I shrug it off, he is nocturnal after all.

I am exhausted. These days off were supposed to give us rest. I feel more drained now than I did doing pushups all day. I head right up to my room. I have to at least try to get some sleep.

An hour or two goes by and I have barely shut my eyes. I keep thinking about the dinner and what was revealed to me. It was all too much to take at once, but now that I've been lying in the quiet darkness of my room for a while some things about our conversation are starting to fit together. I lunge out of bed. I have to get answers and I think there is someone who might have them.

Chapter 24

Vivek answers the door in his bed clothes and robe. His eyes are barely open. He has probably been asleep for hours by the time I started pounding on his door.

"Sigrun, what are you doing here? Are you alright? You're soaking wet," he is utterly bewildered by me showing up at his home, soaking wet on a dry night.

"I'm fine, I'm sorry to barge in on you like this. I know it's late, but I have to talk to you about this," I have a bundle with me and I remove the cloth enough for him to see the cover of the red book.

His eyes grow wide. He covers it again quickly and motions me to come inside. He looks around outside, making sure I wasn't followed, before shutting the door.

"Where did you get that?" he asks.

"I found it hidden in my father's study."

He walks over to the dying fire in the hearth and throws another log on.

"Come, dry off. You must be freezing."

I oblige and sit in front of the fire.

"Why are you wet?" he asks.

"It seemed important that I keep it safe so I hid it, and to get to it I had to go though some water," I explain as vaguely as possible.

"I see," he sits in his chair next to me.

"I have looked through it, but it is written in this language that I have never seen before," I unwrap it carefully and hand it to him. "I was hoping that maybe you can read it."

He opens it carefully. He takes a deep breath as soon as he sees the words on the pages. He seems relieved. "I thought this had been lost forever," he smiles. He almost looks like a little boy, excitement radiates from him. "It has been a long time since I have seen this language it will take some time for me to remember all of it, but I think I can still translate enough to at least get you some answers."

I smile so widely that my cheeks hurt.

He flips to a page and starts to read, "Here, this, it mentions something about the prophecy. A child of fire will be born, and once comes of age a great warrior it will be."

We look at each other. I can see how this could be interpreted in multiple ways. He looks back on the pages. He struggles to find a passage that he fully understands.

"I do see the word dragon, but I'm not sure of the context," he looks disappointed that he cannot understand more. "I wish your father were here. He was probably the only person who could read this entire book."

Eagerly I turn to the page that has the picture with the pendant, "This, what does it say about this."

His weathered hands scroll over the words as he reads, "I think it says something about learning to control something, a gift of some sort."

"Yes, yes it was a gift," I pull a small object from my pocket, and reveal the pendant wrapped in a cloth. I hold it up so he can see it.

"Oh my," he reaches out to touch it and it sparks at his touch. "Yeow!" He says more surprised than hurt.

I cannot help but to laugh. "It did the same thing to Jae," I tell him, hoping he won't take it personally.

He chuckles also, "Well, this is definitely meant for only you." He looks at it closely and then back at the book. "What I meant by a gift is rather a talent. It will help control a gift, you understand?"

"Yes, but not really. I don't have a talent," I confess.

"Maybe not yet, but you did just reach adulthood. From what I understand from this your gifts may lie dormant until then." He flips the pages back and forth, "What does the pendant do now?"

"It seems to read my emotions." He looks at me quizzically, so I expand my explanation, "Like when I'm embarrassed it blushes pink, or I've been told that the rose closes when I sleep, things like that."

His brow is still furrowed, I can tell he does not fully understand. To demonstrate, I touch the marble and the rose blooms for me. His eyes go wide with amazement.

"Why did you stop wearing it?" he asks, his eyes still fixed on the tiny bloom.

"Umm, it was becoming a problem having my feelings out in the open," I smile and feel my cheeks flush.

"Ah, I see," he smiles and stares off like he is remembering his own romantic interludes from his past. "So it reads your emotions?" he asks rhetorically, coming back to this moment. "Perhaps your talent is dictated by your emotions, and this is a tool that will help you learn to control it," he reaches out for it again but he holds it by the cord this time. While I was holding it, the rose was in bloom, as soon as I let it go the rose closed up again.

"Amazing," he says astounded, "your father gave this to you?"

I nod, "Yes, the day before he died."

"It's very special. You should start wearing this again," he pauses and smiles. "A few embarrassing moments aside I think it will ultimately be helpful."

He hands it back to me and I tie the cord around my neck. The rose blooms again.

"Amazing," he says again. "I wish I could be more helpful with the book," he looks down at it again, "maybe if I had more time with it, I might have some old books in my library that may have some translation."

"You can hold on to it," I offer.

"Oh no, I think you were right to hide it. I wouldn't doubt whoever killed your father might have been looking for this."

Instinctively, I put my hand over the pendant to protect it. Vivek sees this and immediately reaches out to console me, "I still think you should wear that. It doesn't seem to have any power for anyone but you, and it doesn't even let anyone else touch it." I nod and lower my hand. "Hide the book, and don't tell anyone else about it or where it is, at least not until things calm down around here."

"Okay," I agree, "thank you, Vivek, and I'm sorry for coming here so late."

"No, I'm glad you did." He wraps the book in the cloth and hands it back to me, "Hide it."

I nod and get up to leave.

Chapter 25

The morning light is threatening to come up and I've hardly slept at all. By the time I made it home last night, there were only a few hours of nighttime left, and I had too much on my mind to find any rest. I give up on sleeping and get out of bed. I wash up quickly and tie my hair back. I put on some old shorts that I love and a shirt and head downstairs.

The downstairs is just as quiet. Khalon must already be out at the field. I grab a large piece of bread and make my way out.

I am looking forward to being back with the group again. They will be a welcomed distraction. Jae and I agreed not to say anything to Ainia, or any of our friends for that matter. At least not until I have decided how I feel about everything. I still feel guilty not telling Ainia the truth. I know even if I don't choose to be with Jae the mere fact that he doesn't love her will hurt her.

I reach the field and sure enough Khalon is already here. He has a large sword that he is practicing with. I stop to watch him for a moment. He twirls it in such a fluid way, he looks graceful. Eventually he turns to see me spying on him. He smiles when he sees me.

I walk past a large stockpile of weapons on my way over to him.

"You and Ravi have been busy," I say.

"Yes, he is very skilled."

"Is this what you were up to last night?" I ask.

"Among other things," he says coyly.

"Did you sleep at all?"

"Did you?" he counters.

"Not much," I answer honestly.

"Are you okay?" he asks me with real concern.

I stretch my arms and wings out and twist from side to side, "I'm feeling fit, and ready to train."

"That's not what I meant," he says arching an eyebrow.

"I know," I spot Jae and Vidar crossing the field. "We'll talk later," I promise.

"Hey, you're wearing the necklace again," he points out.

"Oh, yeah," I feel shy already.

"What made you change your mind?"

"I missed it. It was the last thing my father ever gave me," that is true, but I decided to keep the rest of my reasons to myself, for now.

"Good, it suits you, and I'll be able to know what you're thinking," he smiles at me. "So, I told you I had a surprise for you," he changes the subject. He walks to the other side of the weapon pile and picks up an object wrapped in a cloth. The gesture reminds me of when my father gave me the necklace. It tugs at my heart.

I unwrap it and see a pair of knives, only they are not like regular knives. The handles are long wooden sticks, about the length of a forearm, that have been sanded smooth and the blade is attached at the top curving out and down. They look like scythes that we use for harvesting, but smaller.

I giggle, "You spoil me, sir." I jest, "Most men would give a girl sweets or flowers, but not you. Nope, you go right to gifting knives. What a lucky, lucky girl I am!" I laugh.

He is amused with my reaction. He winks and smiles showing off his white teeth.

"What are those?" Vidar blurts out. He and Jae have made their way over.

"They are called Kamas," Khalon answers. "I want you to practice with these every day," he says to me.

"I don't know how."

"I'll show you," he smiles.

The rest of the group has started to file in as well, and they have brought others. I am pleased that our group is growing.

Khalon gathers everyone and has them choose a weapon that they are comfortable with. Jae keeps his father's sword and Malyn sticks with her bow, but everyone else dives in. Vidar and Soren are the most eager. For them this is better than their birthdays. Remi settles on a pair of long knives. His twin Wren sorts through the pile carefully. She isn't afraid of weapons, but I can tell she is struggling with what she'll be comfortable with.

Khalon walks over to her. He senses her struggle as well. "Let's try this," he hands her a small sword. It fits her petite frame, and a parcel of throwing knives. "I think you will do well with these," he says to her with encouragement.

Looking around at everyone investigating their new sordid treasures I notice that one person in particular is not here.

"Jae," I call him over to me, "where's Ainia?"

He shrugs, "I don't know, I haven't seen her." He starts to look concerned.

Malyn overhears my question to Jae and flits over. "She's not coming today," she confesses.

"Is she okay?" I ask.

"Oh yeah, she's fine, it's just this isn't really for her. She's not really cut out for this type of exercise," Malyn is dancing around the subject a bit, but I understand. Ainia is much more fragile than the majority of us. She is afraid of getting injured.

Khalon came over as we were talking, "I already have something in mind for her. She can be helpful even if it is not on the battlefield."

"What's your plan for her?" My curiosity is getting the better of me.

"You'll see."

"You and all your secrets are getting annoying," I fire back.

He laughs at me. "Come on let's show you how to use those."

Khalon leads me to a less crowded part of the field. He takes one of my Kama and holds it with the pointed end of the blade up and away from him.

"Hold it like this," he instructs.

I take the other Kama and mimic his stance. The weight of it feels good, balanced.

"You're gripping it too tight," he instructs. "Hold it in the crevice between your thumb and index finger. Just use those two fingers to hold it the rest of the hand is going to direct it. Then I want you to let the blade fall forward and roll your wrist so it spins," he demonstrates this and he makes it look effortless.

It is much harder than it looks. It takes several tries before I manage a full spin, but it still looks sloppy. I am supposed to be able to do this with both hands. I can't even manage to do it with one. I picked up archery so much faster.

Khalon knows I'm getting frustrated. Using the flat part of the blade of the Kama he is holding he gently lifts my chin so I am looking at him, "Sigrun, this takes time and lots of practice. Keep working on it."

His encouragement makes the corner of my mouth twist up into a half smile. He hands me the other Kama and then heads off to help the others with their weapons.

I work on twirling my Kama for hours. Blisters start to spring up on the edges of my thumbs and index fingers before I decide to take a break. I look around for the first time this morning to observe the rest of the group. Jae, Vidar, and Remi are taking instruction from Khalon on how to use their swords against several attackers. Malyn is on the other side of the field with her bow, and from the looks of things she has only gotten better with it. Wren has gotten comfortable with her throwing knives but it will take a lot of practice before she will be able to hit a moving target.

Khalon glances at me and notices that I have stopped for a moment. He looks up at the sky and gauges that the morning has gone.

"Okay, everyone, let's take a breather," he shouts, "get something to eat and drink, but don't get too comfortable we are not even close to being done."

The group lets out a collective sigh of relief.

I grab a small satchel out of my pack and fly over to the shady spot where Malyn and Wren are sitting. They are sharing a small loaf of bread. I open my satchel of nuts and dried berries and offer them some.

Vidar comes over and sits with us as well. "Let me see those," he says to me with a full mouth, pointing to my Kamas. I chuckle at his brutish manner and hand them over. "These are wicked," he says staring at the blades. "Can you use them yet?" he asks.

"Sort of, Khalon makes it look so easy, but it is much harder than it looks."

"Khalon makes everything look easy," Vidar says in exhaustion. "My shoulder is throbbing and we aren't even done with the day."

"No kidding, my arm is so sore already," Wren adds.

"Well, Khalon has been training and fighting his whole life, we've only been doing this for a few days," I say diplomatically. "It is okay to struggle a bit," I look over everyone's exhausted faces. "Or a lot," I add with a laugh.

They all chuckle and nod at my assessment.

While they continue to talk about the events of the day, I look around the field. Jae, Ravi, Remi, and Soren are all on the other side of the field they look like they are deep in conversation. However, I can't seem to locate Khalon.

I stand up and take a few steps toward the field.

"Looking for someone?" A deep voice says behind me. It makes me jump a little. I turn and see Khalon standing behind me.

"Whoa, where did you come from?" Vidar asks.

They are just as surprised as I am. Khalon just smiles.

I shake my head and smile at him.

"I can be invisible when I want to," Khalon replies, "It is actually a tactic you all should work on as well, but we'll do that another day. Alright, let's get back to today's training."

Everyone grabs their weapons and heads back to the field.

He was truly invisible to me and everyone else. I start thinking about all of the times that I think I'm alone. I begin to wonder if he watches me more than I know.

Khalon grabs my hand and it brings my attention back to the moment. He looks over my blisters. "Why don't you take a break from the Kamas for now, and work with your bow for a bit."

"Okay," I comply.

The rest of the afternoon goes quickly. Malyn has become so good with her bow that she helps me with mine. Jae keeps his distance from me, but not in a bad way. I can tell we are in a better place, and he is just giving me space. The sunlight is fading when Khalon finally releases us for the day.

* * * * * *

Once I'm home, I wash up and head downstairs to eat something before I go to bed. I'm putting the teapot over the fire when Khalon comes in to the room.

"Tea?" I ask him.

"Sure."

I tear a loaf of bread in half for us to share and set out the jam and honey. We sit in silence waiting for the water to boil. I know he wants to talk to me about what happened with Jae's family last night. Still feeling sensitive about it, I am nervous to bring it up again. Instead, I pick up my Kama from the table and start twirling them again.

"You are getting better with those," he says. "Even in one day I see lots of improvement."

"Thanks," I smile. "It still feels very foreign to me though."

"It will get easier," he reassures. "So, do you want to talk about anything that happened last night?" He addresses the subject directly. In a way, I am glad that he does, but honestly I don't know where to start.

"Well, it was all very surprising," I say in a blanket statement.

"Yes, it was," he agrees. He waits for me to elaborate.

"Did you spy on Jae and me last night?" I ask him directly, now that I know he is a master of being unseen. I want to know if he has been watching me.

He laughs out loud. "No. I thought about it," he confesses, "but, no I did not."

"Do you ever?" I ask.

"Watch you?" he asks me.

I raise my eyebrows waiting for an answer.

"I did when I first met you. That day by the river when I took off," I think back to the day he is referring to. It was the day after he saved me from the Gila. I pushed him to talk about his past. He lost his temper and then left me by the riverside.

"I thought for sure you were going to leave," he admits. "I thought after what I just told you, you would take off the first chance you got. So, I sat and watched you for a while. Then when I realized you were going to stay I felt ashamed for how I lashed out, and I was surprised by your acceptance of me. I wanted to watch over you..." The whistle from the kettle interrupts him. I get up and pour the tea into two cups. When I get back to the table, he continues, "I quickly learned that you are more than capable of looking after yourself, especially in your own village. So, I try my best to respect your privacy."

"You try your best?" I ask. He winks and takes a bite of honey soaked bread.

I laugh and feel my cheeks blush, "Well, I guess that's going to have to do."

"Are you afraid of what I might have heard you and Jae talking about?" He turns my question back onto me.

"No, not really, I would tell you anyway. I just confronted him on something."

"Confronted him with what?"

I take a deep breath before confessing that I had done some spying of my own, "That night in the woods, when we were on our way to see the bees I overheard you and Jae talking about Ainia."

"And, you were giving me a hard time," he starts.

"I know, I know," I put my hand up to cut him off. "I was eavesdropping."

"I think the word you really mean is spying," he teases me.

"I know! I'm sorry," I say irritated.

"That's okay, I knew you were there," he says nonchalantly.

"What? You did?" I feel like I should be mad, but I have no room to be.

"You have not quite mastered invisibility, at least not with me. I asked him those questions on purpose." Before I have a chance to react, he keeps talking, "I thought you deserved to know where he stood with everything. I didn't make him say those things. He offered all of that information on his own. I simply asked a question."

I know he has a point, but I don't know how I feel about him involving himself in this relationship with Jae and Ainia.

"So what did you say to him?" He finally asks.

"Umm," it takes me a moment to regroup, "I just told him that I overheard you guys and that I didn't like what I heard. He has been confusing me with this shift in our friendship and I don't know how I feel about it." I am as honest and as succinct as I can be.

"You deserve more," he says unapologetically.

"What do you mean?"

"Jae is a boy, you deserve a man. You deserve more," he shrugs his shoulders and takes another bite. He has spoken his piece.

His assessment makes me blush again. He might think Jae is a boy, but right now I feel like a silly girl.

"Since we are sort of on the topic," I pause to gather my courage, "have you had many lovers?" I blurt out before I lose my nerve.

The question catches him so off guard that he chokes on his bread. Then he tries to chase it down with his tea which is still too hot. He burns his mouth and spits tea out everywhere. His tan face is now bright red. My sides ache from training, but I can't help it, I laugh so hard I almost fall off of my chair.

"Why would you ask me that?" He coughs and chokes out.

"I don't know," I try to stifle my laughter. "I am just trying to fill in the blanks."

"Fill in the blanks? Those are the blanks that you want to know about?"

I shrug, "Yeah."

"Why?" he asks, but more seriously this time.

"Because, I'm curious about you," I say honestly. "All I know about you is your history of violence. Haven't you ever had a girlfriend?"

"I've never had a friend that was a girl, and as far as what I think you are really asking," he leans back and I can tell he is choosing the best way to answer my question. "I come from a different culture than you," he starts to explain. "A war culture is pretty much void of love. The women of our tribe customarily offer themselves to the warriors as a tribute." He stops to make sure I understand what he is saying, and I do. "And the more skilled the warrior…"

"The more offers," I finish his sentence for him so he doesn't have to.

He nods.

"And, you were the most skilled warrior, so," I decide not to finish my sentence. He has his hand over his chin and mouth and his eyes are squinting, he looks uncomfortable. It is clear we are both thinking the same thing. "Wow," I say finally.

"Sorry you asked?" He looks nervous that he said too much.

"No," I assure him, "not at all." Though I don't know if that is true or not, and he doesn't look convinced. "I am just glad that you are here now. You said I deserve more, well so do you. You deserve to be loved."

He looks me hard in the eyes. His black eyes can be so difficult to read. The few minutes of silence feel like an eternity. Finally he stands and slowly walks over to me. We don't take our eyes off of each other. Unsure of his intentions I hold my breath. Did I offend him? I know he is uncomfortable talking about himself. Maybe I pushed him too far once again.

He is standing in front of me now. Still sitting in my chair I feel even smaller than normal next to him. He extends his massive hand out and holds my jaw carefully. His thumb brushes across my chin. The muscles in my stomach tighten. I close my eyes.

"Get some sleep," he says in his low voice. "We have another big day tomorrow."

He lets my face go and heads upstairs. I open my eyes just in time to see his face before he goes. He looks pained by something.

As soon as he is gone, I breathe again. Feeling lightheaded I rest my head in my hands for a moment before retreating to my room.

Chapter 26

A few weeks later we all arrive at the field like we normally do most mornings, but this time we get there before Khalon. He was not at the house this morning. The door to his room was open and he was not out on his branch. I know it is foolish to worry about him. He is a warrior after all, but the disappearance of Merik troubles my mind.

I am happy to see that Ainia has come back to the field. Even though I still believe a battlefield is no place for her it means a lot to have her support. I fly to her as soon as I see her.

"Hey you're back," I say giving her a long hug.

"Yeah," she sighs, "I thought I would work on my archery a bit more."

"I think that's great."

"Yeah," she mutters out. She does not share my enthusiasm. "Jae came over last night and encouraged me to come back."

I immediately feel ill. Though I'm not sure exactly why. "Jae came over to your house?" I try my best to sound normal.

"Uh-huh," She is not elaborating at all.

"So, umm, what did he say?" I am failing at being normal, and now I'm starting to feel perspiration along my hairline, and it is not from the heat of the morning. Part of me feels jealous. Though I know I have no real right to feel that way. Then guilt sweeps over my body. I'm terrified that he went behind my back and told her everything that has happened these last few months. I glance over at Jae who is across the field. He is watching us. His stare is almost burning, but I doubt it is as fierce as mine.

"Well," She starts.

"Alright, let's get started," Khalon interrupts as he flies in. Normally I would be thrilled to see him, but his timing couldn't be worse today.

She turns her attention to him now. This conversation will have to wait, and I will have to suffer until then. I suppose I deserve to.

"What's the agenda today?" Remi asks. He is smaller than the rest of the boys, but he makes up for it with his enthusiasm.

"Pair up, ditch your weapons. Today we are going to work on hand to hand combat," he instructs.

I toss my Kamas and bow to the ground. Wren grabs my arm. I hadn't seen her before. She must have just arrived as well.

"Wanna pair up?" she asks with a smile.

I smile back, I would like to spar with her.

"No," Khalon shouts. "That one is mine," he is pointing directly at me.

He has a crooked smile on his face. He turns his large hand that is pointing at me. Curling his finger slowly he beckons me to him.

The group is totally hushed as I walk toward him. Neither of us breaks our stare. Once I reach him, I find I can't help but smile my own twisted smile.

"Is this my punishment for what I asked you the other night?" I refer to when I asked him about his romantic history.

He tries not to laugh. "No, but don't think I've let you off on that one," he squints, playfully.

"This doesn't feel like a fair fight," Vidar shouts in a joking way, a few others laugh.

"You're right," Khalon replies, "she is much tougher than me."

A few more laughs ripple along the group. He addresses the group. I keep my eyes on him.

"In all my battles, I don't think I have ever seen a fair fight." Khalon makes a valid point. "You have to be ready to deal with the unfair, dirty, ones. Everyone has strengths," he brings his attention back to me, "and everyone has a weakness." His eyes are menacing.

I suddenly feel nervous.

The group has forgotten about pairing up. They are now in a circle around us, nudging each other for the best view. A few have even taken to the trees to see better.

"Sometimes taking the defensive position is the best tactic. Use your opponents own weight against them," he is instructing, but he never stops looking at me. He grabs my wrist. "If they try to swing at your face," he uses my hand to demonstrate, "you duck under and into them and hit them here." He has his other fist up against my belly right below the rib cage.

He goes through several other moves showing us how to deflect punches and offset the opponents balance. He shows us how to use our wings to our advantage, and how to use theirs to their disadvantage. He expands on how to fight the enemy when they have a weapon and you do not. He uses my body as his demonstration tool for every move.

"Okay, let's do some real sparing," he says. "Ready?" he asks me.

"Yes," that is a lie. I have no idea how I would defeat Khalon in a real fight.

"Okay, come after me," he instructs. I pause, I still see my friend in front of me. How can I attack my friend? "Come on," he urges, this time he shoves me enough to make me stumble backwards.

It makes me mad.

He goes to push me again and I grab the inside of his wrist to stop him and slap him hard with my other hand. It happened so fast I didn't have time to think about it. I just reacted. The group makes a collective gasp, like I have stoked an already angry fire.

"Good, that's good," he says with a smile. "Now try not to be so tame."

He lunges toward me, but I duck and spin out of the way. My heart has accelerated. It is now clear that we are not playing, this is real. He lunges again and I try the same move, but he is expecting that now. He grabs the shoulder of my wing and throws me to the ground. I slide across the grass, but I stand up fast. He comes for me again. I shoot up into the sky just before he reaches me and I twist up and behind him landing on his back. I wrap my arms around his neck to choke him out. He grabs my arms and pulls them apart. He is so much stronger than me. I claw at him. I try to grab his chin and twist his head. I grab at anything to gain an advantage. He moans in discomfort, so I dig harder. This moment of relief doesn't last long. He backs up into the trees ramming my body against one of the trunks. Pain radiates through my body, I go limp for a second. It is long enough for him to throw me off of his back. I land face down in the dirt. I look up and see the wide eyes of my friends. None are as wide as Jae's. I can tell he is fighting the urge to stop this. I get up again just in time to see Khalon charging. I ball up my fist. I wait for him to be within arm's length, and I throw my fist right up to his jaw. He moves his head just enough so I miss, and he punches me hard just below the rib cage just as he had shown us. I have fallen right into the trap without even knowing it.

I fall to the ground unable to breathe.

"That's enough!" Jae shouts, storming through the circle and stands between Khalon and me.

"She doesn't need you to rescue her," Khalon snarls back.

The two of them are getting closer to each other. Khalon's blood is already up, and I suspect it wouldn't take much for Jae's to rise also.

"You're hurting her," Jae shouts.

"She's much tougher than you think, she can take it," Khalon takes a threatening step toward him. Jae matches his step. The two are right in each other's faces. I desperately want to intervene, but I cannot speak yet. The crowd is holding their breath as I'm trying to find mine.

I'm writhing on the ground in pain and finally my body relaxes a bit and lets in enough air for me to speak.

"Jae, stop," I finally utter. I stand up, "I'm okay." I take in my first deep breath and look at Khalon. "I'm ready to keep going," I say firmly.

"Sig you don't have to do this," Jae pleads with me.

"Yes I do," I'm annoyed that he thinks me so helpless.

Jae looks wounded that I have rejected his rescue. Khalon is smirking. I wish he wasn't, but he is.

Jae swallows hard, "Well, I don't have to watch." He takes to the sky before I have a chance to say anything.

"Ready?" Khalon asks me, taking my attention away from Jae's rapid departure.

I nod.

"So, what have you learned?" he asks as we start circling each other.

I think about our fight. He is too big for me to fight face to face, and too strong to go hand to hand with. He attacks rather than defends. Maybe that is the key. I have to go after him, and whatever I do I am going to have to fight dirty.

I charge after him. He looks surprised that I have taken such an aggressive stance, but he plants his feet like he is ready. Just before I am in his reach I shoot up into the air and spin around so I am facing his back. I grab the base of his wing and I kick the back of his knee, hard.

He shouts out in pain, and it just makes me fight harder. I pull on his wing at the same time he loses his balance and falls to the ground. I jump onto his chest, my knees pinning his shoulders to the ground. I reach in my belt for my small knife and with both hands I thrust it down to his throat.

The crowd gasps, some even stepped forward to stop me. But when they get close enough they see me holding the blade above him, barely tickling his throat.

Khalon's eyes are wide with amazement and he has a small smile that looks like pride. My hands are shaking from the adrenaline and still grasping the knife. He gently reaches his hands up to my hips and slides me down his body until his arms are free. I relax a little. He puts his hands around mine and carefully pries the knife away. Once my hands are free, he kisses the inside of my palm.

"Very good," he says quietly.

His praise makes my body melt. I no longer feel the urge to attack or defend.

"What did you learn?" he asks me again.

"Everyone has a weakness," I say.

"And what's mine?"

"Defense."

"Smart girl," he says with a smile. "That's why I always attack first," he explains.

His eyes are playful and also menacing. He puts his hand on my stomach where he punched me. His hands feel rough on my skin, but I like it.

"Did I hurt you?" he asks.

"Yes," I exclaim with humor. "But you were right, I can take it," I reassure him with a smile.

"Ahem," someone clears their throat. I look up to see almost a dozen pairs of eyes on us. I had forgotten they were there. I get up and dust myself off. Khalon does the same.

Ainia runs up to me first. "Are you okay?" she asks.

"Yeah," I stretch out and my ribs ache, "I'm going to be sore for a day or two, though."

"Ah, he let her win." Vidar teases. A few chuckles ripple through the group.

I turn to look at him. He has a smug half smile on his face.

"Oh, really? He let me win." I repeat his accusation.

I walk slowly to him, he stands his ground. Khalon takes a step back to let me pass, and he nods at me as though he were giving me permission to shut Vidar down. Vidar and I stand inches apart staring at each other, both smiling like we each have a secret. Quickly without thinking I slap him across the face, he moves to strike back but before he can raise his arm I have landed a second blow just under his ribs as Khalon had just shown us. Vidar drops down to one knee. He is struggling to catch his breath. I punch him one more time, just hard enough to knock him down and bloody his teeth. The reaction from the group is mixed, but mostly they look at each other not knowing what to think, or what to do. Vidar is on the ground with a look of absolute puzzlement on his face. I squat down beside him.

"Does Khalon strike you as the type of man that would *let* anyone win, even me?" I ask rhetorically. "Besides, I told you

I was going to give you a proper beating. You're lucky, you got off easy." I smile at him and extend my hand to help him to his feet.

He smiles back, wipes the blood from his mouth, and takes my hand.

I spend the rest of the morning practicing archery with Ainia. The majority of the group continues sparing.

Between shots I look around. Jae has not returned to training. It is obvious that he will not be back for the remainder of the day. This is the perfect time to continue my conversation with Ainia.

"So what did you and Jae talk about when he came over?" I ask casually, lining up my next shot.

"Oh, he just told me that he values me as a friend," she says it nonchalantly, but I know she is more upset than she lets on.

"That's not a bad thing," I try to be optimistic.

"He values me as a *friend*," She hits the word friend with an obvious amount of disdain.

"Did he mention anyone else?" I ask, my chest tensing up at her possible response.

"What do you mean?"

"Umm, you know, did he say that he is interested in anyone else?" I'm trying so hard to sound casual.

"No, just that he doesn't feel that way about me and that he felt bad about leading me on."

I'm quiet, I don't know how to comfort her, or if it is even my place to do so.

"All these years I've spent wanting him," she continues, "and now I just feel stupid." She is trying hard not to cry.

Guilt and shame are smothering me.

"Don't feel stupid," I rush to her and pull her into the woods out of sight, "Jae has never been good about showing his true feelings." Though I am trying to comfort her I am also talking about myself.

"What do you mean?" she asks.

"Well, I never knew what he was thinking either, and he's been my best friend since we were kids. I thought the two of you would end up together for sure," that was the truth. I find a piece of cloth in my pack for her to wipe her face, "Just know that this doesn't have anything to do with you, it's about him."

She looks at me quizzically, so I continue. "You're perfect. In fact, you are too good for him," I say trying to build her up.

She chuckles a little bit and wipes her eyes. "You're right, I am," she says with a little confidence.

"Okay then, let's get back out there."

The rest of the afternoon was considerably less dramatic. After a few hours with the bow, I switched to practicing with my Kama. Even in a short time I am getting more comfortable with them.

The sparing continues until the daylight is almost gone. From what I can see Vidar and Ravi were the best of the day, which is really no surprise to me. Vidar has been getting into fights for as long as I can remember, and Ravi is very skilled. He is almost intuitive as to what his opponent is going to do next. Malyn also did well, due to the fact that she is so fast. She is almost impossible to catch.

Khalon did not fight anyone else. He walked around the sparing circle giving instruction and offering helpful criticism.

"Why didn't you fight anyone else?" I ask on the way home.

"You were the only one in that group that could have given me a real fight," he smiles and rubs his wing where I grabbed him. I laugh at his dramatic gesture. I know I surprised him more than actually hurt him, but it was an unexplainable feeling when I realized I had won the fight. Sitting on top of him with a knife to his throat, I had never felt a power like that before.

We sit in the kitchen together and talk about the day, before I know it I find myself gazing off into another place. There used to be nights when I would sit at this table with my father and talk about the events of the day in the same way.

"What are you thinking about?" Khalon interrupts my memory. After a minute or so, my internal thought must have spread across my face. He was able to read me perfectly there was no sense in trying to lie to him.

"I was thinking about my brother and father." He waits for me to continue, and after a deep sigh I do. "Jae always says that the only thing worse than not having a brother is having one like Merik."

"Do you think that's true?"

"I don't know," I confess. "He wasn't easy to grow up with, that's for sure. He is moody and introverted, and sometimes outright mean, but he is my brother," I feel the lump in my throat, "and I was thinking about how he has never been gone this long before, and how he is probably dead," the word dead catches in my throat a little, "and how I have broken the last promise I ever made to my father."

Khalon furrows his brow curiously.

"I promised that I would look after him."

"Sigrun, you cannot hold yourself accountable for him," Khalon speaks forcefully, "whether he left or someone took him it is not your fault, and it is not your responsibility."

His tone surprises me. I feel defensive, "I know what you are trying to say, but that doesn't make it easier for me." He reaches out to touch me but I put my hand up to stop him. I take a deep breath before I speak, "It seems to me that the only thing worse than having a brother like Merik is having him and then losing him."

My head and my heart are aching, and it feels like no one understands.

"I'm tired," I say trying to find a graceful way to excuse myself. "I need to lie down for a while."

I stand up and go upstairs. He says nothing, only watches me as I exit the room leaving him alone in the kitchen.

Once I'm in my room, I fall to the ground. I wrap my wings around me attempting to shield myself from the pain, but it doesn't help. I begin to cry. I cry until exhaustion conquers sadness and then I am surrounded by only silence.

Lying on my floor my thoughts turn from Merik to Khalon. I start to feel bad for leaving him that way.

I head down the hall to his room. The door is closed. I knock but get no response.

"Khalon?" I ask, still no response.

Timidly I open the door. The room is dark and empty but the window is open. Thinking he must be sleeping I poke my head out the window expecting to see him hanging upside down, but he isn't there. Now I feel even worse.

Have I scared him off? Has he left me too?

A twig snaps and brings my attention down to the ground. I see movement down in the bushes, it's Khalon.

Where is he going?

I know that he goes off in the night sometimes, but he never tells me what he's up to. I decide to follow him. I'll brush up on my stalking technique like he suggested. At least, that is how I justify it to myself.

I jump out the window and land as softly as I can. He is far in front of me. It takes me a moment to find him again through the woods. He moves quickly and quietly. I move fast but have to take extra care to be quiet. I even have to control my breathing so it doesn't get too loud.

He is traveling southeast, but I don't know why he is heading this way. There is nothing out here. After a while, I lose sight of him completely. I continue on carefully. Hiding behind the trees I press forward.

Just as I think I should head back I hear something. I hold my breath so that I am perfectly silent. I hear it again. Voices, I hear voices. Khalon's for sure, and another. I move slowly watching every footstep so I do not step on anything that will make a sound.

I crouch down at the base of a tree, hiding in the shrubbery. Between the leaves I see him, but a tree is blocking the other figure. They talk in whispers, making it nearly impossible understand what they are saying. The trees are blocking out what little moonlight there is. I can barely see Khalon's face in the darkness. What I can see is that Khalon looks upset, maybe even mad. What started out as a fun exercise suddenly feels very serious.

In an attempt to see the other person, I move as far to the left as I can without being exposed. Finally I see a part of the figure. He is tall, not as tall as Khalon, but still quite large. He steps forward and I see his full image now. This is not someone I know. His wings are black like Khalon's, but they are feathered. He wears an all-black floor length garment that covers all of his body except his wings and I cannot see his face because his head is hooded.

They exchange a few more tense words. I cannot make them out until Khalon speaks up a bit at one point.

"This is the only way," Khalon says angrily.

I feel my eyes widen.

The other man seems to bow down to Khalon's fury. He tries to calm him. They begin to resume a more friendly exchange when something makes a sound in the forest that startles us all. The stranger takes off into the skies and I withdraw from the scene as quickly as I can without being heard.

Once I feel I am far enough out of sight, I take to the sky as well. Anxious to get within the confines of my home, I fly fast. The closer I get to home the calmer my nerves become, but my mind on the other hand is reeling. Do I confront Khalon? Who is this man? Why is he a secret? Why were they so upset?

He must be from Khalon's tribe, which means we have been found. We have less time than I thought. Panic sweeps over me. I make the decision that as soon as I get home I am going to grab a few things, mainly weapons, and head over to Jae's house to tell him what I have discovered.

I finally get back to the house. It is totally dark and completely quiet. I must have beat Khalon home. I am thankful for that. I don't think I am ready to face him quite yet. I must be quick, as he cannot be far behind. I run up to my father's den to see if there is anything in there that I might need.

I fling the door open and stand horrified. The den is destroyed. Just like the morning I found my father, broken bottles, books and papers cover the floor. The desk and chair are turned over and the shelves have been cleared. A noise behind me startles me but before I can even turn around everything goes black.

Chapter 27

My head aches and my body doesn't feel much better. I slowly start to regain consciousness. I try to sit up but I can't. The pounding of my head makes everything fuzzy, but I am certain that I am lying face down. The ground that I am on is cold and wet, and there is a stench in the air that I do not recognize. It is like burnt flesh and something salty and metallic, like blood.

I try to move my hands but they are tied, so are my feet, and wings. Everything is dark. I can't see anything. After a moment, I realize that I can't see because I have been hooded.

My breathing accelerates. The hood makes it more difficult to breathe. I want to scream out for help. I want to kick and twist my way free, but I don't know where I am. I don't know if anyone can hear me, and if someone can hear me, I don't know if I want them to.

If my wings were free, they would be strong enough to help break the bonds on my wrists. Someone went through a lot of trouble to render me completely immobile.

"I think she's waking up," I hear a voice whisper. I must have moved more than I thought.

"Let the master know," another voice says. The whispering makes it hard to tell, but I don't recognize either of them. My anxiety accelerates rapidly. I have to get out of here and I have to get out of here right now.

I start to twist my hands to see if I can loosen the ties. I can barely move. My hands are tied so tightly that my wrists ache at the slightest change. The rawness of my skin makes me think that I have been tied up for quite some time. The blow to the head was hard enough to knock me out for a long time, maybe even days.

Only a couple of minutes go by before I hear footsteps coming back to me.

"Alright open it up. He wants to see her now," a deep voice says.

"Why is she so special?" Another voice hisses.

"Open it up," the man with the deep voice orders. I hear a clanking, rattling sound and then I hear that someone is close to me. "You two stand her up," the man orders again. I count in my head that there could be at least four of them.

As soon as I feel hands on me, I react. I start resisting them, trying the best I can not to be taken wherever we are going, but with my limbs tied I have no choice. Two large figures drag me across what must be a campsite. I can smell fires burning and several voices holler and hiss as we pass by. There are so many voices that I can no longer keep track of the number.

Soon we are inside somewhere. The ground is no longer soft like the earth it is as hard as stone. I am dropped to the ground, and then forced to kneel. I am breathing so hard that the hood is entering my mouth every time I inhale.

Someone removes the hood. I can see for the first time since I woke up, but it is so dark inside that I can barely see anything. The dwelling that I'm in is one large room completely made of stone. There doesn't appear to be any furniture or anything that would make this a home. In fact, the only thing in the room appears to be some steps on the other side, but I can barely see them or what they lead to.

A rattle from behind me draws my attention away from the room. I see my captors for the first time. They are fairies unlike any I have seen. The rattle came from a fairy that is also a snake. Her upper body looks very much like a regular fairy body except she is covered in gray scales up to her shoulders. Instead of having legs, her lower body is that of a snake and at the very end is a rattle. The man with the deep voice is also a sight to behold. He does have wings, but they are tucked away beneath a hard beetle-like shell on his back.

The structure of his head is remarkable. He has what appear to be horns. They are massive at the base and curve up toward each other, like those on a Stag Beetle. They both have tattoos and brands on their arms similar to Khalon, not as many, but I do not doubt they are very skilled warriors.

So amazed and horrified I almost don't hear the hiss from the other side of the room.

"SSSSigrrrun," he slowly hisses my name as though it got caught between his teeth.

A torch lights up behind me and the Stag fairy carries it over to the voice on the other side of the room. As the light gets closer, I can see the steps lead to a platform similarly to our council building, but this platform only has one chair.

I gasp as the light reveals the one sitting in it. He has several legs and arms, and a massive tail with a large curved stinger.

"Mantus," my voice barely comes out a hoarse whisper.

He smiles when I say his name. He is obviously pleased that his name has traveled so far. His arrogance transforms my fear into rage. It is clear that he is the one who broke into my home and murdered my father, and if Merik is still alive he is probably being held prisoner here. If I could, I would lunge across this room and rip out his throat with my bare hands.

"This is no way to treat a guest. Sarpe cut her free," he orders the snake.

"But, master," she starts to protest. Mantus tilts his head and widens his eyes. He says nothing, because he doesn't have to. "As you wish," she surrenders. She slithers over to me reluctantly.

She is directly in front of me now. Her eyes are orange, but her pupils are different than ours. They are vertical slits, reptilian like. Her white fangs stand out against her dark red lips. She would be beautiful if she wasn't so vile.

She pulls out a small dagger and grudgingly cuts me free. I try not to wince as I peel the embedded rope from my wrists and ankles. She stares into my eyes for a long hard moment before she slithers away. It felt like an unspoken challenge, a challenge that I will not back down from.

"Leave us," Mantus orders.

I sense that Sarpe and the Stag are uncomfortable with that order, but they obey it anyway.

"You trust to be alone in a room with me with my hands free?" I ask a question, but it is more of a threat.

"Sigrun, you are tired, hungry, not thinking clearly," his voice is low and it echoes in this room. I can feel the vibration in my chest. "Even if you killed me, which in the state you are in I doubt you have the upper hand, you would never leave this camp alive. You know this, you are smarter than that," he purrs to me, and it just fuels my hate.

"What do you want with me? Why am I still alive?" I ask directly.

"Direct. I like that." He stands up and I see him in his full form. He is how I imagined him. He stands on three pairs of legs that support his massive lower body and tail. He has a pair of arms that extend from his sides that end in very sharp pinchers and then two regular arms that come out from his shoulders. His skin is deep reddish brown and it looks tough and leathery.

He makes his way down the steps. He does not have feet like we do, instead his legs stab the ground like spears and the stone clacks beneath him with each step.

"Sigrun," he starts again. Every time he says my name my skin crawls, "It is not my wish to harm you in any way. I went through a lot of trouble to bring you here."

"Why?" I demand again.

"You are unique and powerful, I collect unique and powerful things," he walks slowly toward me as he speaks, "I have been searching for a long time for someone I could call my equal, only to be disappointed every time. Then I heard that there was a girl who was born with wings of a dragon."

He circles around me. He sees my wings unbound for the first time. I still remain kneeling on the ground.

"Magnificent," he says slowly as he looks me over.

It makes me shiver. "That is really touching that you want to add me to your little collection, but I don't think I will fit on a pedestal so I will have to politely decline," I say sarcastically.

He laughs so hard it startles me. "No, you misunderstand. You will not just be a member of the tribe, you will be my Queen. You will give me children that will be like the Gods," he crouches down in front of me so that his face is inches from mine. He has very angular features. His chin is very broad and his cheek bones are high and protruding. His lips are black and twist up into a menacing smile exposing pointed teeth, and his red eyes burn into mine. My body is shaking violently. "Don't you see," he coos at me, "you are my perfect mate." He holds my chin carefully between his pincher.

My mouth is dry but I manage to spit in his face. "You murdered my family," I scream at him, "I would only touch you to kill you."

He steps back angry at first. He pulls his fist back like he is about to hit me, but I don't flinch. He lowers his arm and wipes his face calmly.

"I understand it is a lot to consider. Perhaps I have something that will help you come around," he takes a few steps toward the back of the room. "Mordecai!" He shouts.

A man enters from the shadows. He is tall and he wears a cloak with a hood. As soon as I see the black feathered wings, I know it is the man I saw talking with Khalon.

My heart sinks to my knees. It was all a lie. My friend is no friend at all. Jae was right, he used me to acclimate into the village. He is a spy and a liar, and I am a fool.

"Bring him in," Mantus instructs him. Mordecai nods to Mantus and just before he leaves the room his eyes meet mine, he almost looks nervous. Despite my efforts my eyes are welling up with angry tears. He is only gone for a few seconds and when he returns he has another man with him. It is dark on that side which makes it hard to see him. The tears in my eyes don't help either. He takes a few more steps closer. Finally I see something. Yellow eyes shine through the shadows, yellow eyes that I know very well.

"Merik!" I say his name, but I almost don't believe it is true.

He comes closer until his face is fully in the light. His eyes look empty, but he looks good, healthy at least. His light brown hair is longer than normal and his skin is pale, but it always is. He does not look as though he has been mistreated, and I am thankful for that. I scramble to get on my feet, but they fail me. I fall back to the ground. I thank my father in my own silent prayer. At least, my brother is alive.

Merik is in front of me and I reach up to him so he will help me on my feet. He does, but as soon as I try to put my arms around him his hand wraps around my throat and he starts to squeeze. He is holding me up so our eyes are at the same level. He has never been warm and loving, but this is the first time I have ever seen his eyes so full of hate.

My toes are barely touching the ground. I claw at his hand, but he is not budging.

"You see, Sigrun I did not kill your father," Mantus explains calmly.

My eyes look down at Merik's belt and I see my father's sword hanging from it. The blood that dripped down my father's body was shed by Merik, his own son.

The pain of that day comes flooding back. I feel sick. Tears stream down my face and onto Merik's hand. My tears do not affect him at all except that they provide enough lubrication for me to slip from his grasp. I fall back to the ground. I cough and struggle to find my breath.

"You brainwashed him," I manage to garble out.

"No, it was all his idea," Mantus says coolly.

"Why?" I scream out at Merik through my coughing, "Why would you kill our father? How could you?"

He stands in front of me and without warning he kicks me hard in the stomach. I am fighting for my breath again. He kneels down and grabs me by my hair, pulling my face up to his. I see a marking on his forearm. A thick black circle with an X through it. A trophy for an important kill. His reward for killing our father.

"You killed my mother, guess that makes us even," his voice is unmerciful. His mouth is snarling. He pulls his free hand back and releases it hard, punching me in the mouth. I taste the metallic tang of my blood. He has split my lip.

"That's enough, Merik," Mantus stops him before he can hit me again. "Do you want to say goodbye to your sister before you leave?" Mantus asks.

Merik spits on the ground next to my hand.

"I gather that is a no," Mantus snickers. "Mordecai," he calls for the hooded man again. He steps forward, "Put her back in the cage. Give her some time to come around." He nods to Mantus and walks over to me. Mordecai grabs my arm hard and pulls me to my feet. I would struggle, but I'm still trying to catch my breath, and my head is throbbing.

Mordecai holds me tightly under my arm, supporting my weight. I struggle to keep my legs under me. When we get outside, I get my first look at the camp. It is dark out, but I have no idea how close it is to morning. The village is very active for the night. Fires are blazing, people are drinking and laughing. It seems like a celebration. There are several fairies like the ones in my village, with feathered wings, but the majority is completely different. Some have bodies like spiders, or beetles. Some are like centipedes and cockroaches, and then there is Sarpe who is a snake. They are all terrifying.

Their festivities halt for a moment as we come into sight. They all stare at me with sneers and the occasional look of curiosity. Their dwellings are made from stone, clay, and straw. They look cold and dark, and if they left this place tomorrow I doubt anyone would miss this place. The only building of substance is the one where Mantus resides.

We get to the cage, it is an enclosure just tall enough for me to stand in, and possibly lie out fully in, but it is very rustic. Large rods of wood tied together with rope and bound with sap that has hardened over time. It looks very sturdy. I do start to struggle as we approach it. The idea of being confined in that cage sends my adrenaline coursing. I thrash around and use my wings to free myself from his grip, but his hand is iron clad.

"Stop fighting," he spits out through his teeth. He tosses me into the cell and closes the door. He chains the door shut and locks it.

Sarpe slithers her way up to the cage. Her eyes blazing, "What does Mantus want us to do with it?" She hisses.

"Keep her in here for now. He is hoping she'll come around," Mordecai turns and start to walk away, but before he leaves he looks over his shoulder. "Bring her something to eat," he orders Sarpe. She hisses and slithers away.

Alone in my cage I start clawing at the bonds, looking for any weak spots. There are none. Defeat brings me down to my knees.

I would cry, but I am too exhausted. My body aches and my head is throbbing. I feel the back of my head where I was knocked out. It stings with the slightest touch. My hair is sticky with what I can only assume to be blood. More than just physical pain my head throbs with the devastation of my circumstances. My brother has done the worst possible thing I can think of. My friend, who I trusted and fought for and let into my home and my heart, tricked me and had me thrown into this prison. Deceived by both. I cannot decide which one hurts more.

I hear something in the dark. It snaps me out of the torture of my own mind.

"Who's there?" My voice is rickety.

There is no response at first, but a figure soon steps out of the shadows. His yellow eyes give him away. It is Merik. For the first time I cling to some kind of hope. It is possible he is a prisoner too, and was forced to act like one of them. Perhaps he is here to free me.

"Merik," I whisper. The last thing I want is the snake to come back. "Get me out of here," I plead.

He shakes his head slowly. "Where is it?" he asks.

"What? Where's what?" I ask frustrated.

"I know he gave it to you," he persists. He points to my necklace. He must be talking about the red book.

"Merik, I don't know what you are talking about."

Even though I was certain he was talking about the book I won't reveal its location, or that I even know about it.

"You're lying," he looks into me like he is reading my soul. His eyes fix on the necklace again.

"Yes, he gave me this," I hold the marble in my hand, feeling protective over it.

"And, what else?"

"And, nothing else. He gave this to me after my commencement, and then I went to the river with Jae and when I came home he was dead," the words burn as I say them.

He says nothing else. His eyes search mine, his mouth a twisted snarl. Sadness grips my heart. How did we both end up here? This life was supposed to be about goodness and here we are, both in darkness, on opposite sides of a cage.

"What have they done to you?" Unwelcome tears well up in my eyes.

"They have liberated me."

His response baffles me, "Liberated you from what? I don't understand."

"Of course you don't understand, you never did," he walks toward the cage, and extends his hand out to caress the wooden bars. "How do you like your prison cell?" he asks smugly, "Does is feel like the world is caving in, and you can't breathe? Like all of your pain and suffering is on display for everyone to see?" His description is accurate and leaves me perplexed, "I have been a prisoner my entire life."

"What are you talking about?" My hands tighten around the bars in frustration. "Father loved you. I loved you. You have never been caged," I feel sad and desperate. I had hoped to have this talk with him under better circumstances, but I may not have another chance to reach him. "I know we have never been close, and I'm sorry. I know mother died because of me, I know that and I have been living with that my entire life too."

He starts to turn from me and walk away. Anxiety grabs hold of me. I have to make him stay. I have to make him listen.

"She knew she was going to die!" I shout. He stops. It is a small victory so I continue, "She knew she was going to die giving birth to me. Father had a premonition before I was born. They could have saved her by sacrificing me, but they made their choice."

His back is still to me. I wish I could see his face, see if I am getting through to him.

"You lie," he growls. My heart sinks.

"No, Merik, it is the truth. Father told me, I swear to you," I grasp at the bars with desperation. "Don't you think I wish things had turned out differently? I would give anything for her to be alive. To be rid of these wings which have only ever been a curse, but I can't. I can't change it and neither can you."

He says nothing.

"But I am your sister, and I'm here, and we can make things better going forward."

He finally turns around. His expression is unreadable. He walks back to the cage. We are face to face now. Tears are pooled in his eyes threatening to break down his cheeks any moment. Hope swells up in me.

He leans in closer, "Things already are better."

Before I can even comprehend what he means, he takes a small knife from his belt and stabs my hand all the way through, pinning it to the bar of the cage.

I scream.

The pain shoots through my arm all the way to the top of my head.

He removes the blade, and I fall to the ground. I press my hand into my chest, trying to subdue the surging pain. I look up at him. He licks the blood off the blade and then spits it on the ground.

"I would kill you if I had the chance, you should remember that," he whispers before he walks back into the shadows.

I struggle to tear a piece of cloth from my shirt with one hand. Once I have a good sized strip, I wrap my hand the best I can to stop the bleeding. Tightening the bandage is agony, but the hopelessness I feel inside is worse.

Chapter 28

Hours go by before the morning light comes up, and I have not moved. My legs went numb some time ago. The snake never returned with food as she was ordered, but I could not eat it anyway. Pain and sorrow have left me in a wake of nausea.

As the sun comes up, the noise of the camp dies down. Drunkenness has faded into headaches and weariness. The majority have gone to bed. Mordecai comes to my cage. I would tear his wings off if I could.

"Did she bring you food?" he asks.

I only look at him. I say nothing.

"Sarpe!" He shouts.

I hear a rattle in the distance.

She is annoyed, "What is it?" She spits out as she rounds the corner.

"I told you to feed her."

She holds her head high, "So."

"If she dies because of your jealousy, Mantus will have you exiled or worse."

"I'm not jealous of that."

"Then bring her food," he says aggressively. She turns away from him. "And water," he adds. She leaves and he tosses a blanket into the cage, "Here. The nights are getting colder." He looks at me and notices my hand. "What happened here?" he asks, pointing at it. I say nothing. He does not ask again, but only shakes his head, turns and walks away.

He is obviously under strict orders from Mantus to keep me alive, but it seems he hates the task of looking after me. A few minutes later Sarpe returns. She throws a stale chunk of bread on the ground outside of the cage and drops a bowl of water next to it. The majority of the contents spill out onto the ground greedily soaked up by the earth.

I refuse to eat my provisions, and I would like to turn the bowl over spilling the rest of the water, but I hate the taste of blood. I reach out between the bars and grab the bowl. It doesn't fit between the bars. It seems the snake found a loop hole in her orders. My hands are shaking from the pain and dehydration. I hold the bowl up and take in what I can. Swishing and spitting bloody water on to the ground. Indulgence gets the better of me and I drink the last bit.

The daylight passes and I hardly notice. I spend the bulk of my day thinking about how to get out of here, but then what? I don't even know where I am, and I have no supplies.

I keep remembering the conversation I had with Merik. Every time I think about the evil in his eyes my stomach aches. When my mind is not plagued by grief, I fantasize about what Mantus' insides look like, or what sound my knife would make piercing his hard shiny skin. Occasionally one of Mantus' minions wanders over to my cage to steal a look at me. Between the waves of pain and anger I am exhausted.

The afternoon light is coming to an end and the black widow fairy, finds her way over to my cage. She isn't very big but her eight slender legs make her very fast. She is more spider than fairy, but her middle abdomen and head have more resemblance to a girl. Her skin is shiny black and her eyes are red. I also catch a glimpse of a red hour glass on her belly as she crawls around on my cage.

"Pretty, pretty," she says almost in a taunting way, "I think you are very pretty. No wonder Mantus wants to keep you."

A larger male spider walks up to her. His body is similar to hers, mostly spider with a man-like torso and head with two pairs of eyes. His body is thicker and heavier, and he has brown fuzz that covers his body.

"She looks tasty," he says coming up to her.

"Yes, she does," the widow snickers.

"I wouldn't mind spending an afternoon sucking on you," he says and he licks his lips.

My skin crawls.

"Too bad this one's off limits," the widow pouts.

"Yes, too bad," he says. They leave together, but his eyes stay on me until they are around the corner. For the first time I actually feel safer in this cage.

Once it is officially nighttime, Mordecai makes his rounds again to check on me. He looks down at the untouched piece of bread and shakes his head. He squats down in front of the cage and picks it up. He brushes the dirt off and hands it to me. I don't reach out for it.

"If you don't eat on your own, I will force it down your throat," he threatens. He holds it out to me until I reach out and take it, "I'm not leaving until you eat it."

I glare at him while I tear a small piece off and put it in my mouth. It is hard, and tastes bad. My mouth is so dry that I struggle to swallow it. He stands back up and tosses a canteen of water to me.

"Here, drink that too. I'm sure Sarpe didn't give you much water either," he watches me take a few more bites before he leaves again.

The night air is getting colder, and though I hate using anything given to me by these creatures, my chattering teeth force me to cover myself with the blanket Mordecai gave me. I try so hard to fight sleep, I don't trust anything about this place and all I want to do is break free, but I cannot fight sleep anymore. My mind needs to rest and my body needs to heal. I finally close my eyes, and drift off. The whole time I pray that I will wake up in my bed and that this is only a nightmare.

Chapter 29

Something in the dark startles me. I don't know where I am. A beastly growling echoes from the emptiness in the night. It is black as pitch. I can't see anything. I am afraid. Fear latches on to me, but I strain to see anyway. In the distance, I see something glowing, something red. Eyes, I see red eyes.

I startle myself awake. Pain floods in as soon as consciousness arrives. I am still in my cage, everything hurts, and I can't even find solace in my dreams. I ignore my nightmare and focus on the real terror. I have to get out of here. The thought screams in my mind. I start thinking about Khalon being in my village with my friends. What is he telling them? What is he doing to them? The thought rips at my insides. It is so hard to believe that I was so wrong about him. I have to get out of here. The thought continues to reel. I have to warn them.

I start kicking at the bars. Despite my throbbing hand, I hold onto the top and swing the weight of my body at the sides, hoping I will splinter something. The wood is so strong, it doesn't budge. There has to be a weak spot somewhere. I keep kicking. The soles of my feet are raw, but I keep at it.

It doesn't take very long before I hear a rattle approach my cage.

"Knock it off," Sarpe hisses. She looks tired, I obviously woke her, and by the look of it she just went to bed not that long ago.

I ignore her request. I ignore her presence for that matter, and continue to kick. She rattles her tail. My defiance aggravates her. Her rattle is a very obvious indicator. I know exactly when I'm getting under her skin.

She scales the side of the cage. Her eyes are flaming orange. "You'll never break these bars," she snickers, "they've held bigger, stronger, prisoners and no one has ever escaped." She crawls across the cage until she is in front of me. "So you may as well knock it off!" she shouts.

I stop for a moment and look at her. "You don't want me here, right?" I ask. "So, why don't you just open the door and turn around. I'll creep out of here, and you never have to see me ever again."

I can tell that she likes the idea of me being gone. She almost looks like she is considering my proposal.

"It would only be a temporary solution," she says.

"Why?"

"Don't you know?" An evil smile spreads across her face. "We are heading north in a few weeks, heading right to your village. Your men's heads will sit on spikes as a warning. Your women will be given as tributes to our warriors, and only the children who accept our way will be spared," her eyes dance at the thought of destroying the lives of the innocent.

I see the image of Malyn and Ainia beaten and tied up, thrown to savages for amusement, and Jae's body impaled on a spike. My heart quickens. Sarpe can see my distress. The blood has certainly drained from my face, and I'm sure the rose is closed up tight.

She looks satisfied and she starts to leave. Rage bubbles up inside me.

"Sarpe!" I call after her. She turns around to look at me. "I don't know how or when, but I will get out of here," I twist my hands around the bars, "and when I do," I shake my head, "I'm going to use your hide to make myself a new belt."

She sneers at my threat and slinks off to go back to bed. I let go of the bars. I know she is right. The cage is too sturdy to break. The ground is too hard to dig, and the cage too exposed to even try. I sit down in the corner and my put head in my hands. My temples are pounding. I have to come up with a different plan.

I have not eaten in two days. Mordecai has not come to check on me, and Sarpe would never do anything decent for me without being forced.

Evening rolls in fast bringing tumultuous clouds with it. Lightning and thunder crack before a drop of water falls. The Stag comes to my cell with another man. This one has gray feathered wings, but they are tattered and dull.

"The master would like to see you," the Stag says to me as he starts to unchain the door.

For a second I think that maybe I can fly out of the cage as soon as the door opens, kick them in the face to throw them off balance, and then fly hard until I'm free. Excitement starts to course through my body at the prospect of getting out of here. I start to look around, and realize that an impulsive decision will almost certainly be a fatal one. I won't be able to fight my way out of here. I need a different strategy.

"You won't give me any trouble, will you?" The Stag asks, but it comes across as more of a threat.

I purse my lips in a tight line and shake my head. He holds the door open and lets me walk out. I walk between the two of them on my own through the camp until we reach Mantus' dwelling. They stop at the front steps and nod for me to continue on. My stomach is in knots. The last time I was taken into this room everything I knew to be true was destroyed. Each step I take my legs feel heavier.

I enter the room and what was just an empty space now has a long table covered in all different kinds of food and jugs of wine. My stomach betrays me and rumbles at the sight of it. I also see a soaking tub steaming with hot water and I smell rose oil.

"Hungry?" a voice rumbles behind me. I know it is Mantus. The clacking of his feet on the stone floor tells me exactly how close he is to me. "You must be hungry," he says again. I don't turn around but I know he is inches away.

"They said you wanted to talk to me, so what do you want?" I ask annoyed.

He chuckles. I feel his breath on the back of my neck. "I want many things, Sigrun," he touches my hair, rubbing a lock between his fingers. It sends a chill down my back. "Perhaps you would like to take a bath, wash this blood and dirt off of you."

I assume his offer also includes him watching me. Bile rises in my throat.

"No thank you," my words are polite, but my tone is not.

"I insist," he walks around me and goes over to the tub.

He pulls a steaming rag out of the water, and motions for me to come to him. Every part of me revolts, but he is not relenting at all.

I walk over to the other side of the tub and see a large mirror on the wall. It is the first time I've seen my reflection since I've been here. He was right about the dirt and blood. Dried blood is matted in my hair where I was hit and all down the side of my face. My lip is still swollen and bloody from when Merik hit me, and I am covered in dirt. I take the rag and dab at the cut on my lip, it stings. I clean my face and hands quickly. I see his reflection in the mirror as well. Just like I thought he watches my every move.

I set the rag on the side of the tub and turn to face him. He turns and walks to the table where he pours wine into two cups.

"Come. Sit," he beacons.

I have no intention of drinking wine, I must keep my wits about me, but I do walk over to the chair. I start thinking if I play his game enough maybe he won't put me back in the cage, and I'll be able to escape.

The food on the table consists mainly of various kinds of meats, most of which I've never seen before. There is no fruit and a small selection of nuts. They have also set out a cabbage soup and some bread. He makes a plate and sets it in front of me. Despite my surging hunger I don't touch it. I can see on his face he is disappointed, but he chooses not to push me. I'm sitting at his table that is enough for now. He sits on the other end of the table.

I want to ask him about Khalon, but that topic is still very raw for me. I might expose more of my feelings than I want to, and I still don't fully understand the role Khalon is playing in this. I decide to wait.

"Isn't this better than the cage? Food, wine, a hot bath, and that would only be the beginning. You would be the Queen on the arm of the most powerful King in the land. Anything you want would be yours." His words are poison.

I can see how he thinks this plan will force me into submission. Beat me, starve me, and then open the door to food and comfort. All I have to do is give him my mind and body for the rest of my life.

"Anything I want?"

His eyes gleam at the thought of my submission. "Anything," he purrs.

"I would really like my father back," I hiss.

His eyes dull again. He sits back in his chair and clenches his jaw, "That was not done by my hand."

"No, it was Merik," saying the words out loud makes me sick.

"Yes, there is something different about that boy. It has been a long time since I have seen that kind of hate and determination," his mouth twists up into a sadistic smile, "He reminds me of myself when I was a boy."

I feel heat building in my chest. My temper is rising. I have to stay calm a little while longer, "How did you find him anyway?"

"He found us."

The idea that Merik stumbled onto their camp is not surprising. He has been essentially running away from home his whole life, but this time he did it for real.

"My men found him on the border of our camp. He begged to stay. I was going to kill him, but he began talking about his village. We had been planning on heading north anyway, but now we had a real reason to go," he pauses to take a drink. He chuckles to himself before putting the cup down, "That boy really hates you."

Merik really hates me. That has been made excruciatingly clear in the last few days. A vision of his yellow eyes filled with blind fury bullies its way into my mind. I close my eyes tightly trying to force it out.

"Merik wanted to kill you too," he continues, "but I couldn't allow him to do that."

"Why not? You let him kill my father."

"Your father would have only stood in my way. Merik did me a favor when he killed him."

I bite the inside of my cheek to keep from losing my temper. I bite so hard that I soon taste blood. His cavalier attitude toward the murder of my father spikes my anger. My hands start shaking. If we continue on this subject, I will surely do something that will put this meeting to an end, and I still have questions.

"What are your plans for my village?" I ask as diplomatically as possible.

"To rule it," he answers directly. It almost surprises me that he doesn't even try to spin it in some way.

"And, what about my people?"

"Those who fall in line will have nothing to fear, and will live prosperous lives. There is no reason we cannot live together in peace," that is a lie. I trust Sarpe's version is closer to the truth.

"Really?"

He nods with a sly smile.

"You have no plans to enslave the women, murder the children, and stick the men's heads on spikes to serve as a warning?"

His eyes widen. My insight to his plan surprises him. "Where did you hear that?" he asks through a clinched jaw.

I say nothing.

He pauses for a long moment. I can tell he is trying to piece together where I may have heard such a thing. Khalon was the first to inform me of his plan, but Sarpe was the most detailed. He has not mentioned Khalon at all since I have been here, and I wonder if he will finally acknowledge Khalon infiltrating my home.

"Damn that serpent," he says more vexed than angry. "She's always been the jealous type." He does not seem too bothered that his illusion was spoiled. It is more of an irritation that he looks foolish, and an inconvenience that he has to change his strategy. "Well, it seems my guards have been talking more than they should. No matter, you would have been involved in one way or another eventually," he leans back almost relieved that he no longer has to play a specific role.

"In one way or another?" That bit seems dangerously ambiguous.

He smiles. He looks more menacing when he smiles. My stomach clinches, "I have already proposed what I want from you. I want you as my Queen. That would give you *some* say in what becomes of your precious village." It does not take much to pick out Mantus' real meaning. His proposal is actually an ultimatum. I can either be his Queen, living the rest of my life as his personal slave, or I can have my head spiked next to Jae and my other friends.

"That doesn't sound like a very good deal," my annoyance seeps out with my words. It is insulting that he thought I would so easily submit to his will, "You should really work on sharpening your negotiation skills."

His smile fades and sinks into a twisted grimace.

"I will not stand by while you murder good and innocent people," I proclaim. Heat builds in my chest as my anger rises, "I will not allow you into my village while I live. I will never be your Queen, because one thing is abundantly clear to me." I stand up slowly, "You will never be *my* equal."

His fists are clinched.

My body is shaking. I anticipate his wrath. The moment before he speaks drags on for what seems an impossibly long time. I gather he is deciding to whether or not to pluck my wings off himself or have one of his cronies do it.

"Cronus!" He shouts finally. The Stag enters. "Remove her," he orders.

Cronus reaches out to grab my arm but I twist away. I will walk out of here on my own. My eyes remain fixed on Mantus until I am out the door. Things have not worked out how he had hoped, and frustration is spreading across his face. It gives me a small amount of satisfaction.

The rain has come in hard while I was inside. The camp is the quietest I have seen. Almost everyone has sought cover from the storm. Cronus escorts me back to my cage. I go back in without protest. I have accepted my fate. I only regret not being able to save my loved ones from this dreadful end.

The cage offers no protection from the rain. I am fortunate to not have delicate wings. The rain does not bother me much, other than the cold and wet of it. I sit in the dark and wait. I know he is going to kill me, but how and when, are still a mystery.

Hours go by and it seems the darkness and the rain will never stop. The patter of the drops on the ground is almost hypnotic, and at least some of the foul stench that hovers over their camp is being washed clean. I am grateful for that much.

Off in the distance a twig snaps, and my attention comes back acutely. My executioner has arrived. I stand up out of the mud, and decide that I will not go down easily. I will fight back, and hopefully the life that is taken is not mine.

A figure moves swiftly out of the shadows and into sight. I recognized the hooded figure. It is Mordecai. I am not surprised. He seems to be a very trusted soldier, and he likely has more knowledge about me that he gained from Khalon. He'll know my strengths and weaknesses.

He approaches the cage in haste, which startles me.

"We have to get you out of here," he whispers as he starts to unlock the door.

This doesn't seem real. The door is being unchained before me, but I don't understand why.

Maybe this is just one final wicked trick before he slits my throat. Give me the hope of freedom so that the blade stings all the more.

"We have to go before the rain stops. We may not get another chance," he motions for me to exit the cage. He must see the look on my face of absolute confusion, because his body posture softens a bit and he removes his hood so I can see his face, "You have to trust me. I'm not going to hurt you."

His eyes are soft. He reaches his hand out to me to help me out of the cage. I appreciate the gesture, but I don't trust him. I come out of the cage on my own.

I barely have one foot out the door when I hear the rattle approach the cage. Mordecai quickly runs around the corner leaving me alone as Sarpe slithers up to me. It happens so fast I don't even have time to think whether I have been double crossed or if Sarpe just foiled my escape by accident.

"What's this?" She hisses surprised to see me outside of my cage and alone. "How did you get out?" She reaches for her knife. The opportunity to kill me escaping would be too sweet for her to pass up.

I don't have a chance to answer her before Mordecai is back. He drops out of the sky and stabs his sword through her tail, pinning her to the ground. He covers her mouth at the same time so her screams are muffled. He wrestles the knife out of her hand and tosses it to me.

"Before you can make the belt, you have to kill the snake," he says to me. His words echo my own. He has been watching over me the whole time.

His hand still covers her mouth, but her eyes perfectly visible. Two glowing orange orbs wide and unblinking stare at me with fury, disbelief, and I think a little fear.

The knife is heavy in my hand. Now that her life is literally in my hands I don't know if I can go through with it.

"She would end your life without hesitation and with a smile on her face," he can sense my reluctance about taking a life.

I know he is right, she would kill me without a second thought, but now with her helpless the act seems cold and wrong. She claws at his hands trying to free herself, but his hold is iron strong.

I turn the knife around and slam the heavy hilt across her temple. She goes limp in his arms. I have rendered her unconscious and that is good enough for now.

"Put her in the cage," I say to Mordecai.

We quickly tie her hands and gag her then chain and lock the cage door.

Chapter 30

The rain makes it hard to fly so we run out of the camp. Hunger and dehydration make my body feel heavy and tired, but I run faster than I ever have before. We do not speak at all, we save all of our breath for our escape. I push myself hard. My sides ache and I taste the metallic taste in the back of my throat but I do not stop until he does.

Eventually he stops under a low branch. I lean against the trunk so I don't fall over. My head is spinning. My body is trembling.

"We should get you out of the rain," he says.

The rain is cold, but the dehydration makes it much worse. He looks around until he sees some rocks against a hill that form a small shelter. I follow him quickly.

Once inside, he hands me some bread and water, "Here, eat and drink this. You need to regain your strength. We still have a long way to go."

The bread is much better than what I was given in the camp. It is not as good as the bread we make, this bread is harder and a little sour, but right now it might be the best thing I have ever eaten. I drink the water so fast it gives me pains in my stomach. My belly has not been used to this much food for several days and the swelling the bread and water cause is uncomfortable.

"I should look at that," he points to my injured hand.

I shake my head. "It's okay," I say with my mouth still full. I can tell my wound is already healing, and in a day or so it will not cause me anymore discomfort.

I catch my breath once I realize enough distance is between the camp and me. Questions about my new traveling companion start to arise. Every time I think I know who someone is, or what they are capable of, something happens that turns my reality upside down. Mordecai helped me escape. Did he help me because of Khalon or in spite of him? That is one question that weighs heavy on me. He does not know that I saw him that night with Khalon. I fear the wrong question could put my life back in danger.

"Why did you help me?" I ask the simplest form of the question.

He looks at me and pulls his hood away from his face a bit. This is the first time that I have been able to get a good look at his face without being afraid of it. He has long straight black hair, a slender face with a long nose. His eyes look like copper, they shine a reddish brown, and they have compassion in them that I would not expect. Most of his body is covered by his cloak, but I see some of his tattoos peeking out from his collar up onto his neck. Similarly to Khalon he is handsome, but in an unexpected way.

"Many reasons," he answers just as simply.

"Such as?"

He looks down at the ground and smiles a half smile, "Let's just say we have a mutual cause and a mutual friend."

We sit in silence for a long time just watching the rain. The forest feels so peaceful. It is deceptive that we are running for our lives.

My hands finally stop shaking and the dizziness subsides. Before too long, the rain starts to lighten.

"We better keep going," he says putting his pack across his body again. "They will discover that you are gone soon, if they haven't already."

We run through the rest of the night and into the following day. In the heat of the daytime, our pace slows down to a fast walk. We choose not to fly in the day light, because we will be too visible that way, so we stick to the ground. We stop only to eat quickly. The further we get the more familiar things look. We are not far from my village. The joy of this fills me with the will to go faster and harder.

Night falls again and just as we approach the border of my village Mordecai grabs my hand, "No, we have to go this way."

"What? Why?" I don't understand why he won't let me enter my homelands.

"You have to trust me," that is the second time he has said that to me. His eyes are sincere, and he has gotten us this far. I turn to follow him away from the village and back into the thickness of the wood. Though the course we are taking is different I know where we are. We are heading to the field where we train. Just before we reach the field I see the light of a fire just in front of us. There is a large figure sitting in front of it, his head is in his hands. As we step into the clearing, a twig breaks beneath my foot and he looks up suddenly. It is Khalon. He stands up slowly. His eyes fixed on mine. My head feels disconnected from my body, like I have lost all control over it. I cannot move. I still do not know what is true. Did Mordecai bring me back to my friend, or has he led me to my death?

Khalon says nothing and neither do I. He walks fast and then runs to me. I think to myself, I should run away from here, but I still cannot make my body move. He closes the distance between us and I close my eyes, anticipating the worst. His arms wrap around my waist and pick me up so my face is to his. Still holding me up with one arm he puts his other behind my head and he presses his mouth on mine. This almost surprises me more than if he had run a blade through me. My body and mouth are rigid at first. My lip is still sore from when Merik hit me. His body is trembling, and he clings to me desperately. My heart melts, and then so does the rest of me. I relax and let him kiss me. I feel his sharp canine nip at my bottom lip before he pulls away.

"I'm sorry," he says a little out of breath. He has set me back down on the ground, and he holds my face in his hands. "Thank the stars you are all right," he closes his eyes like he is in pain. "I thought... I've been..." he has trouble putting his feelings and thoughts into words.

He turns to Mordecai, "Thank you, brother." He reaches out with one arm, while still holding me with the other, and puts his hand behind Mordecai's head. He puts his forehead to Mordecai's. Mordecai clasps his hand tightly around Khalon's wrist. This embrace of brotherhood touches me deeply.

He turns back to me, "When I came back to the house, I saw the den, and you were gone." He pauses, the recollection causes him pain. "Then Mordecai tracked me down and told me you had been taken to the Skar camp. I've been losing my mind."

He pulls me back into a tight embrace, holding me close against his chest. The warmth of his skin and the slightly accelerated thrumming of his heartbeat makes my legs go weak. I finally feel safe. He touches my face again, almost like he is making sure I'm real. He looks over my face which is dirty and covered with blood. He puts his hand in my hair where I was struck and I flinch at the touch. That spot is still a bit tender. He pulls his hand away and looks down to see blood on his fingertips. The rain managed to dampen the blood in my hair rather than to wash it away. The sight of my blood twists his face into rage.

"I was hit from behind," I explain, "I don't even know who hit me, or how I got there."

"It was Merik who knocked you out," Mordecai says, "Cronus was with him and he carried you back. I did not know about it until I was back at camp."

"The den was tossed, do you know why?" I ask. Now I know he was looking for the book, but I have to find out if Merik told anyone else about it.

"Said he was looking for something, but he couldn't find it, then you showed up," Mordecai confesses.

I wish I knew why he is so obsessed with the book. I doubt he can even read it.

I look at Khalon, "Why are you sitting out here alone?"

Mordecai and Khalon look at each other. They seem to be reading each other's thoughts, and it is a conversation that I want to be a part of.

"Merik is back," Khalon says finally.

I can't breathe.

"He came back two days ago," he has me sit by the fire as he continues to talk. "He is saying that you killed your father." My blood pulses through my body. "And, that he narrowly escaped with his own life." I know Khalon hates telling me this. I can see the disgust in his face. "He is telling everyone that you had returned to the Skars to gather your army."

The story is so absurd it hardly seems true. "Does anyone actually believe this twaddle?" I shout. Anger is rising in me.

"Of course your friends know the truth. Some don't know what to believe," he says disappointed. "He has been very elaborate in his story telling."

I can tell he doesn't want to bring me anymore pain, but he knows I need to hear what is happening here.

"When I came back to the house that night and saw that you had been taken, I went straight to Jae. The kid drives me nuts, but I know that when it comes to you and your safety I can trust him. He, on the other hand, does not feel the same way about me," he stands up again and motions for me to follow him. The three of us start walking toward the field as he continues his story. "I couldn't stand to be in your house with you gone, so I moved out here. Jae was certain that I had something to do with your disappearance, he didn't believe me about Merik."

I stop. "When did you find out about Merik?" I ask dreading his response, wondering if he has known this whole time.

He takes a breath. "I did find out about him before you were taken," he confesses. He eagerly grabs my hand, I suspect out of fear that I might leave, "But I swear I had no idea that he was in the village. I would have never left you if I had known he was here."

"When, Khalon? When did you find out?" I ask more forcefully this time.

"A few days before you disappeared," he admits.

"I had just found Khalon," Mordecai interrupts, "to warn him. I told him."

"I didn't know how to tell you," Khalon says to me. He looks at me, searching and hoping that I will understand.

"No, I suppose not," I say.

I look down at my injured hand. I do understand. I bring my hand up to my chest. I had to see Merik's cruelty for myself. I would have never believed Khalon if he would have told me before.

He takes my good hand and keeps leading me forward. We walk up the opening of the field and I see several campfires and all of my friends.

"No one believed me about Merik," Khalon starts, "but when Merik showed up with your father's sword on is belt they all showed up here." He concludes as all of my friends' eyes find their way to me.

Just like Khalon they take a minute to decide if I'm real or not. Finally like the breaking of a dam they all rush forward. Malyn, being the fastest gets to me first. Flying into me she nearly knocks me down. Ainia, Remi, Vidar, Wren and the rest all crowd around embracing me. I flurry of questions and comments swirl around me.

"So glad you are okay," I hear someone say.

"What happened?" Someone else asks.

"Where did they take you?" Another question from someone.

I don't know where to start, but then I look through the crowd and see Jae standing on the other side. His face looks thin and his eyes are haunted by dark circles. He has not slept for days either. The last time I saw him was the day I fought Khalon. It is not surprising that he did not trust Khalon after that, but I am glad that he is here now.

"What did they do to you?" he asks with such sadness.

I know my general appearance must be very bleak. Blood, sweat, and dirt cover my body. I've barely slept or eaten for days. My clothes are torn, and I have cuts and bruises everywhere.

I swallow over the lump in my throat, "It looks worse than it is," I attempt to smile. My bottom lip quivers. For the first time in days I feel safe and the emotion is overwhelming. I bite my lip to keep from crying.

Jae's eyes drift from me to Khalon and Mordecai, especially Mordecai. I gather they have not been properly introduced.

"Who are you?" Jae asks directly.

"My name is Mordecai," his voice is unwavering.

"Mordecai helped me escape," I jump in. This conversation reminds me of when I brought Khalon home for the first time. This time no one challenges us with more questions. They just observe him silently.

"You must be starving," Malyn says. I am grateful for the deflection.

"I am," I touch my hair and feel the grit of dirt and dried blood. "I would like to clean up some, first." I set my bag down, "I'm just going to run down to the river real quick."

I can tell by their expressions, especially Khalon and Jae, they do not want to let me out of their sight.

"I don't think you should go alone," Khalon says.

"Yeah, I'll go with you," Ainia offers.

"Me too," Malyn chimes in.

"I'll be okay..." I start, but Jae steps forward and cuts me off.

"They are going with you," he says forcefully. Normally his tone would bother me, but I know it comes from love.

"Okay," I surrender, "we'll be back soon."

The riverside is peaceful. The water babbles quietly. Frogs and crickets have come out, now that the rain has stopped, to sing their nighttime lullaby. Ainia and Malyn offered to wash my clothes for me while I bathe. I think it was their way of giving me some privacy, but still being close by.

The water is cold at first. The rain has cooled it down from the afternoon sun. The cold feels good on my head. It numbs the physical aches, if only it worked on my internal ones. I lather the soap that Ainia gave me, it smells like fresh mint. It bites at my wounds, particularly the one on my hand, but I wash my body clean despite the hurt. Eventually the foul stench of rot and decay that overwhelmed my senses begins to dissipate. Soon the smells of pine and lilac from the forest rush in to fill the void.

Floating on my back I see the rain clouds have moved on revealing the moon and the stars. The moon is not quite full but still very bright. The river is black as onyx, but the moonlight cloaks itself around me like a white blanket.

Ainia brings me clean clothes while mine dry out. I almost feel like myself again by the time I get back to the campsite. My friends have set out food and water for me when I return. I eat smoked fish, bread, and berries until my belly aches. Too tired to talk, I listen to my friends talk about the events that took place while I was away. Khalon attentively tends to my wounds as they talk. Before long, I become too tired to even listen. I lie down next to the warmth of the fire. I would have to lie in the fire to melt the chill in my bones.

Khalon lies down next to me rather than seek out a branch. Jae lies down on the other side. Neither one has any intention of leaving my side. Sleep takes a hold of me and I surrender to it with pleasure.

Chapter 31

I feel stronger by morning. My injuries are better already. Even my hand is almost healed. Now that my strength is returning my anger begins to boil. The sadness that I felt is disintegrating. Looking at my friends still asleep on the ground one thought comes to mind. Merik is in my village, sleeping in my house, telling lies and preparing to wipe out everyone that I care about.

I will not let him rest comfortably in my home.

Khalon and Jae both wake as I start getting my things together. Jae rubs at his eyes. He is still sleepy and his hair is disheveled but he looks much better.

"Where are you going?" he asks in the middle of a yawn.

"Once everyone is up, we are going back to the village."

"What?" Jae is clearly nervous about my plan.

"That's a great idea," Khalon says standing up.

He stretches his wings out for flight. Everyone else starts waking.

"I am not going to let him push me out of my home," everyone is listening, but I am speaking directly to Jae.

"Don't you think we should at least have a plan?" he asks.

"I do have a plan. My plan is to go into my village and tell him if he doesn't leave I will bash in his skull," Jae's eyes widen at my candor.

"That sounds good to me," Khalon says, "I wouldn't even give him the option. I would just kill the bastard." He puts his knife in his belt. "Actually, maybe we should beat him first and stick him in a cage to starve, just as they did to you," Khalon's anger is rising too. I like it.

"That sounds like a plan to me," Mordecai says as he walks up to us.

"Me too," Wren says as she grabs her throwing knives.

Before I know it, everyone is up and arming themselves. Most of them say nothing, but I can feel their fortitude emanate in them. It almost feels electric.

"Alright," I tuck Sarpe's dagger in my belt, "let's go home."

* * * * * *

We fly into the village together. It is quiet. No one is out harvesting. No children are out playing summer games. Fear grips at my insides. What if we are too late? I look at Jae, and I can tell he is thinking the same thing.

We go to my house first. If Merik is still here, he is most likely tearing my house apart looking for the book. My hope is to catch him off guard.

From outside my house seems quiet. I look at Jae and Khalon and nod for them to follow me in. I open the door and go in. Sure enough it is a mess inside. The furniture is knocked over the shelves have all been cleared. Broken glass is everywhere. My father's den is the same as it was when I was here last, and my room is even worse. The mattress has been sliced and gutted. Down feathers cover the floor like snow. My dressing table has been torn apart. He has even begun to pry up the floorboards. The only room that has not been destroyed is his old room, though I can tell he has done a good search of it as well. One thing is certain, Merik is not here.

We go back outside and as we do, a figure cautiously comes out from around the corner. Her silver hair does not have its usual luster and her kind face looks worn. It is Beda. As soon as she sees me, her eyes well up with tears. I'm not sure if she is happy to see me alive or afraid of me until she runs up and wraps her arms around me.

"I'm so happy you're back," she sobs.

Normally I would embrace her longer, but I am here for a specific reason.

"Beda," I pull her away, "where is he? Where's Merik?"

She wipes her eyes and nose on a handkerchief, "He is at the council building, they all are."

"What's going on?" I ask.

"He is taking your father's seat," she explains. My hands ball up into fists. "He said he came back to fulfill your father's legacy. The induction is going on now. No one knew what else to do. We have just been going along with the lies. I am supposed to be there, but Akin told everyone I was sick so I wouldn't have to go."

"I don't understand this," I say shaking my head. "Why would Merik take my father's seat if Mantus is just planning on coming in and taking everything anyway?"

"Mantus will come, he will take over, but he has promised that Merik will be the Lord of the Northwoods," Mordecai explains. "Merik is trying to solidify his place here."

"What Merik does not know," Khalon interrupts, "is that Mantus will never let him keep that seat."

Beda looks terrified. Her hands are shaking, "If he killed his own father, and did this to you, what would he do to the rest of us? I am preparing our things to leave. We are planning to sneak out tonight." Tears stream down her face.

"Has anyone been hurt?" Jae asks her. I know he is concerned about his own family.

"No, not yet."

"I won't let anything happen to you," I promise. Trying to reassure her I squeeze her hands tightly. "Go home and stay there until you hear from us. You don't have to leave," I instruct her, "I'm going to fix this."

"How?"

I turn back to Jae and Khalon. "Feel like crashing a party?" I ask.

They both give a sideways smile.

* * * * * *

The energy outside the council building feels heavy. An induction ceremony is usually a joyous occasion. They don't happen often either. Once inducted, a member's term is permanent. In order to lose their seat, they would have to be unanimously voted off by the entire council, voluntarily resign, or die. The terms being as long as they are, make the ceremony a very rare occurrence and usually a very celebratory event. However, the feeling today is dark and portentous. I pull the dagger from my belt and walk up the steps.

Only Jae, Khalon, and I go in. The rest of our friends wait outside. The room is crowded. The entire town is all here. As we enter through the back of the crowd, gasps and hushed whispers begin to ripple through the crowd. Falon is in the middle of his oration, so the commotion goes unnoticed at first. It isn't until we get closer to the front that the mass parts enough for me to see Merik. He is sitting in my father's chair with a smug look on his face. His yellow eyes flicker with self-righteousness. He obviously believes he has won. My hands begin to tremor with fury. I grip the dagger tighter.

"You're sitting in my chair!" I shout. My voice rings out through the crowd and silences Falon.

I never expected to take my father's seat, but I will die before Merik takes it.

Those who were standing in front of me have now moved revealing me fully. Falon smiles slightly and there is a renewed glimmer in his eye, but my focus is primarily on Merik. He glances at Khalon and Mordecai. I know he has never met Khalon, but I'm sure he knows who he is, and the last time he saw Mordecai he was my jailor. His smugness has melted and twisted into confusion and anger. He probably never expected to see me again, figuring I would let myself starve to death, or be killed during escape. He certainly never expected to see me again with an army of my own.

The heaviness that I felt coming into this room starts to change. The air is still dense, but now it feels weighted with anticipation. I can almost feel the heartbeat of every person as I walk past them up to the base of the stairs.

"Did you come back to kill me too?" He spits out in his best theatrical voice.

"Don't even bother, Merik," I say with disgust, "they all know you are a liar. Did you really think they wouldn't it figure out," I point to his belt, "the weapon used to murder our father is hanging from your hip?"

He looks down at the sword on his belt. I watch his face as he puts it together for the first time. In all of his elaborate planning, he forgot one very important detail. I run up the stairs before he fully realizes that his lies have all unraveled. By the time he looks up, I am standing above him with the tip of my dagger at the top of his throat. His body trembles with rage and fear. For the first time my hand is completely still.

The room gasps. No one knows what to do. They prepare themselves to see bloodshed.

Our eyes blaze into each other. "Go ahead," he says quietly and with disdain, "do it. Be the monster you are."

His eyes wince as he feels the bite of the sharp metal pricking the soft part of his chin.

I shake my head slowly my eyes never leaving his. "Only one of us has ever been monstrous," I speak clearly and with certainty, "and it definitely has never been me." I stand up straight but I keep my blade to his throat, "Go. Go back to Mantus and tell him we will meet him at the clearing at the river bend in seven days' time to finish this."

I lower my blade slowly and step slightly to the side. He stands up even slower and starts down the stairs with his head held high. He is arrogant even in defeat.

Once he reaches the bottom, I shout out to him, "Leave my father's sword."

He doesn't look back at me, but he does pull the sword out of its sheath and drops it on the stone floor. The clang echoes through the room. With no one to back him, and an entire village behind me, he obeys. He walks quickly to exit the room, but comes to a halt when he reaches Khalon, Mordecai and Jae who stand firm like a wall of stones. I can see that Khalon is seriously considering taking his head right now.

"Let him pass," I instruct.

Khalon smiles haughtily, he enjoys watching Merik squirm. He moves slightly to the side to allow Merik to pass, but Merik still has to wriggle between Khalon and Jae to get through. Merik takes to the sky once out of the room, and is gone.

I relax a little once he is out of sight. I walk down and pick up the sword. It is heavy, but strangely it seems lighter than I remember.

"You let him go?" Khalon's observation is more of a question.

I nod.

"Why?" he asks.

"Because I want it to end, I want it all to end, and I want it all to end in one day," I say and I put the dagger back in my belt.

I turn to all of the members of the village. Starting with Vivek and Falon they all swarm in to welcome me home. After the initial pleasantries, I sit on the steps and unload my entire story. I tell them every twist and turn, every betrayal, and every awful detail. I see horror in every face looking back at me. I know they have had their realities turned upside down a few times in the last few days. This time I know the pain and threat is much closer.

Finally I stand up and stretch my wings. My legs ache from sitting so long. The morning sun has faded into the dim evening light. I had not realized how long we had been here. I suggest everyone go home and rest. It has been a long day for everyone.

The evening breeze feels good as we step outside. Ainia puts her hand on my shoulder. "What are you going to do now Sig?" she asks.

"Now I am going to go put my house back together," I say, already tired just thinking about it.

"You should just stay with me," she offers.

I appreciate her offer, but I need to go home, "Thanks, but I'll be okay."

"Then we are going to help you put it back together," she says.

"You don't have to."

"Yes we do," Malyn cuts me off.

"I'm going to get some supplies, I'll meet you there," Ainia says as she takes off before I can argue.

"Let's go," Khalon nudges my shoulder and smiles at me.

I shake my head at the stubbornness of all my friends, but I wouldn't change a thing.

I look at Mordecai who has been silent since we got here. "You," I point to him, "you're coming too."

He smiles, it is the first time I have seen him smile, and he nods.

Standing in the main room of my house I'm not sure where to start. Jae hands me a broom as though he is reading my mind.

"This is as good a place as any. Let's get started," he says. I take it and sigh.

Malyn and I start sweeping the floors and picking up broken glass. Jae, Khalon, and Mordecai put the furniture back together and start fixing the floors. By the time Ainia arrives, we have made good progress on the main floor. She comes in carrying two large bags. Mordecai seems nervous when she enters the room. Men often do react to Ainia when they see her, because she is so beautiful, but Mordecai has never seen anyone like Ainia before. She is beautiful, fragile, and sweet. She is the exact opposite of everything the Skar tribe represents. I know that he makes her nervous too, but for a different reason. I think he frightens her.

She empties the contents on to the recently reassembled kitchen table. She brought bread, smoked fish and some vegetables, water and even a bottle of wine. I'm not much of a drinker but tonight I feel like I could use a cup of wine, or two. In the other bag, she pulls out some clothes, soap, and a hair brush. I smile, she thinks of everything.

We spend the night piecing my life back together. Not only by mending the physical objects but by rediscovering our friendships. We share stories from when we were kids, laughing at all the embarrassing moments of adolescence. We spend our night enjoying the past rather than worrying about our future. It is either very late at night or very early morning by the time my house starts to look like a home again. Ainia spent the majority of the time re-stuffing and sewing up my mattress. Malyn and I fixed the shelves in the den and did what we could to salvage all of the plants and medicines. Jae spent a lot of time putting my father's room back together. I have barely gone in there since the day I found him.

I go back downstairs and find Khalon and Mordecai putting the final touches on the living room and kitchen.

"Looks great," I say with awe, "I can't believe this is the same house that I walked into."

Ainia comes down the stairs. She is rubbing her fingers and stretching out her hands. "Your mattress is officially sewn up," she says with pride. It was a lot to sew in one night. "You can go to bed whenever you want," she offers.

Bed. It feels like a long time since I have slept in my bed. The thought is very appealing, but my stomach leads me in another direction.

"You guys hungry?"

"I know I am," Jae says coming down the stairs with Malyn.

"I think we pretty much went through everything that I brought," Ainia says with disappointment.

"Hmm," I scratch my head and walk into the kitchen. I open one of the cupboards and see the bags of pine cones that I put there days ago. Amazingly they haven't been touched. I turn around to my friends and present them with this treat. I shake the cones to release the seeds, and we take handfuls of buttery little morsels. We eat and talk until the sun comes up.

Chapter 32

Weariness shows up on all of us by the time dawn comes. Jae, Ainia and Malyn make their way home and Khalon drags himself upstairs as well. I have never seen him so tired. Mordecai and I are left in the kitchen together. He looks uncomfortable and out of place.

"Come with me," I finally say to him.

I stand up from the table and head upstairs. He follows. Down the hallway past my room and the den we get to the door of my father's bedroom. I lift the latch and open the door. I usually keep this door closed. The air smells of spices. It still smells like my father.

"This is your room now," I say to him.

"Oh no, this is your father's room. I can sleep somewhere else," he protests and takes a step back.

I grab his hand before he can go any further, "My father is gone." For the first time I am able to say that without a lump in my throat, "I have to move on. I want this to be your room for as long as you want it." I squeeze his hand.

He looks down at my hand on his. He smiles, "I see why he cares for you so much." He nods toward Khalon's room.

I look at him quizzically.

"I didn't understand at first, when he told me about you. Then when you were taken," he shakes his head as he thinks about it, "I practically had to tie him up so he didn't storm in there to break you out himself. I have never seen him go through that kind of anguish. We were not raised to care about each other." He is uncomfortable just saying the words.

"But, you and Khalon care about each other, I have seen it."

"That's different. We are soldiers, it's a brotherhood," he says. "You understand?" he asks, but I do not fully understand. He takes a deep breath and searches for the right words, "Soldiers have a bond unlike any other relationship. I know he would risk his life for me, because I would risk my life for him."

"But that's the same thing as our relationship," I argue.

"No, it's different," he shakes his head, "he would risk his life for you, but he would never expect you to risk yours for him," he takes a beat to let that sink in. "He will protect you no matter what."

My head is spinning a little bit. I would like to blame it on fatigue, but the world has been turned over several times in the last few weeks. Trying to decide how I feel about this right now feels impossible. I have too much to sort through as it is.

I look into his copper eyes, and smile a tired smile. "You should get some sleep. Make yourself comfortable, this is your home now," I tell him. I turn and go to my room.

I feel calm in the sanctuary of my room. The familiarity wraps around me like a warm cocoon. My mattress is not as firm as it used to be, but it is the most comfortable thing I have slept on in a long time. The warm daytime breeze drifts in and I finally quiet my mind and let sleep enter.

* * * * * *

I open my eyes and the sun is coming up. I am disoriented. How long have I been asleep? Did I sleep at all? I shiver in my thin nightgown. My wings do not offer much warmth so I wrap a blanket around my shoulders. I sit up and take a look at my injured hand. It is completely healed, so is the cut on my lip. I did heal fast.

I hear voices in my house. It is strange having a full house again. I tip-toe down the stairs still wrapped in my bedding with my hair a mess. Khalon and Mordecai are in the kitchen stocking the cupboards with provisions and setting out food for breakfast. They stop when I enter the room.

"Well, look who's up." Khalon laughs at my disheveled appearance, "You are starting to look more like yourself."

"Oh, be quiet," I roll my eyes and shuffle over to the table where the water pitcher is.

I pour myself a cup. It is so cool and clean. It washes the dryness away.

They are both watching me with smirks on their faces. "So, what day is it?" I ask a little embarrassed.

"It is only the second day," Mordecai says.

I sigh with a little relief that I have only slept one full day away.

"It looks like you have been busy," I nod to their morning spoils.

"We did some fishing early this morning. It is grilling on a fire outside. We found some wild mushrooms and potatoes also," Mordecai explains.

"Yeah, I think we are getting the hang of this whole gathering thing that you have here," Khalon says with a sense of accomplishment, since he has always been more of a hunter, than a gatherer.

"That's good," I validate their efforts. I peek into the bags with the potatoes and mushrooms the salty smell of the earth still fresh on them, "This all looks really good." I go and sit at the table. Khalon puts a piece of bread in front of me, which I eagerly accept. "I could get used to having you guys around," I say with a full mouth.

Khalon chuckles at me. "Not only that, but people have been bringing gifts and food for the last day," he says.

I look around and notice several vases full of fresh flowers, jars of jam and honey, plates of cookies and sweet breads.

I shake my head in disbelief, "I don't understand. I am marching them into war and they are bringing me gifts?"

"War is coming for them with or without you, and they know that now. Merik is responsible for that, not you," Khalon's voice is stern.

"They are bringing you supplies, because they believe you can get them out of this alive," Mordecai chimes in with a more patient tone.

I swallow hard. My body feels heavy. Tremendous weight rests on my shoulders. I knew what I was getting into, and I knew that my friends were going to face this danger with me, but I failed to think about the other lives in danger. The elderly and the children, people like Beda who have never held a sword in their lives. What about them? The color drains from my face.

Khalon sees my reaction and he grabs my hand. He opens it to look at my palm. The cut has healed but I still have a dark pink scar. He kisses my scarred palm and smiles at me, and I cannot help but to smile back.

He straightens up. He does not intend to let me to wallow for too long, "Okay, get dressed we have a lot to do in only a few days."

"Yes, sir," I say mockingly. He squints his eyes and shakes his head at me. "What are we doing today?" I ask more seriously this time.

"We need to put together a strategy plan and get everyone organized."

"Okay, give me five minutes," I run upstairs.

I go through the clothes that Ainia brought me. Most of what she brought is frillier than what I would wear, but I finally come across a pair of olive green shorts and a light gray shirt. I quickly tie my hair back into a loose braid, splash some water on my face and run back downstairs.

We go back to the council building. Many villagers are already there. The recent developments have made everyone seek out answers. The council members look weary. They all perk up when we come into the room. Akin and Vivek smile broadly as we approach. Even Osiris looks pleased to see us. Falon stands up to greet us. His wings hang around his shoulders like a feathered cloak.

"You look rested," he says.

"Yes, but I suspect it will be the last bit of rest I get until this is over."

He nods in agreement.

"We've come to outline our strategy," Khalon begins. "The Skars are very well prepared for war it is all that they do. We need to do what we can to get some advantage."

"How do you suggest that we do that?" Osiris asks.

"First you need to understand who your enemy is," Khalon continues. Falon sits down as Khalon speaks, "They are not fairies like you. Most of them are natural predators, snakes, spiders and worse. Mantus is a scorpion. He is deadly even without a weapon." Khalon moves around the room, pacing back and forth in front of the crowd so everyone hears what we are up against.

"Only about half can fly, but they make up for that on the ground. As strong as they are, they all have weaknesses. It is going to be our job to find those weaknesses. The commanders of his army are Cronus and Sarpe. Cronus is a Stag Beetle. He has massive horns that can toss you as easily as his arms. He is very strong, but he cannot fly for very long and he will tire easily. Sarpe is a rattlesnake. Along with her speed and agility she has a venomous bite, but she is arrogant and she always underestimates her opponent."

I look over the faces of the council and the crowd as Khalon gives the overview of the enemy. They look gray. Khalon has given many rousing battles speeches, but addressing frightened villagers is not his strong point. These people are thinking about their homes and their families being destroyed. They have real concerns that we have to address.

"We are not going to force anyone onto the battlefield," I start diplomatically, "but we do need every able person to do their part, or else the battlefield will come to Northwood."

A flutter of side conversations amongst the villagers begins to arise.

"We will keep the children and elderly here and safe," I talk over them. "We will need volunteers to look after them and others to be ready to help the wounded. In five days, we go to war."

The room is quiet for a long pause. A sick, nervous feeling creeps into my stomach. Without the support of the entire village, we are doomed.

"Well, brother," Falon stands up and looks at Vivek, "what do you say we shake the dust off our wings and end this fight."

A smile emerges on my face. Falon's support means a lot.

Vivek stands up next to his brother, and smiles with pride, "I've been looking for a reason to put an edge back on my sword."

Akin stands and gives me a wink. Then Osiris stands and though he is the least enthusiastic he gives me a small nod. It seems funny to me that Osiris has been the most resistant, but his son, Vidar, is one of the most eager.

"Okay," Khalon starts again, "we need to setup our battle plan."

As he is talking, Jae shows up with Vidar and Soren. Word has circulated about this meeting and soon enough just about everyone is here.

Khalon runs outside for a moment and returns with his hands full of stones. He moves everyone back from the center of the room creating a large void in the middle. Then he rips the large tapestry which is a map of the land off the wall and lays it on the ground so everyone is circling it.

"So this is where we are meeting?" he asks pointing his knife to the spot on the map where the river turns to the west splitting the land north and south.

"Yes," I say definitely.

"It is quite a distance away from the village which is good," Mordecai says, "but we will have to travel a day early and camp just outside of the battlefield."

Khalon nods in agreement. "So we will camp here," he points to a small area in the woods just around the border of the clearing.

I take a moment to consider that we have even less time than I thought.

He kneels on one knee over the map. He sets the stones down that he gathered from outside. "This is you," he shows me an orange-pink stone with metallic flakes. "I want you front and center." I am a little surprised that he wants me that close to danger, "You are the primary reason that Mantus has come this far so soon. His desire to conquer has been enhanced by his fury from your rejection. I want him to see you first. His anger will make him sloppy." He picks up a smooth gray stone next, "Jae, this is you. You are one of the fastest and strongest." Both Jae and I are impressed by his compliment. He does not hand them out often, "I want you on her left side," he sets the gray stone next to mine on the map and then he sets a black stone with chipped edges on the other side, "and I'll be on her right side."

He puts Vidar and Ravi in charge of their flanks on each side, and he thoughtfully places everyone where they would be most effective.

"Ainia and Malyn, along with a few others will be in the trees with bows. They will most likely cross the river before we arrive, but having the water to their backs is an advantage for us."

"Why would he allow us to have the advantage?" Jae asks.

"He won't see the danger in it until it's too late." Mordecai takes the opportunity to chime in. "The idea that we have enough force to push back will never occur to him. He thinks that by crossing the river he is already taking possession of the land and that his troops will push harder to go forward. Also, Mantus, and many others cannot swim they rely on the ones with wings to carry them across. They will want to cross while they still have a complete army."

Khalon nods in agreement and then continues, "But, we will push back and force many of them into the water. We will trap them between our steel and the current of the river. Mantus will retreat to the back of his army once the fighting begins because he is a coward. I don't want anyone to go after him. Mordecai and I will handle him. We know his weak spots, for anyone else he is extremely dangerous."

Though I would love the opportunity to slice Mantus myself, I heed Khalon's warning.

He picks up another handful of stones, "Cronus and Sarpe will be in front," he places the stones parallel to us on the map. "The spiders will be on the sides."

"Spiders?" Ainia asks.

She and Malyn came in so quietly I didn't even know they were here. Her blue eyes are frozen in fear. I know how she feels.

"Yes," Khalon explains. "They move very fast, they have very strong, sticky, webbing that they will use to slow you down and bind you."

Ainia's eyes were wide before he began to elaborate. Now her jaw has dropped, and her skin is positively crawling.

"Oh, and some of them are venomous," Mordecai inserts. The room is silent.

I know what they are thinking. This feels impossible, but there is no other option. We cannot move our village in such a short time. Even if we could move, they will come for us eventually. We have to find a way.

As the meeting ends, I grab Malyn, "I have a very important job for you."

Chapter 33

The next morning we immediately head out to the field. We do not have much time and I need to get comfortable with a sword. I take my Kamas and my bow. Khalon kept them safe for me while I was gone.

The grass on the field shows the wear that has been put on it. It used to be dense and green. Now the many soft blades have been broken and smashed. The dirt has been pounded down hard by many feet. The heat from our bodies and many fires has left the ground warm. This has been a place of rediscovery.

In addition to our usual group, Falon, Vivek, Akin, and Osiris have all arrived with swords in tow. Several others have come as well. Soon the field fills with many others. Strong young boys and girls over the age of sixteen, experienced older men and women, before I know it I am looking at an army. Ragnar and his family arrive with arms full of weapons that they have been forging for the last few weeks. They open the bundles to reveal swords of high polished steel with elegant hilts, and knives so sharp they could split the toughest hide as easily as a single blade of grass. They glimmer in the sunlight. They are beautiful.

Ravi pulls one blade out of a separate cloth. It is larger than the others and the metal is almost black. The blade curves and gets wider toward the end before it sharply comes to a deadly point. He holds it carefully like a sacred object. Ravi and the rest of his family walk toward Khalon as he extends it toward him.

"I used a rare alloy along with the steel," Ravi says presenting the sword to Khalon, "it is practically indestructible."

The gesture that Ravi and his family are making is completely unexpected. At first, it seems Khalon does not know what to do. I suspect the offering of a gift is unusual for him. He reaches out for the extended sword. His massive hands touch the smooth end of the blade with care. He finally wraps his hand around the hilt. None of us could yield a sword that big, but it fits him perfectly. His eyes dazzle as he stares at the blade.

"It is magnificent," he says finally. He nods to Ravi and puts his hand on Ravi's shoulder the same way he does with Mordecai. Ravi smiles and returns the gesture by putting his hand on Khalon's shoulder as well.

Khalon takes his old sword out of his belt and walks over to Jae, "Looks like you are in need of a new sword."

I noticed that Jae had given his sword back to his father now that Falon has joined the fight. Khalon must have noticed too. Jae is stunned by his generosity, and so am I.

"This is Shadow Stealer," Khalon says handing the sword over to Jae.

"Your sword has a name?" Jae asks.

"All great swords have a name, and this is a great sword."

"Shadow Stealer." Jae says the name as he looks over the shining steel.

Jae finally takes the sword in his hand. He swallows hard. I've known Jae my whole life but anyone can see he is truly moved. "Thank you," he says at last, with gratitude.

"Don't mention it," Khalon turns and starts to walk away. "It was too small for me anyway," he turns his head to reveal a sly smile.

I shake my head at him. He always has to have one last dig, but this time Jae laughs as well.

"Ravi, put a new edge on that sword by the end of the week," Khalon points to Shadow Stealer, "I want it sharp enough to split a hair."

Even though Khalon is being very indifferent about it, I know how much it means that he has given up his sword to Jae.

I spend the rest of the day learning to use my father's sword. Mordecai leads the lesson this time. He is even more elegant with a sword than Khalon. It is hard to take your eyes off of him when he is in motion. His movements are as smooth as silk, but deceptively lethal. He makes it look easy, and it is much harder than it looks. It is not just learning how to parry and riposte, or thrusting and cutting. It is about adversarial perception and timing, learning how to use your opponent's movements against them. Even though I start getting the hang of it by the end of the day I feel much more comfortable with my bow or my Kama.

The evening rushes in. Despite the general fatigue of the majority they light fires and opt to continue training into the night. I, on the other hand, decide sleep is more essential for me right now. Khalon also retires with me. Not because he is tired, I think he refuses to let me out of his sight.

"That is a pretty incredible sword they gave you," I say to him as we head home.

"Yes it is," his hand rests on the end of the hilt.

"What's the name of this one?"

"I don't know yet, we'll have to see how she does in battle," he smiles his sideways smile at me.

I touch the sword on my belt, "I wonder if this sword ever had a name. It has been so long since it has seen a fight I bet if it had a name it was forgotten long ago."

"Well, it's not too late. You could give it a new one," he suggests.

"I'll have to see how she does in battle," I give him a sly smile as I use his words.

******

The next day we head out to the field early. The morning air feels clean and the smell of rain clings to it.

Everyone starts to trickle in around the same time as we do. They all gather around Khalon without him even asking us to. We wait for him to dictate what today's lessons will be. Despite some earlier setbacks everyone in the village has learned to trust him completely with our safety.

He kneels down to get into one of his bags and pulls out several small glass jars. They are filled with a milky substance. One of the vials looks very familiar to me.

"Today is going to be for preparing, not training," he starts talking as he continues going through the supplies in his bag. We all start kneeling down so we are on the same level as him. "This is venom," he holds up the jar for everyone to see, "I have been acquiring this for some time. This one came from a very large Gila Monster." He makes eye contact with me for a second. "We are going to dip every arrow tip, and coat every blade in this."

"Will it kill them?" Remi asks.

"Not a dose that small. It takes a lot of venom to kill someone, but it will help slow them down. It seizes the muscles and it will impair their movements enough to give us an advantage," he passes the jars around so that everyone gets a better look at it.

"Will they be using the same thing?" Soren speaks up.

"Many of them have venomous bites, so they don't think about coating their arrows. This is something that I did on my own because I'm not venomous."

"So you're saying don't let them get their teeth into us," Vidar says.

"Exactly," Khalon replies.

"Can you survive a bite?" Vidar asks.

"Depends how much toxin is administered," Khalon explains. "If they drain their stores into you, then that is basically a death sentence. If they bite you on the neck or on a major artery, the venom will travel to your heart more quickly."

I take a moment to look across the faces of everyone. Once again, they all look pale.

"One thing to keep in mind," Mordecai chimes in, "they only have a limited amount of venom. If you get in a position where you have the opportunity, squeeze the glands here," he points to the sides of his face below his eyes and in front of his ears, "this will involuntarily force the venom out and it will take a full day for them to produce more. They may still bite you, but it won't be deadly."

Mordecai's tip helps everyone breathe a little easier, though I certainly do not want to be close enough to milk one of these creatures, but it is good to know that we can take it away from them.

"I want hundreds of arrows," Khalon resumes, "when you think you've made enough do fifty more. We need to do as much damage from afar as possible. I need some of you to get supplies together for the children and those who are staying behind. We are going to turn the council building into one big fortress. I don't want anyone off by themselves once the fighting starts. We need mattresses and whatever else you can think of to make our people comfortable. As soon as you get time, Ainia is going to be meeting with the majority of you today to fit you with your armor."

Ainia nods in agreement. My face tightens with confusion. This is news to me.

"Okay, questions?" he pauses. No one says anything. "Alright, get busy." Khalon releases us.

As everyone settles in on the task they are going to take on for the day, I grab Khalon before he heads off.

"Since when has Ainia been making armor?" I ask with agitation, though I do not know why this irritates me.

"Since the day I realized she is not meant to be on the battlefield, and that she is a genius when it comes to constructing materials. She is really good at this," he looks at my twisted expression and looks confused. "Why? Does this bother you?" he asks.

"It doesn't bother me," that is a lie. "I think this is the perfect job for her," that is true. I do think this is the best occupation for her.

"Sigrun, are you jealous?" He says quietly as he leans in to me. He is grinning ear to ear.

"No!" That is also a lie. Unfortunately, my pendant has betrayed me again. The rose is blushing. He sees it before I can cover it with my hand.

"You are! You're jealous that I went to see her without you." He loves this.

I take a breath and try to control my emotion. Before I know it, the rose returns back to white. I am surprised and pleased with myself. The rose usually holds the emotional color until that particular emotion has passed. This time I was able to return the rose back to neutral before the feelings had gone. Khalon almost looks disappointed.

"Looks like you are learning how to control that," he says.

"Yeah, I'm working on it."

"Good. With what we are heading into, you don't want people seeing what is in your mind," he stands up a little straighter. "Besides I don't need that thing to tell me what you are thinking, I can read you like a book." He is instantly back to being his smug self.

Almost as though on cue, Ainia flutters up to us, "Hey, Sig, come over when you are finished we have something special for you."

She is very excited considering the circumstances of our near future.

"We?" I pick up on that word.

Ainia and Khalon look at each other like they have a secret. I immediately feel foolish for getting so irritated. They have been meeting up to put something together for me.

It is late afternoon before I look up from my task of making arrows, and my fingers are throbbing. I look at the stack next to me and even though I have made so many it still feels like there is so much to do. I stand up and stretch out my aching limbs. Khalon looks at me and carefully puts the cork back in his venom vial. He looks at the sun to see what time it is. He obviously lost himself in his duties as well.

He stands up, "Okay everyone." He signals for everyone to gather, "In two days' time, we will be heading out of here.

Even though we could spend all day and night killing ourselves preparing, I want you to spend tomorrow with your families and loved ones. I want you to remember everything that you will be fighting for."

A new resolve sweeps across everyone. Khalon has a gift for keeping people motivated by any means necessary.

Ainia's house is quiet. Her parents will be staying behind. They also have delicate wings similar to hers and Ainia's brother is still too young to be left alone. They have already gone to the council building to help set it up.

"Hey," she pops up from around the corner, "you came at a good time. This place was packed a couple hours ago. Okay, wait here I'll be right back."

She disappears around the corner again.

I look at Khalon who cannot help but grin. "Should I be worried?" I joke with him.

"I think you are going to like this," he says back.

Ainia comes back into the room with a large wood box. She is so petite she struggles to carry it. Khalon helps her with it the rest of the way. He sets it down in front of me and steps back so I can open it. I look at them and they are both clearly eager for me to open it. The box alone is so lovely and so grand I cannot imagine what its contents could be. I open it completely unsure of what I am going to find inside.

Black and shining objects glimmer in the afternoon light. I pick it up and see it is a beautiful breast plate. The material is a hard black scaly material that has been polished to a mirror like shine. It comes up high on the neck and falls to the natural waist. There are straps and buckles on all four corners, which is how it is secured, but I am clueless when it comes to dressing in armor.

I am speechless at first. It is beautiful. After a moment of looking at it, something stands out to me.

"This looks sort of familiar," I say to Khalon.

He nods with a smile. "It is from the Gila," he says.

"You're joking," I am amazed at how beautiful it is. The Gila was dull and dusty looking when I saw it. It was nothing like this. I cannot believe this is the same hide.

"I went back for the skin. As you know its hide is extremely tough, but incredibly light. I thought it would be ironic that the thing that almost killed you would now protect you," he smiles wryly.

Ainia comes over and holds it up to me, "So the straps come over the shoulders and then cross between your wings and then attach here at the bottom."

I look in the box and see something else. "Oh, and I made you matching leg and arm guards," she explains as I pull out each piece, "and this is what is really special." Her eyes light up as she pulls out some kind of harness that has a series of loops down the back. "This was Khalon's idea," she looks at him with a smile.

He takes his cue and comes in to explain, "This goes on your back and through your arms and wings." He straps and buckles me in it carefully. Once it is on, he explains what the loops on the back are for, "These hold your Kama," he puts my Kamas in the harness between my wings so that they make an X and follow the curve of my wings without cutting me, "and then your sword goes in the middle." He takes the sword from my belt and slides it down between the Kama, along the line of my spine, so that the hilt lines up with my neck perfectly.

I rotate my wings and arms fully. I can feel that the weapons are there, but they do not interfere with motion or flight.

"How does it feel?" Khalon asks with some concern that I might not like it.

I run my fingers on the smooth scales, "It's perfect."

Chapter 34

I insist that Ainia stay at my house since her family is still at the council building. At first, she has reservations about staying in my house. She has obviously become comfortable with Khalon, so I am led to assume she is still very nervous around Mordecai. Eventually, despite her nerves, she concedes that it is simply is not safe for her to be alone at night.

Both Khalon and Mordecai offer up their beds, but I know Ainia would be the most comfortable in my room with me. We had many sleep overs when we were little girls. This might be fun, like old times.

We sit on my bed together, cross-legged, in our nightdresses talking in the candlelight. We haven't really had any kind of light conversation since before the summer.

"He really likes you," she says out of nowhere.

I swallow hard and stop breathing. I don't know who she is referring to and if she is talking about Jae, this might lead to a conversation that I am not prepared to have. I focus really hard to keep my pendant from changing. Amazingly it works and the bloom stays the same.

"What? Who?" Acting stupid seems to be my best plan.

"What do you mean, who?" She laughs and playfully pushes my shoulder, "Khalon. He is crazy about you."

I breathe finally, feeling relieved, "Oh, I don't..." I stammer out. I am still uncomfortable talking about any of this.

"No, he totally is," she interrupts me. "I know I wasn't really," she searches for the right word, "receptive, to him when he first came here, but when you went missing I don't think I have ever seen such grief and worry from anyone, except for maybe Jae." She smiles at first and then her eyes go off into the distance for a moment like she is searching in her memory for something.

A nervous knot twists in my stomach.

"Khalon has been a mystery since I met him," I redirect the topic away from Jae.

"Yeah, mysterious, that would be the perfect word," she abandons whatever thought she was having. "Tall and dark, and those pointy canines," she touches her own tooth while thinking about it. "They're kind of sexy, right?" She looks at me with a big smile. I know she is trying to pry some kind of salacious gossip from me.

I shake my head at her, but I cannot help but smile back. She looks at my pendant, which must have blushed, because she points at it and her mouth drops open.

I cover it with my hand. I have to give her something. "Well, he did kiss me once," I mutter quietly.

"I knew it!" She pounces on me, very pleased with herself and her ability to needle information out of me.

"It wasn't a big deal," I manage to get out through my laughter. "It was a reflex he had when I came back."

"Sure it was," she says sarcastically.

My body temperature is starting to rise. I have to change the subject fast, "So why does Mordecai unnerve you so much," I divert drastically.

She sits up and gets serious again, "I don't know. He just gets under my skin and he is just, so intense." She shakes her head as she thinks about it. I listen to her, and even though I want to defend Mordecai, I keep quiet. "I know he helped you escape, and I am grateful for that, but it might take some time to get used to him being here. It was the same with Khalon too, but we all came around, eventually."

I nod at her revelation.

We both sit there in a comfortable silence for a moment. I think sleepiness grabs a hold of both of us.

I hug her, "I'm glad you're here," she hugs me back. "Let's get some sleep."

"Okay, good night," she says as I blow out the candles.

******

The morning sun wakes me. Ainia has already gotten up. I find her downstairs drinking some tea. Even first thing in the morning she looks flawless and every hair is in place.

"Tea?" She offers.

"Please."

She pours me a cup and sits back down. "What are you going to do today?" she asks.

I hadn't really thought about it until now, "I'm not sure."

I have no family to spend time with, and I do not want to be with anyone else's family today. Khalon and Mordecai are still sleeping and I think it would be best for them to sleep as much as possible.

"I think I would like to spend as much time in our woods as possible. Maybe lie in in a meadow, try to find some peace," I say finally, but I shrug my shoulders at the impossibility of the idea.

"That sounds nice," she says sweetly.

"What about you?"

"I am going to help my parents out and spend some time with my brother."

"That's a good idea," I take a sip of my tea. "Well, I'm going to get myself together. I'll see you back here tonight, right?"

"Yeah, I'll be back in time to help with dinner. I think we should make something special," she suggests.

"Great idea, I'll see you later," I run upstairs and get dressed.

The day is beautiful. The sun is bright but occasional cloud cover keeps it from getting too hot. At first, I do go out into the woods and lie in a meadow, but before long my thoughts turn to another place and I have to go there.

When I arrive at the waterfall, I see Jae's clothes down by the water's edge. It seems he had the same idea, and he beat me here.

He smiles at me when I surface. He is sitting on the edge of the pool. His hair is still a little wet. He has not been here for very long. He looks a little surprised to see me.

"What are you doing here?" he asks, but by his smile I know he is glad I'm here.

"I thought of the place I wanted to be more than anywhere and this is what I came up with," I say while hoisting myself up onto the rock ledge next to him. I squeeze the water out of my hair.

"I'm glad you came here," he moves my hair off of my shoulder.

"Why did you come here?" I ask him.

"I had something here that I wanted to come and get before tomorrow."

This answer surprises me. It seems we both use this place for our secrets.

"I was going to give this to you later, but since you are here now," he says.

He opens up my hand with one of his and then drops something on my palm with the other. It is an amethyst. One of the amethysts from this cavern I suspect.

"I chose this one because it matches your eyes." He smiles at me. I pick it up with my other hand and notice it is on a chain. "I thought it would look nice with the necklace that your father gave you, like you could wear them together," I can tell he is nervous. "Do you like it?"

I look at the stunning violet crystal. It is flawless, and when I turn it in the light, flashes of blue and red catch my eye.

"I love it," I look at him and say again, "I love it."

He looks relieved and elated. He takes it out of my hand and places the chain around my neck. It falls just below the other pendant on my chest.

"Thank you," I lean over and kiss his cheek. He leans into it hoping for more, but he doesn't act on it.

"I guess we both hide things here," I say.

He looks at me a little confused. I get up and grab the book from behind the rock that I had it stashed.

"I want to show you this," I unwrap the book. The red cover is as alluring as ever.

"Whoa, what is it?" He touches the cover carefully.

"It is a book about me, I think, and about this," I point to my rose pendant. I flip through the pages to show him, "The language is so old I can't read it. I took it to Vivek and he could only translate a few words. I hid it out here because I think it is what Merik was looking for." He looks at the pages with the same kind of wonder that Vivek and I had when we first saw it. "You are the only other person that knows it's here. If something happens to me...." He looks at me and tries to speak, but I cut him off, "if something happens, you have to keep it safe. Promise me."

I know the last thing he wants to promise is anything that pertains to my death, but the importance of my request takes precedence.

He takes a breath. "It will always be safe," he says finally.

* * * * * *

I take my time going home. I enjoy all of the sights, smells, and sounds of the forest. It is late afternoon by the time I get back. Ainia arrives at just about the same time. I hide my new pendant under my shirt. I am not sure what Ainia might think if I tell her about Jae giving me such a gift.

Since the men did all of the gathering Ainia and I prepare dinner for us all. The evenings have been getting cooler, so we settle on making a stew, something warm and comforting.

She cuts the potatoes and puts them in the pot to boil, and then starts cleaning and chopping up the mushrooms and some young carrots. I go out to gather the right herbs. By the time I come back, the vegetables are starting to get tender. We add some of the smoked fish and the herbs, and some wild onions that I brought back. Soon the house is filled with the savory aroma of our upcoming feast.

Khalon and Mordecai sit at the table like eager children. They did spend the majority of the day sleeping so they are ravenous with hunger. I break out some bread to appease them for the last bit while the stew thickens up.

We serve them hot and steaming bowls with large plates of fresh bread. We are all very quiet during dinner. We enjoy the food and savor the effortless silence. By the time I serve dessert and tea, we are all laughing and teasing each other. Even Ainia has relaxed with Mordecai.

I bring out some of the baked goods and sweet breads that were given to us, along with jars of jam and honey. I want this to be the most indulgent meal of their lives.

Eventually, under Khalon's advisement, we all retire to bed. We will be leaving early tomorrow morning. The jovial mood that we felt during dinner begins to shift as we get ready for bed. Both Ainia and I change into our bedclothes and wash our faces. She sits on the end of the bed brushing her golden hair and I sit at my dressing table and look at my own reflection. I feel anxious. This is the face that my village will be following into battle, but nothing about me looks like a leader. I feel like I need to do something that proves I am fully committed to this plan. I look down at the table. It hold various objects, lip and cheek stain, a hair brush, scented oils, a few ribbons and the knife I took from Sarpe.

I pick up the knife and turn to Ainia, "I need you to help me with something."

Chapter 35

"No!" She refuses.

"Ainia, it's not a big deal."

"Well, if it's not a big deal then you don't need to do it," she replies clearly pleased with herself, like she found the loophole.

I shake my head at her stubbornness. By her smirk, I gather she thinks she has won. Unfortunately, for her she seems to forget how stubborn I am as well. The knife is still in my hand, so before she can protest I grab the majority of my hair and cut it off in one swipe.

She reaches out to stop me, but it is too late. I am already dropping my wavy brown locks on the floor.

"Oh, Sigrun," she looks utterly defeated, "what did you do?"

It is funny to me that this is a real tragedy for her.

"Well, now you have to finish it," I say to her. "You can't send me into battle looking such a mess," I smile and turn the knife handle toward her. She reluctantly takes it.

Hours later I find myself sitting at my dressing table again. I had tried to sleep. I laid there for hours trying to turn my mind off, but it was no use. Surprisingly Ainia is sleeping soundly in my bed.

Sitting still and quiet at my table, I hold the dagger I used to cut my hair. The point of it digs into the wood and I balance it upright with one finger at the end of the handle. I am frozen, staring at the blade while my mind reels. The gray early morning light starts to filter in and even though I know morning is here I cannot bring myself to move. It takes a soft knock at the door from Khalon to force me out of my stasis.

"We'll be out in a minute," I say just loud enough for him to hear me.

Ainia begins to stir. Though she got some sleep, I know she will be tired. As she starts to get out of bed, I look at my reflection in the mirror. The face I recognize, but now without hair I look very different, harder more severe. I think back to the dream I had where my eyes were red and my head was covered in scales. It was a bit of a relief when my hair came off and I saw regular flesh. There is nothing sinister here. I run my hand across the soft stubble that covers my head. The sensation feels good, and makes me smile.

I go downstairs while Ainia gets ready. Khalon and Mordecai are already downstairs getting the last of the things together. Khalon is kneeling on the ground tying up a large bundle of arrows. He hears me come into the room, but he has not looked at me yet.

"I hope you got some sleep last night," he says as he secures a knot in the rope. "You should eat something..." he was going to say more but he looked up and saw my recent transformation.

He is stunned at first, his eyes wide, but then the corners of his mouth twitch upwards into the beginnings of a smile. He stands up and reaches his hand out to touch the top of my head. His fingers lightly trace the contours of my naked scalp.

"She made me do it," Ainia blurts out as she enters the room.

He smiles broadly and laughs a little at her bitterness. I think he knows it was more of a struggle for her than it was for me. His eyes never leave mine, I don't know if it is pride or amazement, but he looks awed.

"I'm glad she did," he leans in, "I like it."

Mordecai clears his throat. I look over Khalon's shoulder and see him standing in the doorway. He points to his head and winks at me. "Looks good," he says with a smile and then takes off. My brow furrows with confusion.

"I am sending Mordecai and Ravi out ahead of us to scout out the area, so if there are any surprises we will be better prepared," he explains Mordecai's rapid departure.

"That seems smart. What can I help with?" I look around to see what else needs to be done, but it looks like he has been up for a while and there is not much left to do.

"I think we are pretty much ready to go. Just get your things together," he says to both me and Ainia, "and make sure to eat something, we are going to have a long trip today."

We both nod in compliance and prepare to leave our home.

The sun is up, but it is still early by the time Jae and the others reach my house. We are walking out of my front door when they land. Khalon is in front of me.

"You all..." Jae stops talking as soon as he sees me. His eyes are as wide as Khalon's were, but he does not share his positive undertone about it. In fact, he looks destroyed about it. "Sig, what-what happened to your hair?" he asks. He looks at me and then Khalon, then back at me. He thinks Khalon is responsible.

"Don't look at me," Khalon puts his hands up in the air, laughing again.

"I take it you don't like it," I ask him, but I don't particularly care what his response is. I did this for me.

"No, it's not that I don't," he stutters a bit, "it's just different."

"We better get going," Khalon interrupts.

Our small group continues to grow in size as we make our way through the village. Every home we pass more people fly up into our swarm. The trip is harder with arms full of weapons and supplies. We cannot travel as fast, and we tire much faster. We only stop for a few minutes at a time. The urgency to get to the clearing and get settled in takes precedence over resting.

By the time we make it to our destination, the sun has traded for the moon and stars. We perch on the trees until Khalon gives us the signal that it is safe on the ground. He makes a bird call and then waits. A few seconds later we hear one back. It is Mordecai. He and Ravi come out of the brush. Khalon lands to meet him.

"They are not far," Mordecai starts, "Maybe ten minutes flying time that way." He points off behind him.

To hear that they are so close makes my chest tighten.

"They have something big with them, but I don't know what. I couldn't get too close, but I could hear that they are definitely getting ready."

"Getting ready? What does that mean?" I ask as I land next to them. Everyone else follows my lead and comes down from the trees.

"Rituals that they perform before battle, things like that," Khalon gives me a blanket answer.

"Are we safe here?" Falon steps into the conversation.

"Yes, they may have scouts out so we will post watches through the night, but they won't come out this far in the night. We would have the advantage in the trees," Khalon explains. He takes his sword out of his belt and plunges it into the ground, claiming this land as ours. "Okay, let's set up camp," he orders.

We build fires and organize our supplies. I take the food that is given to me, but I am not hungry. My stomach feels like a rock in my body.

I am sitting next to Mordecai, which is convenient since I was planning on seeking him out anyway. His black feathers shine in the flickering light of the fire.

"I'm worried about you," I say to him.

His face contorts in confusion, "You are worried about me?" He almost sounds flattered.

"You were on the other side not that long ago. In just a few hours, you will be killing those who you once called brothers."

"Khalon is the only brother I have left."

I pause and look at him. I am not fully convinced. "Why did you leave them?" I finally ask the question that has been in the forefront of my mind since he broke me out of their camp.

He takes a slow breath in, "You've seen their cruelty first hand." He looks at me but I say nothing and let him continue. "I was brought into the tribe like Khalon, I was very young, and I excelled with the sword. I became numb to the killing. I never realized another life was possible until Khalon left, and that gave me courage. Once I found Khalon, I knew I could never go back to that life. I stayed only long enough to help gather information and then get you out of there." He pauses to stoke the fire with a long stick he found on the ground. "Now that I have met you and your people I feel fully alive for the first time in my life. I will not give that up."

I smile. His answer pleases me. I care for him and I am scared for his life. "Since you have defected, are you not afraid that they will seek out your death at any cost?" I cannot hide the concern in my voice.

"Have you ever seen a dead crow?" he asks me rather than answer my question.

The question seems a little odd. I tilt my head and furrow my brow at the question, but I do try to answer it honestly.

"No, come to think of it, I have not," I admit.

Now that I am thinking about it, all things in nature do meet their end, but I cannot think of one time, whether it is from natural causes or unnatural, that I have seen a dead crow.

"That is because I, the crow, am the one who takes them to the underground." he is smiling but his eyes are serious.

I smile back at him just as Khalon comes back from his first watch.

"You ready to take watch?" Khalon asks Mordecai.

Mordecai gets up and starts to walk away.

"Mordecai," I shout out to him, "you are wrong about one thing," he turns back around to look at me, "every person here would call you brother."

He looks to the ground. I catch him smiling before he turns and slips into the night.

"What was that about?" Khalon asks.

I shake my head and blow it off. Khalon doesn't press me further, but he does see the uneaten bread sitting next to me.

He sits down. I am preparing myself to hear a lecture about how I need to eat and keep up my strength. Instead, he picks it up and takes a bite of it like it was left there for him all along.

"I remember I couldn't eat before my first battle either," he says with his mouth full. "As you can see, I have gotten over that," he smiles.

I feel slightly relieved that he is not going to make me eat it, "How long ago was that?"

"Many, many years," his ambiguity suggests he was quite young when he shed blood for the first time.

"How old were you?"

He takes a breath as he remembers, "I was maybe twelve."

"Twelve?" The number shocks me, "So young. Do they all start so young?"

"No, I was bigger and stronger than most of the others my age, but I was still only a boy," bitterness seeps out of his voice.

I sit there quietly with him until he reaches out for my hand and places it on the eye-shaped tattoo on his forearm.

"You asked me about this once," he says.

"You don't have to…"

"I want to," he cuts me off.

The noise from our camp seems to disappear. The impending doom of tomorrow fades beyond reach, and for now, it feels like it is just him and me and the fire.

"Many years ago," he starts, "we were crossing into a territory that Mantus wanted to take for himself. There was already a tribe living there. These fairies were not all that different from your kind. They were not as evolved, I think they were a very simple sort, but I believe they were good."

I barely breathe as he speaks.

"The day that we marched in, they had no warning, it was just another day for them until we were at their doors with our swords," his jaw clenches at the memory. I want to comfort him, but I don't want to interrupt him either so I remain still as he talks. "It was my job to seek out the leader and eliminate any possible threat for Mantus. Threat," he shakes his head at the word, "there was no threat for *us* in this place. These were peaceful creatures. The leader was a man just a bit older than I am now with a wife and a young son. I murdered this man. I did not speak his tribal language but I understood the word he kept screaming. *Why*. I murdered his wife and the child – the young prince – crushing their bloodline before the sun set on that day.

"Later that night, once we had secured our position and the celebrating had begun, Mantus branded me with this mark. This was the village's most sacred symbol. For them it harnessed the idea of being watched or protected by something bigger. For me it was to mean that no protector could save them from me. It was meant to be a marking of pride. Now, I look at it and the other marks and have only shame and regret. I wish I could take back all the awful things that I have done, but I can't, and these markings serve as my penance.

"I will never be able to make things right for those I have wronged, but tomorrow I will end the cruelty of Mantus."

My hand still rests on his arm and his fingers intertwine with mine.

I take the bread out of his other hand. "I truly believe this will be the last battle you will ever be in," I say as I take a small bite.

He smiles at me. Whether he is smiling simply because he is pleased I am eating, or if it is the thought of closing this dark chapter in his life, is unclear.

"I have set up a tent for you," he says after I have finished my dinner.

"You have?" I was expecting to sleep on the open ground or up in the trees tonight.

"I know you will have a hard time sleeping, but it is important that you get some rest," he stands and pulls me to my feet.

We walk around the corner and he shows me the tent that he has set up for me.

"This is just for me?" I feel a little selfish sleeping in the tent by myself, not everyone has a shelter for the night.

"It is just for you. You are safe. Get some rest, and I'll have Ainia dress you for battle in the morning."

This treatment seems strange, but before I can ask him anymore questions he nudges me into to my tent.

I lie down on the blanket he laid out for me. I know Khalon is right about me not being able to sleep, but I close my eyes anyway. I try hard to think about the things that are important, the reasons that we are here. I think about preserving our way of life and saving the lives of our innocent children. Every time I think of something that makes me feel righteous, images of Merik's hateful eyes spring up into my mind and then I am filled with vengeance. My tent feels hot, stifling in fact, but I find comfort in the heat and, strangely, I drift off to sleep.

Chapter 36

The morning light has not come up yet when Ainia comes into my tent.

"It's time," she says quietly.

I sit up as she comes in with a couple of bags. She says nothing else and neither do I. I put on a simple dark gray undershirt and long pants. She pulls out my armor one piece at a time. She handles it carefully like it is made of gold. She straps me into my breast plate first. Then she laces up each leg and arm guard one at a time. We don't usually wear shoes in the summer time, but I put on boots also. Finally, she helps me into the weapon harness. The armor feels hard and ridged but it fits me so well I can easily move in it.

We put each weapon in its place one at a time. My Kamas cross between my wings and my father's sword fits down the line of my back. My old dagger hangs from my belt and Sarpe's dagger hangs from another harness around my thigh. I pick up my bow and look at her once I am fully dressed.

"Well, how do I look?" I ask trying to be somewhat jovial.

"Intimidating," she smiles.

We walk outside and discover everyone else is just about dressed themselves. Khalon and Jae are just outside my tent, right where I would expect them to be. Jae is dressed in orange-brown armor and brown pants. His new sword at his hip, he looks almost regal.

"Wow, Sig, can you even move in all that?" Jae asks as he pokes around all of my straps and loops.

I twist my body at my hips, stretch out my arms and wings, and squat down to the ground, "Amazingly, yes, I can."

"She looks great. She looks like a leader," Khalon says.

Khalon is not wearing body armor. His chest is bare. He does have arm guards on his forearms and leg guards on his shins, but that is all.

"You are not wearing armor," I make more of an observation than a question.

"Slows me down," he replies arrogantly.

It makes me nervous that he is so exposed, but if there is one thing Khalon knows how to do, is survive a battle. I smile at him rather than argue, because I know it would do no good.

My smile slowly fades away as reality creeps in. Everyone has gathered around us. They are all dressed and holding their weapons. They are waiting for orders. It is time.

Falon and Vivek make their way to the front of the crowd. Their armor matches Jae's and they have their family crest painted on their chest plates. They are the leaders of our village so I wait for them to give instructions. A minute goes by before I realize they are waiting for me to lead.

I turn to Khalon. "Let's go," I say a little hesitantly.

That simple phrase electrifies everyone unanimously and they all shout out in unison. It startles me at first, but then their fervor penetrates me. We do not have to be quiet anymore.

We fly out to the edge of the clearing. We land just before we lose the cover of the forest. Khalon points to the trees where he wants Ainia and the other delicate winged individuals to position themselves. They take to the trees with bows and bundles of arrows.

He looks at me, "You ready?"

That is an impossible question to answer, but *no* is not an option.

"It is time to end this." As I say the words, my heart beats faster and my eyes open a little wider.

I look at Jae and he gives me a much needed nod of encouragement. It means a lot to know he will be at my side. I turn to march out onto the field. As soon my feet hit the open space, I see the outline of their army all the way on the other side of the field. I walk slow and steady. I look to my left and see Jae. His face looks focused. His eyes dart quickly. I suspect he is trying to get an accurate picture of the enemy, and right now he truly understands how fearsome they really are. He does not look afraid, which surprises me.

It is just how Khalon said it would be. The spiders are on the outside of the formation. His fliers are in the center. Sarpe is in the front, slithering anxiously in one spot back and forth wearing out the ground beneath her. Her tail is still bandaged from where Mordecai stabbed her, and her eyes are fixed on me. I do not see Mantus and Merik, which worries me.

I glance at Khalon on my right, true to form, he is positively snarling. I'm sure images of ripping Mantus apart are dancing through his mind, and his absence on the field likely has him even more agitated.

I walk out ahead of everyone and then I stop. Everyone takes their cue, stops marching, and remains in formation. I spread out my wings so the Skars will recognize me across the field. Maybe Mantus wants to confirm I am here before he shows himself. The sight of me excites the Skars. They begin chanting and grunting in a beastly way. They stomp their feet, and they clang their swords against shields, and knives against knives. The pulsating sound makes the ground tremble.

The Skar crowd begins to part. That is when I realize they were not making the ground tremble, it is something bigger. Mantus, Cronus, and Merik come through the crowd riding on Gilas. Black and orange beasts, like the one that attacked me, sharp needle like teeth dripping with poison. Their giant feet shake the ground. I know now what Mordecai meant when he said they have something big with them.

I look at Khalon, my eyes wide. He looks at me and raises his hands up to a stabbing motion and then a twisting one. He makes me remember how he killed it. Stab it at the base of the skull, then twist the blade. I nod as I remember.

Mantus has a self-righteous grin twisting up the corner of his face. He obviously feels victory is assured. His smirk turns into a rage filled grimace when he sees Khalon and Mordecai standing next to me. I'm sure Merik reported back to him that they were with me, but seeing it himself has ignited his fury.

Merik just looks hateful. His face is screwed in a hard frown, his yellow eyes almost glowing in the rising sun.

Falon and the rest of the council are positioned directly behind me.

"Do we attempt to negotiate?" Falon asks, clearly unaware of the brutality of our opponent.

"Mantus wants our land, and our women and children. We want him to promise to leave this place and never come back. Those are two absolute conflicting goals," Khalon explains with his eyes still focused on the enemy. "There is no point in even trying with him."

"I still think we should," I say, "I know I will feel better sinking my sword into them, knowing we gave them every opportunity to leave." Khalon's mouth twitches into the beginning of a grin at the idea of killing Mantus.

Jae, Falon, and I start to walk toward the enemy line. We leave Khalon behind since he will be too volatile to bring to this meeting. Mantus looks at Cronus and then at Merik. He was not expecting any show of negotiation.

The three dismount the monsters and head out to the middle of the field where we have stopped. Seeing Mantus walk toward me, his legs all quickly moving, sends a chill down my spine. Once he is in front of us, his army quiets.

"I'm giving you one last opportunity to leave this place, Mantus. Go home," I try very hard to keep my voice from shaking.

"That is where you are confused, Sigrun, home is where I am headed. I'm giving you one last opportunity to save yourself, leave this disgrace of an army, and be my Queen," his voice rattles and hums through my armor.

I feel nauseous at the thought of his proposal. Jae also tightens up. I feel his energy shift at the suggestion that I succumb to Mantus' desires.

"I have an additional demand," Mantus continues. "Those two," he points to Khalon and Mordecai, "are to be tortured and executed, and their heads will sit on spikes as a reminder for what happens to traitors." The bitterness of his anger is almost palatable.

The fear and nervousness that I was feeling has now funneled into rage. His arrogance is like a poison, and it is time to rid this world of it.

"I will have to vehemently decline your offer," my voice is still shaking, but now it is with anger.

He snarls. It seems he was hoping the sight of his army, and the prospect of my death, would change my mind.

Both sides take several steps backwards, staring at our opponents, before we turn to walk back to our sides. As soon as he turns, he raises his hand up to the sky and shouts one word, "WAR!"

His army begins chanting again, but louder this time. We return to our side. Khalon and Mordecai are at the front.

"I take it he did not agree to the terms," Khalon tries at some humor. Falon actually chuckles, which surprises me. He is much more relaxed than I expected.

"That would be an understatement," Jae responds.

I am worried about Jae. His resolve is quite low. I can see in his eyes he has already accepted our defeat. He looks at me and takes my hand. He begins what I expect to be a farewell speech, but before he gets a word out a noise in the distance cuts him off. A faint humming rises above the tree line.

"Do you hear that?" He says instead.

"I do," Falon replies.

"What is that?" Mordecai asks. The humming has intensified and is now so loud that it begins to drown out the grunting and chanting of the Skar army.

I look at Jae and then at Khalon. I cannot keep from smiling. "Reinforcements," I say.

"Malyn," Jae says. He finally smiles for the first time today.

Just as he says her name she shoots up from the tree line with a massive swarm of worker and drone bees. There must be hundreds of them.

She lands next to us. We take a quick moment to welcome her, and tell her how glad we are that she made it. The lead drone that I met at the hive also lands with her. The rest of the swarm hovers above us.

"Queen Asherah sends her regards," the drone hums to me. "She of course wishes she could be here, but as you know she is difficult to move."

"I understand," I say to him, "I am just so glad that you are here. I want you to be used primarily as a distraction." I explain, "I do not want anyone to use any fatal stings unless you absolutely have to. We did not call you here to commit suicide for us."

He nods to me out of respect. I nod back.

I look back out across the field. Manus' smile has weakened now that our army has grown exponentially in the last minute. He still carries a look of superiority. He still thinks he will be victorious, but now it will not be as easy as he thought. He raises his hand up once again, and gives a signal to his troops. They change their chant to a single word that they shout out over and over again. I do not understand it. It is a language that I do not know. Out from the sides of the flanks an army of shiny red ants march out onto the field.

"Looks like Mantus brought his own reinforcements," Khalon says.

"Fire Ants," Mordecai announces.

"Don't worry, they are easily dealt with," Khalon encourages the rest of us. He starts talking quickly because they are heading right for us, "They are blind, but their senses of smell and sound are superior. They move very fast, but their bodies are fairly fragile. Do not get into a position where they can overtake you, they will strip the flesh from your bones if you let them. An air defense is best. Do not waste your arrows on them, and if we can misdirect and herd them into the water they will drown easily, and be carried off by the current."

I sling my bow across my body and reach behind me to grab my Kamas. Everyone stands easy holding the line with their swords in hand.

This is it. The ant army approaches fast. There is no time for rousing battle speeches, war is in on us.

The bees spring into action. They swarm in all together, as if they are of one mind. They dive down and scoop up ants two at a time, thinning the colony dramatically, and fly way above the Skars reach and drop the flailing ants into the river. Then they circle back around as the next group picks off more and more. Occasionally the spiders shoot webbing and snag down one of the bees, but they move so fast, and they dance erratically in their flight pattern that they are not caught often.

The remainders are easy enough for us to handle. I spin my Kamas so fast that they become metal propellers at the end of my arms. The first ant reaches me. Comparatively they are much smaller than us, but they have huge mandibles. I figure they hold their prey with those while they sting over and over again with venom. I do not let fear dictate my actions. My Kama connects with him and I easily slice him into bits. Then the next one comes. I dig my blade into the top of his head and pull down, splitting it open. One after another, I destroy with little effort. Khalon takes out three or four at a time with his massive sword. I hear a couple of screams, a few of ours were bitten, but nothing that they couldn't get away from and nothing that would be considered a serious injury.

Soon I look around and we have slaughtered their first wave, with very few injuries on our side. Once everyone else figures that out, they all shout out a shatteringly loud victory cry.

I do not celebrate yet. I look out across the field. Mantus' eyes are burning. He is furious that his first attack yielded no real damage.

He raises his hand and gives another signal to his troops. He backs up his Gila and begins to retreat to the back of his flank, just as Khalon said he would. Just before he is out of sight Khalon drops his sword picks up a spear, draws it back, takes a few quick steps and releases it with tremendous effort.

My first thought is, they are so far away. Why would he waste a spear? Then I see the spear go further than what seems possible. It soars gracefully through the air until it reaches its destination, which in this case turns out to be the neck of Merik's Gila. The Gila dies instantly, falls over on its side, and throws Merik to the ground. He is not hurt, but the shock of the kill has him clearly rattled. If that spear had just been a little higher, it would be Merik lying lifeless on the earth. Both sides are silent in disbelief. Then after a beat, our side rises up in jubilation.

My eyes are wide, and my breathing is rapid. "Can you do that again?" I ask eagerly.

He chuckles at my excitement, "I would not hold your breath for it."

"That was a one in a million shot," Mordecai says squeezing Khalon's shoulder with pride and exhilaration.

Our excitement has brought on outright rage from the other side. Mantus' army starts running toward us. Khalon has done it. In one throw, he has sparked the emotion necessary to bring them to us, right into range of our arrows.

I shoot up into the air and give the signal for them to start firing. We shoot arrows as they run across the field. They are all very good at blocking our shots, but we do get a few down.

The Gila that Cronus is riding takes fifty arrows before it even slows down. Cronus is swinging an iron spiked Morning Star above his head. It is such a beautiful name for such a barbaric weapon.

They are only feet away front us. I drop my bow and pull out my Kama again. I fly up into the air just as the first wave hits. I am only interested in fighting one person: Merik.

I see him fleeing to the back of the squadron. Just like Mantus, he is a coward. I start to fly after him, but I only make it a few feet before I am snatched out of the air.

Sarpe throws me back to the ground. Her orange eyes are as wild as ever. She still has a scar above her left temple where I hit her. She is clearly furious about it.

"I have been dreaming about the different ways I was going to filet you into tiny pieces," she hisses.

She lunges at me with her sword. I hook her blade with my Kama and force it away. I get back on my feet. She swings her blade and I block with mine. She tries several different combinations and I block them all. We are very well matched. She lunges at me again this time I spin using one wing as a shield. I feel her blade connect and scrape across my scales. Surprisingly it only produces the same discomfort as fingernails scraping down flesh. I can feel it, but the pain is certainly tolerable, and it does no real damage to my wing. As I continue to spin, I extend my other wing to hit her hard on her side. I manage to get her off of me, but not for long. I have to find her weakness and soon. She slowly advances toward me. We circle each other blades up and ready. Her tail starts to rattle. That is my signal. I know she is about to strike. I beat her to it. It happens so fast, but to me everything feels like it is moving in slow motion. I hook her sword with the Kama in my left hand and jump up and kick her in the face with the heel of my boot. Her head goes back and I take that moment to sink my blade into her body. I feel, and hear, the pop of her flesh. I swing around her in a full circle and by the time I get both feet back on the ground I see her torso slide off of her lower body.

Though I have cut her in two she continues to wriggle on the ground. Her arms carrying her, she manages to grab hold of her sword again. Confused and panicked I look up until I see Khalon. He is removing his sword from his own fallen opponent. He sees me and instantly knows what is happening.

"The heart or the head, that is the only way to kill her," he shouts and signs across the field.

I nod and grab her dagger from the strap on my thigh. I kick the sword out of her hand and I kick her in the face again so she is on her back. Standing over her, I slam the dagger into her chest all the way until she stops moving; that seemed the best way to return it to her. I stand up, draw out my sword, and I take her head as well.

I look up at Khalon. His eyebrows are raised. He looks impressed that I took off her head.

"Just in case," I say to him before returning my sword back to my harness.

I look around to see where Merik is. He is still at the far end with Mantus watching from a distance. Khalon and Mordecai continue to battle their way out to them. I start to head that way again, but a scream from behind me draws my attention away.

The spiders have located Ainia, Malyn, and the others in the trees. The Black Widow has lassoed Ainia in her webbing and has pulled her out of the trees. Ainia is screaming and struggling to get away, but she is helpless against the widow who is much stronger and has eight legs to hold her with. Malyn and the others continue to fire arrows, trying to help her, but the spiders move so fast they deflect them easily. I start to run to her, but Mordecai is already there.

He knocks the widow off of her, but the widow is up fast. She hisses at him and shoots out webbing every time he moves. She lunges onto him and webs his hand with his sword to the ground. He holds her the best he can with one arm, but her face inches closer and closer to him. Her fangs drawn, milky white liquid drips from them. She just needs to get a little closer so she can sink her teeth in.

Ainia finds her courage and jumps onto her back. Ainia grabs the widow's head and feels around until her fingers locate the oval glands on the sides of her face. She presses hard. Mordecai moves his head just enough for the milky venom to expel onto the ground and not on his face. This gives him enough time to free his hand and his sword. He slices off all four legs on one side and stabs her in the abdomen. Once he is certain that the widow is dead, he orders Ainia to get back into the trees and keep firing arrows. Then Mordecai turns back to his course across the field, back on his mission reach Mantus.

Jae is in the middle of the field with Vidar and they have their hands full with Cronus and his Gila. Jae is bleeding, but nothing more than some cuts and scratches. Vidar is definitely showing signs of fatigue. I fly to them to help give them an edge. The Gila is injured, it has probably taken over a hundred arrows, but none of them have pierced its hide enough to be fatal. Cronus swings his Morning Star and it connects with Jae's chest. The power of the blow knocks Jae down to the ground. His armor protected him enough that it was not a fatal blow but he is on the ground and incapacitated for the moment.

The Gila recognizes this opportunity. It steps forward. It has Jae's leg pinned to the ground. Jae screams out in pain. I know how heavy a Gila is and right now it is crushing his leg.

Vidar is trying to help him, but every time he gets close Cronus throws the Morning Star. Cronus has dismounted and is now facing Vidar one on one. It takes everything for Vidar not to be injured himself.

Jae rams his sword into the Gila's mouth as it tries to bite him in half. The Gila screams out a high pitched squeal. He is hurt, not enough to stop, but it buys me just enough time to land on its back and plunge my sword into the back of its neck. I feel tough hide break around my blade. The Gila rears up screaming, giving Jae the room to roll away. I grunt as I twist the blade hard. Then I feel a snap as its spine breaks and suddenly the beast stops and falls lifeless to the ground.

Jae and I both look at each other and breathe for a second.

"You okay?" I manage to say.

"Yeah," He says as he assesses the damage of his leg, "I don't think it's broken." He says finally, "you?"

I nod, breathing hard, unable to speak.

I look around. The last time I looked, Cronus was in this area with Vidar. Now Cronus is heading toward Mantus. It seems Khalon and Mordecai have finally made their way to Mantus, and Cronus is on his way to even the odds. Vidar is nowhere in sight, but we do not have the time to look for him now.

Merik is retreating further and further back. His sword is drawn, but he makes no attempts to fight. A fair fight frightens him. Jae and I do not need to speak. We both know what we need to do.

We fly as fast as we can to them. Mantus is brutal in battle. He is so big and strong. His pinchers and tail can be lethal on their own, but he is also masterful with a sword. It would be certain death for any man that faced him alone, but his hands are full with both Khalon and Mordecai fighting him.

Jae and I work hard to keep Cronus away from them. We want to give Khalon and Mordecai the opportunity to take Mantus down. This is not easily done. Cronus is much bigger than us and he does not have many weak spots. He uses his horns just like any other weapon.

Cronus swings the Morning Star at me, I move just out of the way from the strike. He swings it up in the air in a circular motion. He moves forward slowly, the propelling hum pushing Jae and me backwards. Our eyes fixed on where it may land.

He throws it again. Everything slows down like it did the day I shot the fish. My senses are heightened. I move my head just enough for the ball to miss me, but I swing my head back around so the chain wraps around my neck and the ball changes course, pivoting back around toward its master. The unexpected force of it rips the chain from Cronus' hand and the ball swings around and hits him in the chest.

I take pleasure in the moment his eyes grow wide just as he realizes he is about to be struck by his own blow.

Cronus is on the ground. The wind is knocked out of him for a moment.

My attention is brought to Khalon, Mordecai, and Mantus. The fight between them is like a game, or a dance. Khalon and Mordecai take steps forward and backward, they jump up into the air, trying to disorient him. They want him to tire, to get sloppy, so they can deliver that one deadly blow. Mantus knows this game too, but this might be the first time he has been a player in years.

Mantus has Mordecai caught up in one of his pinchers. Khalon takes a hard hit to the face from the other pincher and is knocked to the ground; his sword is thrown just out of reach. Mantus steps up onto Khalon, because of his weight it takes everything Khalon has to keep Mantus' pointed legs from stabbing through his body. Khalon groans, he is struggling, but he tries not to give Mantus the satisfaction of a scream.

"You are a traitor," Mantus hisses. "You do not deserve a soldier's death."

He rises up his tail to strike. Khalon is defenseless. Mordecai wriggles free just enough to kick Mantus hard in the side, knocking him a bit off balance. This gives Khalon enough of a distraction to move his head as the tail stabs into the ground rather than his flesh. Khalon manages to shift the spear-like limb off of him and reach his sword. He swings and severs the bulbous stinger from the rest of Mantus' tail. Mantus screams a beastly roar in agony.

Both Mordecai and Khalon free themselves from his grasp. Seeing his own blood, Mantus knows he is injured, and his confidence starts to wane. He not only starts to back down, he actually begins to flee. So does Merik. Mordecai and Ravi chase Mantus into the forest. Khalon looks at me.

"Go after Merik," he urges me, "we can handle this." He nods to Jae as they advance toward Cronus.

It is the first time I have seen Cronus look scared. I imagine Cronus never thought he would have to fight Khalon. Jae has a fire in his eyes that I have not seen before. I think he is going to enjoy taking Cronus down.

I take Khalon's order with pleasure. I run after Merik. He gets up to the water's edge. I see him begin to release his wings to fly away. Anger surges through me. His cowardice is an insult; for him to take everything from me and not give me a fair fight at the end is the greatest offense.

"Merik!" I shout as loud as I can.

He slows down once he realizes I will never stop chasing him. He turns to face me. He has his sword in his hand, and I have my father's sword in mine.

We have already said everything we needed to say to each other. I know I will never get through to him. He is rotten to the core. He must feel the same way, because he lunges at me fast. I deflect and get ready for the next move.

Our swords clang and grind on each other. I block him then he blocks me. We both know each other so well. I know how he moves, he knows how I move. We have been studying each other our entire lives. I don't know when he became so skilled with a sword, but he is quite good.

I have been fighting all morning and my arms are getting tired. Sweat is dripping off both of us. His breathing is labored I know he is tired too. He comes after me again. I block him. Our swords and hands lock up between our faces. We push on each other hard. The blades tremble as they get closer to my throat, then I push back and they get closer to his. He gives a burst of strength and hits me in the face with the hilt. I spit out a mouthful of blood. I have several cuts from this battle. I have been bleeding all day, but for some reason the blood from this hit is the most bitter. I am flooded with rage. My body feels hot, and I attack.

Blow after blow, I swing my sword at him. He works harder trying to block me than when he is attacking. I push him further back toward the water. I'm screaming out as I swing my sword, he blocks again, but his heel catches the edge of a rock and he falls into the water. He loses his sword as he goes down. I take my sword in both hands and rise it up above him. I stand ready to drive my sword into his chest. His eyes are wide with fear.

Hovering above him, my hands tremble.

"Go ahead, Sigrun," I hear a voice behind me. It is Jae. Both he and Khalon are there.

I stand a little taller, my hands steady a little. The support from them gives me validation. I scream out as I drop the sword down toward Merik's chest. I stop myself just as the point is about to touch his body. Though my body has stopped I keep screaming, because this moment hurts more than any other pain I have felt. I physically cannot force myself to bring the sword down. Merik still looks like that scared little boy. I take pity on him.

I step away and drop the sword to the ground. I turn my back to Merik. I do not feel good for sparing his life. I feel like a failure.

Khalon steps to my side and puts his hand on my shoulder. I can tell he is proud even though I let Merik live, maybe even because I did.

Jae is standing in front of me. I put one hand on Khalon's hand and I reach out my other hand for Jae's. Suddenly I see Jae's face contort and his eyes widen. He starts to shout something. I don't realize what is happening in the moment. Khalon shoves me so hard I fall to the ground. When I turn to see what happened, I see Khalon falling to his knees with my father's sword in his chest. Merik is on his feet with a twisted grin. He has thrown the sword aiming for me but Khalon pushed me out of the way. Merik is disappointed he missed, but taking down Khalon is still a feat for him to be proud of.

I look at Khalon then at Merik. My friend is dying. My hesitation, my failure, has caused this. I hear no sound but the sound of my own heart, which is surprisingly steady. My body feels hot. Tears spring up in my eyes, but they evaporate away before they can roll down my face.

I stand up and start walking toward Merik, like I am being pulled to him. My eyes sear into his. The world slows down around me. Every shred of loyalty or compassion that I felt for Merik is gone. My focus on Merik is so impenetrable that I barely even notice when my shoulders burst into blue flames.

Merik's face changes. The arrogance drains out of him. He is more terrified than I have ever seen him. He does not understand how I am doing this. I do not understand how I am doing this, but I keep walking toward him. By the time I make it to him, my entire upper body is on fire. I can feel the heat, but it does not burn me. It feels like standing close to a fire on a cold winter night. It feels good.

I reach my hand out and grasp his throat. I am stronger than before. He is squirming hard to get free, but my grasp is unbreakable. I watch his expression. His eyes follow the flames as they slowly make their way over my shoulder and down my arm toward my hand that is holding his throat.

"You have taken everything from me," I scream into his face. My voice is different too: deeper, rougher, it almost echoes.

He begs, pleads, and screams, but I hear none of it. All I hear is the soft roar of the flame, my own heartbeat, and the crackle of his burning flesh.

My rage pools in me feeding the flame, like a river of oil. I look into his eyes, mine burning into his. I do not look away, and I do not let go until he is nothing but a pile of ash at my feet.

Once the flames stop, I look at my own hands and I take a deep breath, and remember what has happened. I run to Khalon. Jae is frozen in place his mouth and eyes wide. By the look of Khalon's gaping stare even he has forgotten that he has a sword through his chest.

"How-How did you do that?" Khalon struggles to get out. I put his head on my lap.

"I don't know," I try to shush him and get him to save his strength. "Jae," I shout to him, "Help me."

He runs over to the other side of Khalon.

"You were on fire," Khalon remarks, almost un-phased by his own dire circumstances.

"Shh," I try to quiet him again.

The sword is in deep. I am at a loss I don't know what to do. I have only bandaged small wounds. This is something that needs a real healer, and proper supplies, which we do not have out in this field. Even if we did have supplies the likeliness that he would survive is low.

"It must have missed his heart, or else he would already be dead," Jae assesses.

"Help me get it out."

I hold Khalon down as Jae grabs hold of the hilt and pulls on it hard. Though I can tell Khalon is trying hard to fight through the pain, he cannot help but to scream as the blade is slowly pulled from his chest.

The blade is gone, but now the wound is bleeding so fast. I hold my hand over the wound and press hard. Khalon winces.

"Jae, I need something to put on this, we need to get this bleeding to stop," I look to see if I can use my own shirt, but it has burned up, only the armor remains.

Jae gives me his shirt. I press it on his wound. The shirt is soaked within seconds.

"Sigrun," Jae says quietly, "we can't stop the bleeding."

"No, we have to find a way," I snap.

Khalon's teeth start to chatter. He is getting cold. We are starting to lose him.

"Sigrun, I don't know what to do," Jae says, "If we can't stop the bleeding..." He does not finish that sentence, but I know where it was headed.

I shake my head. I refuse to give up on him.

"S-saving you w-was w-worth dying f-for." Khalon stutters and trembles.

"No, no, no," I resist, "you cannot leave me." I look into Khalon's dark eyes. They are starting to get darker, more lifeless. I look up to the sky. Dark clouds are rolling in. A storm is coming.

"Please help me," I say so quietly only the spirits can hear me. I take a breath and then feel a glint in my chest.

I look back down at Khalon. His eyes are struggling to stay open. My heart aches. I feel overwhelmed with emotion. I kiss him. The last bit of life stirs in him. I feel his hand on my face, and I pull away to look at him. He looks surprised, but happy.

"Why did you do that?" He struggles to speak.

"To distract you," he furrows his brow in confusion. I kiss him again before I continue, "Because this is really going to hurt."

I look at my palm, covered in his blood, and I recall all of my emotions that I have felt today, fear, rage, loneliness, love. I focus hard until my hand ignites. Blue flames flicker on my hand, on only my hand. I press it down hard on his chest. He screams.

Chapter 37

My room is cold. Frost clings to the ground outside despite the early morning sun. Autumn has come and gone, and winter is rushing in.

I look down at the clothes spread out on my bed that Ainia made for the ceremony. They are beautiful and amazingly enough she followed my wishes for them.

Steam from my tea swirls around my face as I recall the debate we had regarding them.

"Sigrun, you should wear a dress," she argued.

"I don't like dresses, and it is going to be cold."

"I'll make you a new fur, but I think it would be more appropriate if you wore a dress," she was so adamant, but I was not going to waiver on this.

I shook my head. "No dresses," I said with absolute conviction, "but I'll take the fur."

When she finally accepted that I would be wearing pants, she swore they would be the nicest pants she ever made, and they are. They are black and made from the softest blend of cotton and silk. The silk made them shimmer a bit in the sunlight. She studded silver beads down the side seams and across the waist. She also made me a matching black Y-back shirt with a high neck, arm warmers, and a new gray rabbit fur shoulder shrug with a high collar and a long cape. However, I was most impressed with the boots.

I remember being shocked when she brought them to me. The silver scales shining the same way the Gila armor did, but this hide came from Sarpe. A way for me to "walk all over her forever," she said as I stared at them with disbelief.

Beautiful clothes, beautiful sentiment, anyone would be thrilled for this day, but I find myself almost dreading it. Even though it has been months, the memories are still fresh with me. Though it was a victory we did lose several of our own, grief had clung to the village, and Mantus is still alive.

Mordecai and Ravi chased him into the forest, but he ultimately slipped through all of our fingers. His stinger is severed, but he is still dangerous.

I finally quit procrastinating and get dressed. My hair has grown out some, but it is still very short, so I am very thankful that Ainia made my fur collar high enough to cover my neck. I still wear both necklaces every day. They both serve as reminders about love and what is good in this world.

I look at my reflection in the mirror. My face has already lost its summer tan. My violet eyes look bright.

I found out later, after the battle, from Jae that while I was on fire my eyes turned red like the dream I had the night my father died. My eyes were red, my head was bald. Though there were still some differences, some things make more sense now, some things make less. I am not fully monstrous like I was in the dream, but I understand why many people stayed away from me for a while.

Several people were afraid I would burn them if I got upset over anything. It was silly really. I have been working very hard to learn and understand this new gift, and my pendant is now mostly just a beautiful charm. It rarely changes on its own anymore. I have learned to control it and my emotions.

I am still eager to learn more about it and myself. After the freshness of the battle had worn off, I went back to the cavern to retrieve the book. I gave it to Vivek. He felt it was safe enough for him to have it, and he has been working on translating it ever since.

I decide to leave a little early this morning to go see Vivek. He has been one of the few that has not treated me differently since that day on the battlefield.

He is surprised to see me standing at his door.

"Sigrun, shouldn't you be getting ready. It is a big day for you," his brow furrowed.

"I know. I just felt like sitting with you for a bit before the ceremony," I explain, "if you have time."

"Of course," he invites me in.

We sit in the front room and Yoana comes into the room with a cup of tea for me. She is as quiet as ever, but in the last few months I have learned her unspoken language.

"Actually," Vivek starts, "I am glad you stopped by." He walks over to his desk and picks up the red book. "I finished translating the section with the picture that looks like your pendant."

He opens the book to that page and sets it on my lap.

"So this phrase above the picture," he points to the words, Օբյեկտ կրակի. "This reads An Object of Fire."

"The pendant is an object of fire?" I ask, thinking that this why I have my strange new power.

"No, I don't think so," he shakes his head, "I think the object is you."

I don't say anything, so he points to the opposite page that has the description.

Երբ մաշված մի երեխայի հրդեհի օբյեկտ շեշտում է հուզական վիճակը։ Այն լույսերը կրակը շրջանակներում. Այն տալիս է ուժ է արժանի. Այն ուժեղացնում ներուժ է հաղթահարել չարը.

Երբ մաշված մի երեխայի, որ չար չարաշահման իր իշխանության կարող է ոչնչացնել բոլոր լավ է այս աշխարհում.

"It says, *When worn by a child of fire, the object accentuates the emotional state. It lights the fire within. It gives strength to the worthy. It intensifies the potential to overcome evil.*

When worn by a child of evil, the misuse of its power could destroy all the good in this world."

He looks at me. I am picking apart the lines piece by piece. So many questions rise.

"A child of fire?" I ask, but I know that it means me.

"I think this was the prophecy about you," he cuts to the point.

"Well, I can see why Falon didn't like me," I try to make a joke. "*The misuse of its power could destroy all the good in this world*," I repeat the last line grimly. I shake my head, which is suddenly aching.

Vivek closes the book and takes it back to his desk. "Lucky for us you are only good and nothing evil," he says with a warm smile, "so good in fact I had always hoped that maybe you and my nephew would." He stops talking and raises his eyebrows.

I blush at the suggestion, and giggle at his candor. I shake my head. "I love Jae, but it's complicated," I say as I stand up.

"It's complicated?" he asks, "Or, someone has complicated it?"

My embarrassment is surging. I get to the door and turn back to him, "Let's just say I seem to also have an affinity for the misunderstood." I smile at his confused look and I head out through the door.

The cold air bites at my lungs. I decide to take my time and walk to the council building rather than fly. The frost crunches beneath my new boots. The looming cold makes everything feel so still. Most fairies dread the winters. We cannot be outdoors as much, some fairies like Ainia have to be very careful in the cold, but it never bothered me all that much. I almost like having a reason to keep cozy inside my home. Sitting by the fire with a cup of tea, that sounds very good to me right now. By the time the forest thaws out in the spring, I will be ready again to be outdoors. It seems to be the perfect balance.

I am so wrapped up in my own thoughts that I don't realize how close I am until I hear a voice from up ahead.

"Sigrun, I was looking for you," I look up and see Khalon.

He looks a little relieved to have found me before the ceremony. Ainia also made him new clothes for today. He also has black pants and a new shirt that finally fits him properly. His wings are draped around him like a black cape.

"I left early to talk to Vivek," I explain.

"Are you feeling okay, about today?" he asks me with concern. He moves the hair off of my forehead with one finger.

"Yeah, I'm good," I lie.

"That didn't sound very convincing," he squints his eyes like he is looking into me.

It makes me smile.

"No, it's just I'm not sure if I'm ready," I finally speak the truth.

He looks at me with the kind of patience that I will never have. He holds my hand in his and kisses my palm. He looks into my eyes.

"You're ready," he says confidently, "not just because of how you lead your people onto that battlefield, or more importantly how you lead them off of it, but because you are someone that they listen to. They believe in you. They chose you." I look down for a moment, but he tilts my face back up, "I never met your father, but I know he would be proud. You are ready to sit in his chair."

I put my arms around his neck and hug him tightly. He puts his arms around my waist hugs me back. When I let him go, he holds my face and kisses the tip of my nose. I take hold of his hand and look at it. It is so much bigger than mine. The fresh scars from battle have all healed leaving only faint pink lines.

"You know I think we could get some of your older scars to fade like these have," I say examining him.

"Think so?"

"Yeah, I'll look around the den when we get back to the house."

"Okay, but I think I want to keep this one," he puts my hand on his chest and holds it there. It is the spot where I cauterized his wound. It saved his life, but it left a very large scar.

"This one means a lot to me," he says.

I smile, but say nothing, because I don't have to. He has always been able to know what I am thinking.

"Okay," he says finally, "let's go, they'll be waiting for you."

Just about everyone is already inside the building. Everyone is wearing their best clothes and furs. I hear the band tuning their instruments. The smells of the food waft out all around the building. They are certainly getting ready for a celebration. The energy is joyous. It is a much different scene than the day Merik was going to be inducted.

I see Jae, Ainia, and Malyn standing out front. Mordecai and Vidar walk up to them just as we do. They all smile when they see me. Ainia takes a good look at her handy work. I play it up and spin around theatrically for her assessment.

"Looks good," she says, "for pants that is." She has to give at least one playful little jab.

I give them all a hug and thank them for being here. I hold Vidar a little longer than the rest. He lost his father, Osiris, in the battle. That day when I turned and Vidar was gone, he had run to help his father, but by the time he made it to him it was too late. Osiris had been run through by an enemy sword. Though Vidar did get his revenge I know seeing his empty chair today will be hard. It means a lot that he has come to support me.

Malyn is probably the only reason that he is coping so well. They have been inseparable ever since, and they have just declared their intentions to marry as soon as winter breaks.

Ainia has been spending a lot of time with Mordecai. I was surprised at first at how her feelings changed, but so many lives did change that day at the clearing. She began to look at him differently afterward, and he continues to look at her with such adoration.

Jae and I are still as close as ever. We have never readdressed any of our feelings. He has not pursued anyone else, which leads me to believe that he is still waiting for me to, as he put it, catch up, but I am too much of a coward to ask him directly. I wasn't lying when I told Vivek that it was complicated.

Falon walks up to our group. He gives me a hug, which I was not expecting. He has kept his distance since he saw me on fire.

"Are we starting?" Jae asks.

"Soon," Falon says.

Falon looks up at the sky like he is looking for something. I look up also. I only see the naked trees, the sunshine, and the fog of our breath on the cold air. Then I hear a buzzing sound that is all too familiar.

The head drone bee shoots out from the trees. He is accompanied by two other drones. I am so surprised to see them all I can do is smile broadly. They land in front of us.

"What are you doing here?" I ask.

Before the drone can respond, Falon jumps in. "I was beginning to think you weren't going to make it," Falon says to him as he bows respectfully.

"You knew they were coming?" I ask Falon.

"We would not miss your induction," the drone answers instead, "and of course Queen Asherah wishes she could be here, but knows you understand that she is unable to attend. She asked us to bring this." He holds up a beautiful wooden box with intricate carvings. "A gift for you," he holds it out to me.

Falon reaches out and snatches the box before I can touch it. "I'll take this for now. Let's get started," Falon ushers everyone into place.

The music starts playing. It is a formal, ceremonious piece of music reserved for prestigious events. Falon stands on the platform at the other end. Vivek and Akin stand on either side of him. The head drone is also on the platform as an honored guest. All of my friends have been positioned at the front near the platform.

I begin walking down the center aisle. Jae and Khalon walk just behind me. I feel shy with everyone's eyes on me. I fix my eyes on Falon which is my ending point, and walk at a comfortable pace until I get to the steps. I stop once I get there.

Falon makes a speech about honor, family, and loyalty. Each member of the council drinks wine from the same cup and makes a speech of their own about what being a member of this council means before passing it along. The cup is finally handed to me for me to drink from. I was afraid my hands would tremble, but they are steady as I take the cup. The wine is sweet.

"Sigrun Livingstone," Falon starts, "repeat after me…"

I take my vow to put the colony first, to protect the people, and honor tradition.

The ceremony is quite short, and moves fast, which I am thankful for.

I take my cue and walk over to a silk pillow with two shining metals on it. I pick up one and walk up to Khalon.

"Khalon Blackburn," he smiles at the new family name I have chosen for him, "you are my General." He bows down as I slip the ribbon over his head, "May you carry this title in name alone and enjoy a time of peace."

"I am honored, and I am looking forward to peace, but will remain vigilant, just in case," he winks at me. I bite my bottom lip to keep from smiling since this is a serious event.

I walk back over to the pillow and grab the other metal. I walk over to Jae.

"Jae Redwood, you are my High Counselor," I slip the ribbon over his head. "I will look to you for advice and support regarding every major decision for this village going forward."

"I accept this position with gratitude, and I vow to always support you, this council, and our village," he says seriously.

I also award gifts and metals to Malyn, Mordecai, and Ravi for their bravery, and to Vidar and other the families who lost loved ones.

Before the completion of the ceremony, which ends as the inductee sits in the chair for the first time, Falon takes the box from the head drone and stands in front of me. He nods for me to open it.

The top lifts open, hinged on one side. The insides are lined with purple silk and the object inside is covered by a matching silk cloth. A note rests on the inside.

Falon picks it up and reads it aloud, "*Every Queen needs a crown. Signed Asherah.*"

He lifts the cloth away. It flutters in his hand and reveals a solid gold crown. It looks like golden branches all woven together creating peaks all the way around, and in the center sits a large vibrant emerald. It is almost a glowing green.

The crowd awes as it is lifted out of the box by Falon. He hands the box to Vivek and he walks behind my chair holding the crown.

"Your majesty," he says nodding for me to take my seat.

He smiles at me. His eyes are sincere. I look around and see the smiles and anticipation on everyone's faces. Both Jae and Khalon nod for me to go on.

My mouth goes dry. My skin shivers at the suggestion. I know I am not ready to be a Queen. I am not equipped to lead this colony solely. This is a much bigger responsibility than I am ready for.

My heart is beating in my chest. I feel like I might fall over. I close my eyes and take a breath. I steady my body.

I never lived for this. I know I'm not meant to be a Queen, but I sit down and agree to let him place the crown anyway. It is heavy, but my shoulders are strong enough to hold it. As the crown settles, I find myself smiling, because who knows, maybe I will grow into it and surprise myself.